JOEY W. HILL

VIRTUAL REALITY

ELLORA'S CAVE
ROMANTICA PUBLISHING

D1484484

VIRTUAL REALITY
An Ellora's Cave Publication, June 2005

Ellora's Cave Publishing, Inc.
1337 Commerce Drive, Suite #13
Stow, Ohio 44224

ISBN #141995184X

Edited by: *Briana St. James*
Cover art by: *Syneca*

Warning:

The following material contains graphic sexual content meant for mature readers. *Virtual Reality* has been rated *E-rotic* by a minimum of three independent reviewers.

Ellora's Cave Publishing offers three levels of Romantica™ reading entertainment: S (S-ensuous), E (E-rotic), and X (X-treme).

S-*ensuous* love scenes are explicit and leave nothing to the imagination.

E-*rotic* love scenes are explicit, leave nothing to the imagination, and are high in volume per the overall word count. In addition, some E-rated titles might contain fantasy material that some readers find objectionable, such as bondage, submission, same sex encounters, forced seductions, etc. E-rated titles are the most graphic titles we carry; it is common, for instance, for an author to use words such as "fucking", "cock", "pussy", etc., within their work of literature.

X-*treme* titles differ from E-rated titles only in plot premise and storyline execution. Unlike E-rated titles, stories designated with the letter X tend to contain controversial subject matter not for the faint of heart.

Also by Joey W. Hill:

Virtual Reality

Chapter One

Her palms were damp, and her heart rate had increased exponentially the moment she sat down on the upper deck of the ferry. It struck her as odd that, after all the life-altering decisions she had made over the past few months, crossing lines she wasn't supposed to cross, she was experiencing nervousness for the very first time. It was somewhat like a soldier worrying about getting shot after he had picked up his gun and charged the field.

She'd broken federal privacy laws to be here. She'd taken the week off from work, because she had no idea if she'd be home tonight or in several days. Because she hadn't told anyone where she was going, her friends or family would say she was risking her physical wellbeing. Now that she'd committed herself, stepped on the boat, she knew the greatest risk of her bold move was to her emotional wellbeing. And she supposed therein lay the main reason for her sudden and unexpected lack of composure. If she came home sooner rather than later, she'd need the balance of those vacation days to pull the pieces back together, because that would mean she'd been rejected.

It was a beautiful day. As the ferry mates shouted out the all clear and the passenger vessel for the triangle run through Ballentyne and Morehead Islands pulled away from the dock, the sun glittered off the water in the marina and the white hulls of the well-maintained yachts in their marina slips. October was still a warm month in coastal North Carolina, the water often holding enough summer heat to allow swimming. A seabird, dark head sleek from his underwater fishing, dove again, and came up fifty feet away from his original spot.

She wore sunglasses, so she could take all this in and still keep an eye on the stairwell to the upper deck. She knew he was here. She had heard someone call his name as they were boarding, heard him respond, the cadence of his voice muffled by the chatter of day-trippers. She'd wanted to turn then, seek him out, but she didn't. She wanted the first time she saw him to have the isolated perfection of a painting in a gallery. She could look upon him, separate from his surroundings, and get a good, long look, not a desperate glimpse at him among other milling bodies.

Footsteps scraped on the metal stairs to the upper deck. He'd told her that he always sat along the starboard rail, so she had placed herself about fifteen feet away, on an anchored center bench, her profile to that position. If she looked toward him with the concealment of her sunglasses, he would think she was studying the shoreline, the tourist attractions of the island beach strands and the opposing lighthouses of Ballentyne and Morehead Islands that had guided ships from the ocean into the waterway and river for decades.

Nicole swallowed, forced herself to relax as she saw a man's form enter into her peripheral vision, take a seat exactly where he had described he sat.

He'd forbidden her to do this. That was another reason for her nervousness. To disobey one's Master, not for the pleasure of punishment, but because she knew she had to do it or lose her mind, didn't make it less nerve-racking.

He'd also told her if they ever met face-to-face, she'd be disappointed. With a casualness she was far from feeling, she turned her head so she could capture him fully within the frame of her vision.

He was just sitting down, in the process of leaning back against the rail that ran behind the metal bench, comfortably situating his ankle on the opposite knee. He had his notebook out, balanced on his thigh, and he took a sip from a Diet Coke can, his head tilted back slightly, showing her the arch of his throat. Placing the can in the crevice between his thighs, he slid a pen from the pocket of his cotton button-down shirt, a soft, faded teal color.

She'd ceased breathing, living. Her heartbeat had stopped. That was the only thing that could explain the stillness that descended as she set eyes on the man she loved with every part of her.

For the very first time.

He reminded her of a wrestler. Not the big flamboyant artists of WFW, but a finely proportioned, stocky Olympic athlete. A bear. Strong, solid, built square and muscular. His shoulders alone looked like they could carry any trouble offered to him, and his quiet, steady expression inspired confidence. Not a tall man, he was perhaps four or five inches over her five foot three.

His dark brown hair was mixed with silver, early gray for a man not quite forty. It was a rich pelt that lay smooth against his scalp, but she thought it might get curly if it got longer. He would not be the type of person who wore his hair longer, denying the advance of time with the foolish vanity of a ponytail, though his thick locks would have been beautiful as a mane.

She had imagined the pieces of him, studied his two-dimensional photograph until her fingers had turned the corners soft and smooth as cloth, no matter how carefully she handled it. Now she had the opportunity to study him as a whole, absorb the physical and metaphysical at the same time. Particularly as she moved to his face.

He didn't wear sunglasses, but the early morning sun denied her as good a view of his eyes as she wished, since they were half closed against the bright light. But under the dark silk of his eyebrows, she discerned the rich brown color of his irises, vibrant eyes that seemed to notice everything around him. Firm lips that were a little thin, suggesting a formidable temper when riled.

While his body and demeanor suggested a bear, the shape of his head, his profile and the silver-streaked hair reminded her of a wolf. A combination of two strong totems, both of whom steered clear of direct contact with humanity as long as their habitat was not invaded. Fierce when cornered.

He was writing in the notebook now, intently, and she wondered what words he was putting to paper. She liked his arms, the forearms in particular, the soft down of brown hair that lay on them and on the top of the broad, strong fingers with short trimmed nails. Only the top button of the faded shirt was open, and the sleeves were carefully, equally folded back past his elbows, the sign of a man who expected to get his hands dirty every day. He wore his jeans not tight, but snug, as Southern men did, so she could see there was good muscle tone in his thighs. He'd lifted the soda can to his lips again, and she was unable to stop her eyes from lingering on the shape of him in the crotch area, making her thankful for the sunglasses.

This was him. The man she'd needed, wanted and thought about in a million different ways for the past eighteen months. She could stay where she was, do a round trip in the boat, never identify herself, never make a move in his direction. Her impression of him would remain intact, enhanced now because she'd seen him, fleshed out the image she'd built within her mind. She'd have no illusions shattered.

But she wouldn't have anything more than that. Each drastic step she'd taken to come here reflected that she'd made her choice. All or nothing. And there was only one direction to go for that.

She gave herself one more moment to look at him. She lingered on the shape of his lips, and the artistry of his hand, resting along the rail as he studied his surroundings. Other than the greeting to the ferry mates, he did not entertain other company, though she guessed that most of the regulars on the boat knew him. Several gave him a cordial nod as they passed him, seeking a seat on the rear deck.

His head turned toward her and she averted her gaze, inadvertently casting her vision over the nearby passengers. She registered how the eyes of several of the women flickered over him, went past, then came back. They probably didn't consciously know why they felt so drawn to him, but she knew his magnetism for what it was. She had experienced it directly. Not as fully as she intended to, but enough to know he was capable of stripping a woman down to full, wanton surrender if he chose to do so.

Nicole reached into her purse, smoothed her skirt. Taking a steadying breath, she rose from her seat and turned toward him.

He was looking over his shoulder at a passing freighter, the Diet Coke can balanced on his knee beside the notebook on his thigh. She made the eight small steps to stand before him and reached down. Resting her index and middle finger on the opening of the drink where his lips had been, her other fingers overlapped his, grasping the can. His flesh felt warm and rough. Thoroughly male.

He looked toward her and up, startled, and she found she was right about his eyes. Rich and brown, almost amber in the bright light. The eyes of a wolf.

"Do you mind if I have a sip?"

* * * * *

Mark noticed her right off when he first sat down, the woman sitting in the middle of the upper deck, her profile to him. From the way she was dressed, he assumed she must be a new administrative employee on one of the islands.

He liked women who dressed with style. He wondered if this woman knew the amazing things that a tailored summer linen skirt could do to the female backside when sitting. The fabric under her drew taut, and each slight shift as she recrossed her legs or bent to look for something in the purse leaning against her leg molded the fabric to one ass cheek, then the other. He visualized the indentation between the buttocks, the soft skin and heat just inside the milky curves. He knew how sensitive the nerves were around a woman's anus, knew stimulating that area would cause her to moan and writhe. Her thighs would tremble open, seeking him, loosening her internal grasp on inhibitions and fears.

That skirt she wore was likely lined with a silken under layer that ensured the fit would be smooth over her hips and thighs. It embraced her body rather than constricted it with stray seams or a pull of fabric across the pubic area. When she stood, he was sure it would fall smooth to the hemmed end, just above her knee, and there would be a small double-stitched slit in the back, just enough to give him a glimpse of her thigh, the creases at the back of her knee. The light silk of her blouse blew against her body, outlining sweet curves in a demure way that was more titillating than a strip show, because of its clean, innocent sexuality.

What was it, he wondered, that made twenty-first century females of all ages put on tight tiny T-shirts and hip-hugger jeans that barely covered their crotches and the cracks in their asses? Hell, a few years ago a man would have assumed any woman who dressed that way was a twenty-dollar-a-hit streetwalker. Such, he supposed, were the vagaries of fashion.

The man looking for quality, for the woman who was a true sensual feast, wouldn't linger in that kind of candy store. Either the outfit said the girl was available to any man, or she was a tease, both turnoffs to him.

But the woman who dressed to make a statement of quiet elegance and style over a body she kept healthy and fit—that woman would stir an erection for him faster than a legion of tiny T-shirt clad cutouts.

This woman seemed to be such a person, because he was having trouble tearing his attention away from her. When she rose and began to turn in his direction, he shifted his attention politely over the rail. He studied the freighter leaving the river for the distant port of Cairo, according to its transom, but his mind remained on her.

She projected a serious mien, like most of the quiet women he saw ride the ferry to and from their jobs. Wearing clothes that said they were self-sufficient, intelligent and kind of heart, those women still sometimes looked away from their books or magazines to gaze out at the passing water, in a way that told him they were something else beyond all that. Wishful. Wishful that something would happen to them that they could embrace, pull to them and cherish as a last-forever kind of memory.

"Do you mind if I have a sip?"

Mark looked up at the soft, feminine voice. Standing before him was the woman he'd been studying. She had a short cap of hair, professionally styled to be shiny and thick, revealing shell-perfect ears and framing a gamine face with dark eyes and lips painted in burgundy. As he suspected, the skirt gripped the curves of her lower body in smooth lines, and her shapely calves were accentuated by stockings and a pair of short black heels that enhanced the delicacy of her ankles. A woman who took a great deal of care with her appearance to project calm elegance, but he sensed something else under that, a yearning that somehow touched him, pulled a reaction from his heart and mind, a sudden, intense interest in her.

"Pardon me?"

"Your Diet Coke." She had placed her hand on it, on the top of the can, her fingertips resting where his lips had been. "I'm supposed to take some medicine right now, and I don't have any change for a drink. Plus, I'm not really thirsty. It seems silly to buy a whole drink for that. Would you be bothered if I took a sip of yours to swallow it?"

"No. Not at all. Except there's practically none left. Hold on." He set aside the notebook, rose before she could protest, and went to the drink machine against the upper deck cabin.

When he turned, a new Diet Coke in his hand, she was standing where he'd left her, her head tilted at an angle that shone the light of the sun on the white column of her throat, illuminating the faint, fine down along the line of her cheek. She was reading what he had written about her.

She had no way of knowing she'd been the subject of his writings, of course. He had used no names, and many women coming from the mainland to do the few administrative jobs on one of the islands wore tailored skirts. Even so, knowing she'd read his thoughts about her made him uncomfortable.

When she raised her head and looked at him, he knew what she must be seeing. An average guy approaching middle age. Average height, brown hair, brown eyes. Average everything. Smiling ruefully, he let his tension go and went back to her. He popped open the top so she wouldn't have to risk her well-manicured nails.

"I'll drink the rest," he said. "Just take what you need, or keep it, if you find you're thirstier than you thought you were."

"Thank you," she said. She surprised him by sitting down next to where he had been sitting. Picking up the notebook from his seat on the bench, she offered it back to him. There was room, but she didn't scoot over. When he sat and took the notebook from her hand, his denim-clad thigh pressed against hers. He leaned forward, so as not to crowd her, but she extended her hand for the soda, so he had to lean back.

"Thanks." She opened her hand, revealing a light pink pill, and placed it on her tongue. He watched her raise the drink to her mouth, the press of metal against soft flesh, the tip of her tongue touching her upper lip.

"Nothing serious, I hope," he said.

"No, just an allergy pill." She smiled, handed back the can. Her lips glistened from the drink, and he wanted to lean forward, touch his tongue to that moisture. Have her part her lips and hold them still while he traced them, nibbled on the succulent inside of the mouth. Feel her breath grow hot and erratic on the bridge of his nose as she obeyed, despite the desire to respond. That was how it would be. He knew what would please her.

God, he had to write that down. His fingers itched to do just that.

Since she seemed to be looking out at the passing wake now, he fished his pen from his shirt collar and began to jot down the thought, thinking he would just transcribe a few words to remind him later. But when his pen touched paper, the words flooded from his brain to his fingers, out through the pen, and would not let him go until he completed the thought in all its wonderful detail.

When he was done, he clicked the pen up and replaced it in his collar, and found she had been watching him write. She smelled of a rich fragrance, applied so lightly that it was like catching the whiff of a harem on a desert breeze at twilight and losing oneself in the imaginings of the paradise that could be found in such an unattainable place. Her leg warmed his, and he wished he could feel her. Not just in this indirect way, which was not really touching her at all, but his own skin growing warm from the proximity of hers.

"What do you do?" she asked.

"I'm an engineer."

"So you look at an idea, and make it real?"

"I look at an idea and design a way to make it real." His shoulder was against hers, and when he shifted, it brought him the feel of a narrow point of bone and the press of soft flesh under the fabric of her cream silk blouse.

"You don't get to be the one who makes it real?" She smoothed the skirt over her knees, not a nervous gesture, but more as if she were petting herself. "Isn't that frustrating?"

Mark looked down at his lap, at the notebook. "Sometimes. But you have to have a reality to test your design on, and that takes money, people, equipment. I usually get to be there to see it happen, though. To help make it happen."

While silence stretched between them, Mark tried to understand what he saw in her eyes as she gazed back at the horizon.

It was a perfect day to be on the boat, the breeze with the heat of a lingering southern summer in it, sunlight glittering off the white foam of the ferry's wake. There were just a handful of passengers, midmorning on a weekday not being a high traffic time for the passage between islands.

"Are you going to work?" he ventured.

"No. I just couldn't be there this week. Does that make sense?"

Mark nodded. "Perfect sense."

"I'm not lazy," she added. "But sometimes when you go, day after day, you start to feel like you're on this wheel, and your feet are becoming welded to it, so you're just the wheel. You have to break out for the day."

"I think the appropriate corporate term is 'mental health day'." Mark smiled.

Her attention snapped to his face and stayed there, intent, even as his mouth settled into a more serious expression. "Is something wrong?" he asked.

"Not a thing," she said after a moment. "My name is Nicole." She extended her hand.

"Mark." He took it, folded slim fingers into his hand. She had soft skin, and a cool, narrow palm. People shaking hands when they met was unusual, except in business. And shake was not even the correct term for this. It felt more like a crossing of barriers. Flesh meeting flesh, an invitation to some as-yet-undefined level of familiarity. The wind shifted, and he smelled that fragrance again. It took him into her home, her vanity, where she stood before a mirror getting ready for work. Clad perhaps in nothing more than a bra and panty set. His attention flickered to her blouse. She'd want something pretty and comfortable, something that made her feel feminine under her clothes. White, because of her blouse. A cushioned undercup made of crushed velvet material that would support and cradle at the same time. A white filmy overlay, a pale leaf pattern. The cushioned undercup would just cover the nipple, while the transparent overlay would frame the top curve of her breasts. The panties would be the same filmy leaf pattern, styled with a flared leg, the kind that were not quite bikinis, but not quite tap pants, with the rippled sides showing the smooth crease of thigh to hip. They would also reveal the curve of her mound when she took a wand to apply the fragrance to the line of her throat, the high inside of her thigh, the pulse at her wrist. Lips applied to that pulse point, just there, would make her lose all sense and reason. Little flicks of the tongue, stray nibbling kisses, while her fingers curled against his face in helpless desire.

"Here." Nicole leaned forward. Her fingers touched the front of his shirt, a light pressure on his chest as she drew his pen out of the placket. "You have that look again. Write it down before you lose it."

Mark wondered why it was that the lightest brush of another's fingers was felt so acutely, when one's own touch was barely noticeable. It was as if nerve endings were flames, leaping closer to the skin's surface when fueled by excitement or the anticipation of touch by another. Fire could not feed itself.

She reached across him, placing the pen in his hand, her breast pressing into his arm. She had noticed he was left-handed.

Mark bent his head and wrote, aware she sat beside him, watching the flourishes and curves of every word. He wrote very deliberately, letting the movement of the pen stroke out each word as if he were caressing the image they evoked.

When he looked up, she swallowed. A lovely flush had tinged her cheeks, and he didn't think he was imagining that the pulse in her throat was beating more rapidly. Which told him she could read his handwriting.

"So," she said. "If you had someone willing to test your design on reality, Mark, would you take the risk? If she agreed to step into your scenario, and follow your direction faithfully, your every...command, could you do it? *Would* you do it?"

His gaze shot to hers, and at the sudden deepening of her blush and the tremor that ran through her hand, he knew.

"Please don't be angry." She held his gaze, refused to look away, though he could tell by the clench of her fine, slim hands folded in her lap, the quiver of her jaw, that she was frightened.

Shock rendered him without voice for several moments. His gaze roved over her, taking in every detail of her appearance again, because this apparent stranger was suddenly someone he knew. A woman whose heart and mind he knew better than anyone in the world. He'd just never seen her face. Until now.

Ironically, he realized he had noticed everything about her except for the tiny cat's paw earrings in her second ear piercing, a discreet whimsy to the hoops she wore just below them.

"Shy Kitten." He used the login ID she'd given herself. When he'd first interacted with her, he'd thought it had been an erotic innuendo, but in their very first chat he'd known that she'd not intended such a seductive reference at all. She was a shy kitten in truth.

Her flushed cheeks, the concerted effort to keep her eyes on his, only underscored it. Knowing her as well as he did, he didn't have to guess how much courage she'd had to gather to make this bold a move.

His kitten. After meeting eighteen months ago and playing online with each other two nights every week for well over a year, she'd broken the rules of the game. She'd come to find him.

Chapter Two
Eighteen Months Earlier

So, why do you use the logon ID, 'Shy Kitten'?

Her fingers were cold and shook as she typed. *Get a grip, Nicole. He doesn't know you. He can't see you. If you make a fool of yourself, it doesn't matter.*

She wasn't really certain she was a submissive, or if she was just intrigued with the fantasy. She'd haunted the sites for several months at first, then dared some apprehensive conversations with those in the D/s lifestyle, becoming more confident as she found they weren't serial rapists trawling for victims or escapees from Mad Max films, but people like her. People exploring an alternative form of sex that drew them to it like a natural craving.

It had taken nearly half a year, but at length she'd risked a "date" in a private chatroom. The Dom she'd chosen had been almost as new to this as she was. She'd deliberately chosen him because of that, because he seemed safe. The friendly but lackluster interaction made her feel silly and unsatisfied, and afterward, she knew what she needed to do. She'd never been one to waste her time. If she truly wanted to figure out if this was something that ran deep in her soul or was just a passing fancy whose time for indulgence was at an end, she needed to deal with someone who knew the ropes, no puns intended. She'd chatted with her new online friends, those deep into their submissive roles, and they told her to extend an invitation to "The Master".

That wasn't his calling ID. But these women passionately claimed it fit him. If their amusing accolades were to be believed, he had earned the title in the same manner that God had been given the capital form of the generic term, as the supreme representation of all beings of omnipotent power. He was the best at what he did.

She'd never thought she'd have the bravery, but she had done it. Resolving that she would stop altogether if her interaction with him was as lukewarm as her prior one, she'd sent the invitation before she could lose her nerve. So here they were.

```
    I need you to be honest, and respond to me
immediately when I ask you a question. Don't
think   it   through,   don't   edit   it.   No
backspacing. You send it as you type it. You
will be as open to me, more open to me, than
you are to your own mind.
```

The words, just letters strung together, hit her low in the solar plexus, thrummed through her fingers on the keyboard. In that first statement, she understood why he had the reputation he did. It was the difference between meeting pretty women on the street and a movie star, all that beauty honed to an artistic perfection.

```
    I just started doing this, so I'm nervous
about it.
    You've tried out at least one Dom on the
list.
    Yes.
    Yes, Master.
```

Goose bumps crawled up her spine, gave her a shiver. Yes, Master.

```
    Yet you asked for me. I liked your
invitation. It was simple, elegant. Like you, I
suspect.
```

She flushed. How do you know? You've never seen me.

```
    I can see you right now. I'm in the room
with you, Kitten, the moment you begin typing.
Can't you see me, feel me? I'm standing right
```

behind you, the heat of my body almost touching yours. No. Don't turn around. You will stay still.

Nicole jerked to a halt, almost laughed at what she'd been about to do, but when she realized how he had anticipated it and her body had obeyed him, amusement was supplanted by something else. When she shifted, her thighs were damp.

My hands are on your shoulders. My fingers trace the lines of your collarbone, the sensitive valley of skin between them. Learning you.

Nicole tilted her head before she realized she had done it, feeling the touch of the words.

Tell me what you're wearing.

A silk robe, as you…commanded, in your instructions. Nothing else.

Mmm…lovely. I am sliding my hands down your arms, coming forward. I'm cupping your breasts through the silk, lifting them so I can play with the nipples, watch them, feel them grow hard for me. Are they hard for me, Shy Kitten?

"Yes," she whispered. Then she remembered to type it in, missed a keystroke, but sent it anyway, mindful of his order.

Good. I'm getting you hot. You're a responsive submissive, very responsive. I like that. Take off the robe and sit before me naked.

Feeling absurdly self-conscious, she did it, laying the robe aside. She'd left the gas logs on, and so the room was warm with their flame, as well as her own heat.

Why am I going this fast, Kitten?

She moistened her lips. Because I belong to you. She typed it without thinking about it, without hesitating, and was then lost in amazement with herself, staring at the words.

There was a pause, the cursor blinking.

Because you belong to me, or because you
want to belong to me?

Both.

She didn't know if she was riding an impetuous wave of
lust and emotional turbulence that would embarrass her
tomorrow, but he had indicated she should type what she felt,
no matter what it was. It was the exact opposite of the type of
dating she'd experienced in her world, the pretentiously
civilized rituals of social interaction between men and women
that masked true desire. In her limited attempts at dating, she'd
found herself impatient, wanting to give everything of what she
was to the man, to beg him to open himself up and offer the
same to her, so they might see whether the connection was there,
or if they were just wasting each other's time. She couldn't,
though. To do as she wished would be an unforgivable breach of
mating code.

They all learned how to play hard to get, to be circumspect
in admission of their feelings. It was a trap that had a double
snare, because in the process there was the danger of losing sight
of what the heart truly wanted, distracted and drained by the
energy of the strategy. Oh, she was tired of those types of games.
Of any games. She wanted something like this, where the rules
were on the table, and clear to understand. Where the man
wanted everything she felt, up front and immediate.

Describe yourself to me.

She looked at herself, and a dozen possibilities ran through
her head, stymied her.

The truth. Or you'll earn a spanking, and it
won't be a pleasant one.

She stifled a nervous chuckle and a little bit of a gasp,
because she sensed a serious warning behind the words that had
a touch of playfulness to them.

I'm not quite five and a half feet tall. My
hair is to my shoulder blades. She ran her
fingers through its dull length, noting the
split ends. I'm afraid it hasn't been trimmed

in awhile. I used to be... I've gained some weight, these past few months.

What are your nails like? Do you do manicures?

She smiled. No, Master. They're pretty chewed. Nervous habit, I guess.

Have you always done that?

No. **She shifted.**

Do you wear makeup?

Sometimes. Not so much anymore.

Who took away your joy in yourself as a woman, Shy Kitten? Women are vain creatures.

Before she could type an indignant response to that, his words stilled it. Men like it that way. I like a woman who attracts me, excites me with her appearance, even if she has no intention or awareness of me.

Then I guess I'm wasting your time.

You're misunderstanding, **he responded immediately.** Don't view every word from me as the stroke of a sword that you must combat with a return strike. You must listen with your heart. Not your mind, your fears or your pride. Pride that is only a shield against your fears has no place with your Master. You must be open to me in all ways, speak with your heart.

That leaves me very vulnerable.

Yes, it does. Again, Kitten. Tell me who has made you lose your joy in yourself.

I'm not a basket case. I'm not one of those pathetic nutcases seeking therapy and friends on the Internet.

But was she? She wasn't sure.

What are you seeking? It's not an idle question. A fantasy, a limited indulgence, a way to achieve orgasm once a week with another

person in a way that's safe? You could have
stayed among the masses, surfing from Dom to
Dom, one weeknight to the other, but you
didn't. You specifically sought me. What do you
want? What are you hoping to find with me?

She swallowed back the pain, wished she had enough pride
left to shut down the computer and tell him to go to hell. Of
course, she'd have to reverse that process. She choked out a self-
deprecating laugh.

I don't know. Something I'm afraid I'll
never have. Something that may or may not be
here in this…way of relating to someone. But…I
didn't… I never planned to visit places like
this, but something about it always intrigued
me. I thought I was just looking for kicks,
trying to break out of a 'good girl' mode, but
I think that was just the way my subconscious
talked my conscious into coming here. Now that
I'm here, there are things in me that
want…something. God, I sound like an idiot.

No, you don't. You sound like someone
honestly trying to understand what she wants. I
sense you're brave, as brave as you are lovely,
and you're willing to risk your heart to find
yourself again. Something in your heart has
compelled you to choose the path of a
submissive.

It was a full minute before she could type a response, and
he waited her out, that cursor patiently blinking.

You sound like you've been there.

This path has been both my hell and my
salvation. So I've realized that I'm at the
center of my Fate. I'm attracted to you, Shy
Kitten. You're going to do something for me.

Yes?

The cursor stayed in place, no answer. Nicole thought it
through, took a deep breath. Overcame trepidation, reworded
and re-punctuated.

Yes, Master?

This week, you'll go get a manicure. You will get your hair done. I want you to go buy a new outfit. You won't pay for this yourself. You'll tell me how much it costs and we'll set up a double-blind post office box, to keep your location and identity safe. I will be sending you the money.

But you shouldn't—

His words scrolled across the screen before she could finish.

You're mine now. I'm claiming you, and I will take care of what's mine. If, at any point, you don't wish to belong to me, you'll tell me so, and our time will be over. Don't buy the outfit in the size you want to be. Buy something you like that fits you now. I want you to look in the mirror and be happy with what you see. Tell me what size your breasts are.

Thirty-four C.

A very nice size, just on the plump side. I like a woman with a soft, pretty ass, Kitten. Do you have one?

Yes...I think so. **Her throat was tight, and she was lightly perspiring.**

Do you like cats, or are you telling me your pussy is as shy as the rest of you? Coax your legs open, spread them for me so I can see. Are you shaved?

No.

When you go to get a manicure, I want you shaved. A full waxing so you'll feel your pussy rubbing against your panties when you walk. I want you to feel your sensuality, know that somewhere out here I am thinking of you, seeing you, my cock getting hard thinking about your body being prepared for my pleasure.

Y...Yes, Master.

You'll find there are a wide range of definitions for the term 'good girl', Kitten. And I think you'll be a very, very good girl for me. Do you want to be a good girl for me?

Yes. Yes, Master. **Her mouth was dry. She wished she'd thought to bring water into the room.**

Then do as I tell you by Wednesday. I'll talk to you this same time every Thursday night, as long as you accept my Mastery over you.

Chapter Three
Present Day

"You said you were overweight and had a complexion problem, but you liked your shoulders and ankles. That your mother didn't like your hair long, that it was frizzy." His gaze passed over her. "You lied to me."

"No, I didn't." She raised her chin. "I told you that eighteen months ago, the first time we met in our chat room. I…you made me want to be prettier, made me feel prettier, so it was easy to decide I wanted to start taking better care of myself."

"You were always beautiful here." He tapped his skull. "In my mind."

"Then I hope the reality doesn't disappoint you. I lost the weight, and decided my mother was right." She lifted a defensive shoulder when he withheld a response. "Chopped it all off. And amazingly, when I started going to bed with fantasies of you, instead of potato chips and ice cream for company, the complexion took care of itself." Her words were matter-of-fact, direct, though he was very aware that her hands in her lap were trembling, the nervous reaction sweeping up her arms.

She lifted her mouth in a shy, nervous smile. She was more fragile than he expected, and he already knew most of her vulnerabilities.

"You don't know what I'm capable of," he said in a low voice. "No matter what you think you've done or experienced in D/s play before."

"I've done nothing, experienced nothing, except what I've experienced with you, every week," she said. "I'm scared. But

27

I…I'm here. And I'll do whatever you tell me to do. Just don't ask me to leave."

Though his mind screamed at the foolishness of the action, he took a mental step closer toward reins that hung just beyond his grasp, waiting to be used, taken. "Are you offering yourself to me, Nicole?"

"You know I am."

She firmed her lips in defiance, and he wanted to jerk that stubbornly set mouth to his and plunder it, almost as much as he wanted to find the courage to shove her back to her safe world, where he could have her without hurting her. His words had teased her past her inhibitions, roused her with images. Brought her here. All actions had consequences.

"Did you tell someone where you were going?"

She shook her head, and he scowled. He was still, in person, a stranger. She was a woman alone on a one-day spontaneous adventure without the knowledge of friends or family.

"Kitten, that's just stupid. I could be a murderer. The least you should have done is lie to me, tell me that someone knows where you are, even if they don't."

"I'll never lie to you, Master. You forbade it." A touch of a smile flirted around her lips. "And I did tell my cat. Besides, if you were a murderer, I'd be dead before they came looking for me anyway, wouldn't I?"

Correction. He'd like to follow up that plundering kiss on her sweet mouth with a savage spanking. He stilled his mind, shut down every skittering doubt and fear, and focused just on her, and the notebook in his lap, filled with pages and pages of imagined possibilities. The chance to see those possibilities become reality sat in front of him.

"Maybe we could start with something small, then. A microcosmic experiment," he said, not wanting to think about what he was doing. He had no right to indulge even the slightest of his personal fantasies. He leaned back against the rail, gauging the best profile for her from his view.

"Nicole, uncross your legs and cross your feet at the ankles for me."

She moistened her lips, a sign of anxiety in cats, and he suspected for her as well. But she stopped smoothing her skirt and slid her thigh off her knee with a whisper of fabric. She straightened, as he knew she would need to do, to align her calves and settle that foot at an angle cinched in before the other.

"Keep your back straight, and fold your hands in your lap," he murmured, soothing and quiet as the wind ruffling the fine down of hair on her nape. "Do you like that pose?"

A half smile was his answer. She was uncertain. He imagined his words were his pen, she his paper, accepting them, giving the ink a canvas to script an image. An image that would swell and become even more of a creation than its original intent by the fusion of the two elements.

"I like this pose," he said. "It draws attention to the most beautiful parts of a woman's body. The small of her back." His hand left the rail and he touched there, lightly, just a graze of his fingers that made her catch her breath, her stomach drawing in for a second, a quick jump. "Her neck." His fingers trailed up, a brief impression of her spine, the fragile bumps that allowed her movement and her skin sensitivity to his touch. The down at her neck was as soft as he expected it to be, and he wanted to stroke the close-cropped hair above it, but he didn't. He took his hand away. "When you're sitting like that, so elegant and perfect, it makes a man desire to have you. He wants to kneel before you, slide his fingers onto your thighs beneath the hem of your skirt, feel the muscles quiver under his fingers. But some part of him also wants to sit, just like this." He settled back again now, his arm along the rail behind her. "And not disturb you, so he can observe how every breath raises your shoulders. Linger on the shape of your breasts beneath your blouse and bra, enjoy the way the folds of your skirt pull across your hips where your thighs bend so you can sit. Watch the fabric shift under your ass as you turn your head to look around you."

"Is that permitted?" she asked quietly.

Mark swallowed. She hadn't run, and she'd asked the perfect question. She had taken her first step over the threshold into a real Wonderland, and he found himself unable at this moment to deny her entry. They were just on the ferry, he told himself. What was the harm? Was it really much different than the computer?

"Yes. But keep your hands in your lap, and your ankles crossed."

She looked at him, and her eyes were vulnerable, but alive and bright as well.

He could see how his words affected her. Her nipples pushed against the fabric of the bra, faintly visible beneath the thin blouse, two points that focused him on every ripple the blouse made that accentuated them, the silky fabric stroking her as his fingers burned to do.

"So what do you like about sitting this way, Nicole?"

He knew that the act of keeping her thighs in that straight seam, the knees touching, compressed what lay between her legs and made her all that more aware of it. It pressed her center flat to the bench's surface, whereas crossing raised it. Sitting as she was sitting now, she would absorb every vibration of the ferry's engine through the sensitive nerve endings in her pussy.

"It…" She wet her lips again. "It feels like butterflies, here." She cupped her palm over the slight swell of her lower abdomen, a part of her he'd like to bare by sliding that cream-colored blouse up. He'd unzip the skirt, tug it down to lay his lips on the flesh just below the navel. Most women weren't comfortable being touched in that area unless they were very relaxed, too self-conscious about their weight, whether they were fat or thin. But he would make her lie still while he nuzzled and licked, admired every soft inch.

"If you were writing about me sitting this way, what would you write?"

He considered her. "I'd imagine you just as you are, only you'd sit here before all these people, bright under the sunshine, in a silk teddy." He watched the color climb in her cheeks, and fire licked at his insides, goading him. "You'd be in this same position, only I'd loop a pale pink ribbon around your ankles to make sure you stayed that way. I'd take the ends up to your wrists and tie them so you could only sit and be beautiful and worry about nothing else.

"The teddy would be the type you'd buy for a wedding night. It would be mostly transparent, with wire cups and a stretch in the fabric so it would shape and mold to every graceful curve of your body, give where it was needed at your hips—"

"I'd need a lot of that—"

"Hush." A stern look silenced her as effectively as if he'd shouted. "You won't do that again, Nicole. You're a lovely shape. The way you look, your mirror, is only what I see and feel about you, and what I can make *you* feel and see. Tell me you understand, and I'll go on."

At any moment, she could spook, say she'd had enough, move away. He didn't want to move too fast, not only because he wanted to keep her here, but because he was fascinated with watching a dream literally sculpted into reality. Like any creation, every step had to be carefully examined for the perfection of the stroke, or the molding of the clay. Until the act would take on a life of its own and throw in something spontaneous, unexpected, the spark of soul, as if the designer's hands and the subject had combined to inspire it. Another part of him, the part that knew the dangers of this meeting, wanted to push hard, make her break and run. The two sides warred within him.

"I understand," she said in a soft voice, looking at him, the shift of her eyes telling him that she was still trying to figure out where they were going.

If he had time and did it right, she would relinquish that need to control, and trust him enough to follow where he led. She had reached that point with him online, but this was a whole new area, as much as if today was the first time they had ever met.

When he noticed his palms were sweating, he deliberately opened them on his jeans.

"The teddy would be embroidered with seed pearls and sewn with satin petals. Through the sheer sides I would be able to see the crease in your skin, that curve on your rib cage caused by the weight of your breasts resting there. The embroidery and satin embellishments would only cover as much of your breast as a low shelf bra, so the swells and that valley between them would be visible, traceable, with my finger."

Her lips parted as he spoke, those breasts rising and falling a little more rapidly. He noticed a flush on the soft skin revealed by the vee of the blouse. Mark was glad for the notebook he'd slid over his lap to conceal his own reaction. That might spook her in truth. Not that he had more than the average man's equipment, nothing to make a woman run screaming. Or laughing either, thank God. Even so, women didn't initially equate a guy's hard-on with their more romantic fantasies. He'd found women were very self-absorbed in their sensuality, welcoming men and their raw physicality into their secret folds only once the flower had swelled, the petals opening, kissed with dew.

No, it was too soon. To let her see his erection at this point would be too much like flashing her.

"So, that concludes this particular design experiment," he said.

"So soon?" She drew a deep breath, settled back. Her reaction—hesitant, as though she almost didn't want to settle back, wasn't sure if he'd granted her permission to do so— moved him.

In just a few short moments, she had accepted his yoke. It was amazing to him, deeply humbling. He wanted to cherish her, hold onto this moment somehow without progressing, where it could not be tainted by a misstep. He should leave it here. Move away. Send her back behind a monitor screen where it was safest for both of them.

"You've done this before, haven't you?" Her shoulder blades and the fragile base point of her neck pressed against his arm, stretched along the rail behind her. Flirting, or just comfortable familiarity, it felt equally welcome. "A lot."

There was little to read in her voice, which meant she was covering something. Hurt or jealousy, or something else, he did not know, but he watched her face carefully. He shrugged, which slid his biceps against the silk covering her shoulder. "Never in person, face-to-face like this."

"I guess you've known a lot of women...like me, online."

"Less than you think." When Mark touched her shoulder, she looked up at him. "There are lots of places online you can go to talk dirty to someone, or have someone do the rebellious slave act. It's interesting, but pretty melodramatic, like reading a comic book. But moments like the ones we've had online... They're the real thing." He had to be honest with her. Jesus, he had to get her back to the mainland. The sooner the better, and even that might be too late, since he couldn't seem to keep from saying things he shouldn't say. "They're rare. You have to have a person willing to stop all the chatter and worries in their head, and just listen and trust you, even on the Internet. It gets under the skin when you do it that way. The rest is just sex, and practicing being good at it."

"It's more than practice for you." She reached up, tapped the hand at her shoulder. "It's the way your mind works. Who you are."

Something tightened in his chest, tearing him between the desire her words provoked and the pain they roused, scraping against unhealed wounds. He managed a smile, but he could tell she'd caught both reactions.

To defuse things, he should route them to an easier discussion, something inane. Their respective careers, the weather, but his lips could not form the words to push her back from him that way, send the obvious message to back off. Not with her this close physically and mentally inside his boundaries. She'd broken through with that first bold move with the Diet Coke.

"So have you ever wanted to try it on someone for real, like that?"

"Of course."

"So how would you feel if you had someone willing to…participate in what you write…all day? No promises or strings beyond that…unless you want them."

The words sunk into him, the possibility offered like a troublesome spirit visiting the dim, dark recesses of Faust's study in the most desolate hours of night. She had leaned forward, so their faces were very close. He studied the way her teeth worried her bottom lip. In her dark eyes, he sensed something very close to the natural world. The shy wildness of a deer, able to bound with joy through the forest, privy to so many mysteries of the moist Mother Earth that men could only experience vicariously, through their grounding in a woman's body. She wanted to play, play with dead earnestness, and savor the joy of a day away from the expectation of the expected.

"I'm scared," she admitted, and her voice shook a little. He relented, reached across to grasp her fingers in her lap, his knuckles pressing on the slope of her thigh.

His desire won out over good sense. "I know. I think I want you a little scared. The good kind, like when the Ferris wheel stops at the top. Just for today, Nicole. That's all I can give you. Okay?"

"Okay."

"I mean it."

She nodded, a quick jerk of her head. She was accepting what he offered, yet he knew she wanted more, so much more than he could give. Which is why he had lost his mind giving her this much, but there was something threatening to erupt inside of his soul, a demand that her proximity was calling forth like the offer of drugs to a lifetime addict. With no strings attached.

He pushed aside the comparison viciously, rejecting it along with the shadows it evoked in him. Her eyes saw too much, for her hand crept forward, touched his forearm, a touch of comfort.

"All right, then." He leaned back, set her hand from him, though he squeezed her fingers a moment in reassurance before laying her palm back on her leg. "Go back to sitting up straight with your ankles crossed." He kept his voice calm, easing her back to where they were, though he felt like falling on his knees before her and worshipping every inch of her skin. When did he get this greedy? His own demands were rising in him, filling his mind, directing him, and he had to tighten the reins on his own reactions, his desire to master her in ways she was not prepared to face. He'd yoked it in, sat on it, letting it out only in a digital world. He'd done that long enough to know how to control it. So he'd thought.

She nodded, assumed that same position. Mark glanced around, taking stock of their immediate neighbors. He found they had this part of the deck to themselves, with the exception of a family of day-trippers, hanging over the rail and pointing at seagulls and the passing coastline.

"I want you to shift toward me, keeping that posture and your ankles crossed," he ordered. "Your knee should be touching the point of mine, just a light contact."

She turned, sliding her round ass in a crescent path along the surface of the metal bench.

"Now, I want you to place your right hand against your throat. Close your eyes."

She did, on both counts. He liked the way the soft shade of brown eye shadow and slightly darker liner enhanced the fringe of lashes fanned against her skin. She laid her hand against her throat, the palm flat, fingers curled, like a nervous farm wife worrying the collar of her housecoat.

"I want you to touch your neck the way you'd want me to touch it." He curled his fingers loosely around hers, molded them so her index finger was extended, and used the pressure of his hand to have her trace her esophagus, trail her knuckles along the jugular. Then he squeezed her, warning her that he was letting go. "Forget about me watching. Your hand is my hand, touching you the way that you like, fingertips caressing your throat. Every delicate bone, the fine hairs, just under the ears..."

Was he leading or following? It seemed they were moving together, him anticipating her desire, knowing how sensitive a woman's neck could be, at the same moment she lifted her chin for better access to her own touch. What greater instruction manual was there to a woman than that delicate column, arched up in passion, or curving to turn the head and answer a question with a smile or frown, bending to consider a task or problem? Rounded to nestle her cheek into a pillow and find dreams.

"Now, down. The fingers, just two of them, outline that tender pocket where the collarbones meet, and trail onward, tracing the lapel of your blouse. Slide your fingers just under it, where you can feel the slope of your breast, its curve outward. Feel the contrast between baby soft skin and the lace of your bra."

He leaned forward, clasping his hands between his knees, and lowered his voice to blend with the warm breeze brushing her cheeks. "I can see the outline of your fingers, just the tips, tracing your left breast beneath the blouse. Your nipple is growing tight, blood swelling the breast, because it recognizes your touch, recognizes that you know best how to pleasure it. Would you like to touch your nipple, Nicole?"

"Yes, Master. How?" she asked, a breath of sound.

"Your fingers will slip that top button above the front clasp of your bra. You'll slide your hand into your blouse, your fingers under that left cup, and knead yourself."

"Will people see?"

"Do you want them to see?"

Her eyes opened, startled, but he kept his expression unreadable. "I..." She licked her lips. "I want to do what pleases you, but...no."

He inclined his head. "That's what I want as well. I don't desire to share you, Nicole. No one will see but me. I won't expose you to others. Not at any point. I'll make sure others aren't looking, even if we're out among others as we are now. Everything we do is just for us. Exhibitionism is not part of the design, unless you specifically ask for it." He lifted a finger, touched her chin. "Unless you ask nicely for it, and then I don't think I could deny you anything."

She managed a smile, some of her tension apparently easing at his reassuring gesture. The possibility of being seen would add to her excitement to a certain extent, but he knew she wasn't into public exposure, and the fact she trusted him to protect her stoked the fires within him. Despite that, he kept his expression serious, calm. His heart might be slamming through his chest like a cartoon character's, but he knew it was crucial for a Master to project confidence, dominance with an equal dose of protectiveness, so the tenuous emotional connection was not lost.

Her gaze locked with his and slowly her fingertips descended, the polished short nails sliding the button free, then revealing a hint of lace as she pushed her hand under the light silk covering and into the cup of her bra. He blinked, shifted his gaze down to watch the outline of her fingers as she found herself, the small undulations of movement under her clothes, a lift of the whole breast as she tugged and drew in her breath, catching her bottom lip in her teeth.

"Stop," he murmured. She did, her nostrils flared with her more shallow breathing. "Make the other one harder now, with your other hand, so your arms are crossed. You'll probably have to free another button to have room for both your wrists. Stay sitting up straight, your knees pressed together," he admonished gently. "And keep your thighs still. I don't want anything pleasuring you yet except your hands on your nipples."

Anticipation, along with a bit of wildness, reflected from her eyes as she swallowed and loosened another button, showing him a ripe curve cradled in white silk. He suspected the fabric of the bra was sheer enough to show him the flushed color of the aroused tip, but he wasn't taking her that far that fast. As much as he would like to have her move her hands, hold them at her sides while he leaned forward and licked that valley, nuzzled the full breasts held up and together by the undergarment like an offering to the gods of the ripest, most succulent of all fruits, he wouldn't. Not yet.

She was fondling herself, doing it slowly, carefully, cognizant of the people behind them, which made it even more torturous, he knew. "What kind of bra do you like to wear for yourself, Nicole?"

Her fingers stilled.

"Keep going while you speak, Nicole. I didn't tell you to stop."

She drew in a breath, obeyed.

He could keep her doing that for a while, rousing her to a tremendous level of intensity, and her self-consciousness would keep her to that pace. She would be unable to come, only driven to mindless arousal, open to further suggestion like a person under the influence of hypnosis, only this was far more honest. This came from her own sensual, natural instincts, instincts she was taught to suppress or use in a calculated fashion, rather than simply enjoying them as they were meant to be.

"I like the shelf bras," she said, her voice a little uneven, unfocused. It made him want to catch that full bottom lip in his own teeth, suck on it, tongue the crevice between it and her teeth, explore the part of a woman that was so like her pussy that a man could almost, but not quite, content himself in either orifice. Both were preferred, if the truth be known. For a man like him, plunging his cock in all her openings would be the triumph of full possession. Her pussy, her mouth, her ass, serving him, a triangle of submission that encompassed all of her spirit. When a man was in a woman's cunt, if he did it right, he had her full attention. She would open up like an angel's wings, surrender and bring pleasure to him at the same time, in the same act.

"Why?"

"Because...when you put one on—"

"But *I've* never worn one," he said.

Though he couldn't help smiling, his request for correction was clearly a demand, a gentle reminder of what he'd taught her online. He wouldn't permit her to distance herself from her vulnerability.

Her lips curved, and she nodded. "When *I* wear one, put one on, I like how it looks, the way it holds my breasts like...like a man would, and they look so pretty, perfectly curved on top, quivering with every step I take." She slanted him a glance. "Sometimes in the morning before work, I put on my underwear, the stockings and my heels, and just walk around like that for awhile, watching the way my body moves, knowing it's moving like that under my clothes all day."

Which explained the sensual grace of her movements, a woman aware of her sexual value to the men who watched her.

"It makes me feel very sexy."

It made him hard as a rock just imagining it, and from the slumberous smile in her eyes, he knew she knew it. She was getting brave enough to tease him, and he loved her for it. He loved her, period, and that was the most dangerous thing of all.

"Take your hands from yourself, put them back in your lap. Folded, left over right, fingers straight. Don't fix your blouse."

He liked the way the wind rippled the separated cloth, giving him glimpses of her breasts held in the cups of the bra like a man's loving hands, as she had suggested. The movement of the fabric was like clouds passing over the pearlescent moon, giving him the gleam of a pale orb one moment, hiding it coyly the next.

"Lean back, just a little, and toward me."

His arm was behind her again, so the change in position pressed her against his side, cradled her in the shelter of his arm and chest. She was stiff, unsure of the sudden intimacy. Touching this way could be more disturbing than choosing to follow a sensual command, he knew, because the latter was delivered from outside her personal sphere of space. He ran a finger along the line of her opposite shoulder, soothing her.

"Tell me something interesting, something you've never told me. Take your time."

The hum of the ferry engine that covered their intimate conversation, the swish of water running along the sides, the calls of the seagulls following in their wake, looking for fish, filled the long silence between them. He watched her face, her lowered eyes as she processed her own thoughts, sifted through the items she could choose. As if she was choosing something to wear, something that would define who she was for today. When he'd first met her, she'd been at the point that she'd choose anything out of her closet, making her decisions based on functionality. She'd lost any interest or pleasure in her uniqueness, or in decorating herself. She had flattered him by telling him once or twice that he had helped her rediscover it, but he had known it was always within her. That it had been even more her doing than his that brought it back to life over the months they spent online.

She'd increased her understanding of the world around her as well as her wardrobe, so that he wished he could be inside her mind, watching her pause over each thought, examining its colors and determining whether its expression suited her mood for today. Whether it would please him. He'd love to watch her go through that process, internal and external, choosing what she would wear, be and express, every day of her life. And how that would change on the days he chose the clothes out of the closet for her, how she would adapt her mind and body to his demands, how that would sculpt and expand her spirit.

"When I'm on the bus, going downtown to work," she said, "I always wish I could turn and look into the faces of the people next to me or across from me. Without them feeling the need to say something, or stare back. I wish they'd just keep gazing out the window, or looking at their book, and I could look at them."

"What would you be looking for?"

"Nothing in particular. I just want to send them this mental message. I see you. I care." She raised her gaze to his. "But they throw up that wall. They look up, see me looking and need to say something that means nothing to either of us. I think in their hearts, they'd rather just look back at me, study me as I'm studying them, without being self-conscious. Maybe we'd smile, maybe we wouldn't. We'd just be still, and know we matter to each other, though we're strangers. Knowing that if one of us stumbled going down the bus steps, one of the others of us would try to catch them, because we're connected. But they don't do that, so I keep my head down and don't speak, for fear of being caught up in some inane conversation. All the time...well, no, maybe for a moment or two, I'm thinking, 'Maybe they're sitting there in a lonely place, feeling disconnected from everything, needing to know someone is out there and cares'. But I don't lift my head, I push the thought away, and try to send this little warm wisp of energy out of the corner of my eyes, hoping it will help, but feeling like it's not enough, and we're both empty."

"You're so full of life, Nicole, the world can barely contain you. But let's do this." He took her hands, tugged her so they were facing, her outside knee meeting his, and forming a connecting triangle between their diagonally opposed bodies.

"Just look, Nicole," he said. "And I'll say nothing. I'll just look back at you."

Chapter Four

Looking at him was like looking at the ocean slipping by the boat in the early morning, the sunlight so bright with promise it melted on the waves. Everywhere she looked was more, more to take in, swelling the heart with life and all its facets, like the jewel it was.

His hair was soft under her fingertips when she reached out to touch it. His eyes registered that he hadn't given her permission to do that, but when she paused, just short of making contact, his eyes warmed, and she knew it was okay.

She had registered pieces of him up to this moment, but now she had the opportunity to study him as a whole, without the fragmented impression that stealing glances had caused.

His lips curved at her touch. Oh, that smile. That was what had stopped her heart and voice within five minutes of their first face-to-face meeting. She could tell he did it rarely, which hurt her, but knowing she had coaxed one from him warmed her in all the dark places of longing.

That smile did something to his face. It was a handsome countenance with the amber brown eyes, long lashes and heavy eyebrows, broad forehead. But the smile opened a door inside his soul, let her see the best part of the person within, and that best part was wonderful enough to sustain a woman for life. She was certain the women who had interacted with him on the Internet had been well satisfied by the experience, with his gift for words that made her shiver, but they had not gotten the best of him, which was contained and represented by that smile, all at once. It was intangible, but when he smiled, she actually felt her knees weaken and warmth spread from the knees to her neck, cozening every organ and system in between. It wasn't romantic; it was life sustaining. It was comfort and hope, a shelter against the things in life that stripped those things away. He smiled, and it restored her.

He closed his eyes as she moved her touch over his forehead, down over one eye.

"Don't fall asleep," she murmured. That smile broadened as he reached out, found her other hand on her lap.

"I could," he said, in that gentle and deep male voice that reminded her of the whir of a fan in the summer. "I feel like I could stay in this moment forever, even when I want to go on and see what the next one brings. As an engineer, I'm sure there's a way we could do both."

"If there is, you'll be the one to find it," she said, and believed it.

Mark opened his eyes and studied her for a long moment. He had done this a hundred times on the Internet. At the fetish sites he frequented most often, women were always sending him requests to take them on as a cyber submissive playmate, because of the skills he demonstrated in the stories he posted. The offers that were beautifully penned, that moved him, he usually took for a limited amount of time, seeking someone who felt as he did. That the intricacies of D/s behavior were just a primal way of seeking that moment beyond sex, where one spirit opened to another.

But until this moment, he had never tried to be a Master without a machine between him and the woman on the other side of it. If he thought about that too much, he would lose his edge. It was the first time the gift had been offered to him, and he realized, whether for good or bad, he wasn't going to turn from it. Especially since it was Nicole offering. He'd just have to be sure to keep it in perspective, and just as he was careful to do online, make sure she understood the boundaries past which they could not go.

"So do you want to know where we're going?

"I'd like to know," she said.

"There." He pointed. "Ballentyne Island. Have you ever been?"

"A long time ago." Nicole smiled, lifted a shoulder, which gave him another view of the slope of her breast. "You know how it is. I live only a couple hours away, but I don't ever take the time to play tourist in my own state."

"Instead, you just hop a plane, pay a few thousand to go spend a week somewhere that looks just like it."

She chuckled. "Yes."

"Ballentyne is a nice place. Very quiet. Only golf carts and bicycles allowed, lots of places to hike in the maritime forest, kayaking." He considered her, took his time. "I'll have to get you a change of clothes."

"Oh, I have money. I can pick up—"

"No." He shook his head, closed his hand over her purse before she could touch it. "You remember the rules, Nicole. Today, I'm taking care of you. Of everything." Putting his thumb against her lip, he caressed it enough to allow the pad to touch the moist inner area. He cradled her cheek with the rest of his hand, making sure his smallest finger pressed against her pulse, so he felt the jump there. "That's the way it works. Understand?"

"Okay." She parted her lips slightly, gave him better access. He took advantage, outlining the slick interior, touching the edge of her front teeth. Her breath teased his skin.

"Do you work on the island?"

"No." He shook his head. "I work on the mainland. But when I started to ride the ferry for relaxation, I explored all these islands, to see what new things I could discover just by wandering. It's peaceful. Particularly during these mid-fall weekdays, when there aren't many tourists anymore."

"So you ride the ferry all by yourself? Alone."

"Not today."

She moved her face against his hand, a quiet gesture of compassion. He knew she was asking to move into an area he was not offering to open, for her or any other woman. Though truth be told, she'd come closer to tempting him to do it than anyone else in his life, and that had been in the deceptively safe digital world. In person, she'd be far more dangerous to the world he'd had to create to keep his sanity. He told himself that, charged himself with it, and still got lost when she turned her head, nipped lightly at his palm before drawing back.

"So, I'm your latest discovery, then?" she asked, shifting the topic, as if she could read his withdrawal.

"No. I think I'm yours." He tapped the top of the Diet Coke can.

A flush rose in her cheeks, and the rush of emotions made his chest feel tight.

"You're a lot like that heron." He nodded to one of the white, graceful birds, stepping slowly through the marsh bordering the waterway. "You're already part of what's beautiful all around me. There's no discovery involved, just noticing the gift. And discovering how hungry I am to have something that beautiful and powerful in my life, if only for an afternoon..." His hand closed over hers. "That's not playacting, Nicole."

"The game isn't about pretending to be someone you're not, but uncovering who we are under all the disguises we wear." She quoted his words from one of their nights together. "'The pure form of the invention, without any extraneous material."

"You've got a good memory, but I'm more interested in what's going through your mind, from you."

She looked at their linked hands, then up at his face. "When I'm with you...I never feel like I have to say anything." She withdrew her hand, her palm damp to his touch. "I'm not sure... Why do you ask that, right now?"

"Because the best games aren't games at all. I don't want you to have any illusions about what this is." He took a breath, made his gaze hard and steady on her face, raised his touch to her face, gripped her chin. "To play this game right, you're going to get stripped to the bone in an afternoon. I've decided to accept your gift, but only for today. And that's it. That's all I have to give to you in the real world. I've got something powerful in me, Nicole, and I don't let it out to play, but you're teasing it out. If you don't think you can handle it, I need to know now. But if you trust me enough, I promise you, what's left when all else is stripped away will make you want to stretch your arms out and embrace the sun, not hide in shame. As long as you don't press it, and you're willing to walk away when the sun sets."

"How can you know you'll make me feel that way?"

"I don't. But looking into your eyes, and at the beautiful day, spoken in a thousand tongues around us, I can't see how any other outcome could be possible."

Her serious expression eased, a light coming to her eyes and curving her lips. "You're magic."

"No, that's you." He lowered his hand, moved it along the rippling edge of the blouse, not touching her skin, just hinting at it. "You may button one button, but keep the other open so I can see the curves of your breasts from this position next to you. You don't know how gratifying it is to a man to get a glimpse of something like that. The cashier looking down the V-neck of your knit shirt, watching your breasts, heavy and plump, all their weight resting forward as you bend and turn, unloading your groceries in the checkout line. Or to the man standing behind you in the teller line at the bank, watching you write a check. Your arm holds the checkbook pressed hard against your body to give it stability for writing, the breast lifting up out of the bra cup, pushing the flesh so it stretches the fabric of your shirt. To your co-worker, sitting next to you in a business meeting. You lean back in your chair, take a sip of your coffee, and the breast shifts away from the bra as your collar gapes, showing him the outline of it."

The smile was still in her eyes, even though the dark color had heated. "With all the young girls hopping around in almost nothing these days, why would any man go to all that trouble and eyestrain?" She slid the button closed and laid her hands back in her lap.

"Because one is being provided indiscriminately to the whole world. It's merely surface, goods she might or might not be willing to let you have, but nothing of herself in the offer except desperate insecurity. The other is an intimate, quiet area, a glimpse of a hidden place. The difference between a carnival and a secret garden. One you'll get tired of, or sick, if you overindulge. The other one never stops giving sensual pleasure, in more ways than you can count.

"Seeing that curve—" His finger rose, paused in the air just above her collarbone and then followed the line of the silk. He did not touch anything beneath it, just hovered over it while her lips parted, and her fingers curled into tight buds on her thighs. "—just a glimpse of what hides beneath the clothes... It's like standing in the desert at night, seeing a silhouette of a harem girl in her master's tent, preparing herself. You see nothing but the exquisite, intimate promise, but it's such a propulsion to the imagination that you can feel that dusky skin beneath your mouth, your lips pressing it, teeth giving it a light scrape as you suck with your lips, just enough to bring it to your tongue and hear the whisper of a shuddering breath feather your hair as she lies still, looking down at you with eyes the color of the most delicate, flavorful chocolate."

"Wow." She shifted slightly, her body as well as her gaze, and he let his touch drift over her cheek.

"What were you thinking, Nicole?"

She made a nervous face. "What I just said."

"No. That's not true. You won't lie to me, remember? The exact words that entered your mind, that made you look away from me." He gauged her response, and tightened his fingers on her face, made her hold his gaze with will alone and his confidence in his will to hold her. "Tell me." He made it gentle. The game of removing layers was as much persuasion as order, until it was impossible to tell which was which.

"You're...making me wet, with just words. Really wet. I..." Her fists got tighter, the line of her shoulders more tense. That becoming flush was almost to her hairline on her neck.

"In my eyes, Nicole. Right here. Look at me as you finish saying it."

"I thought...I'm glad I wore a lined skirt today, because my panties are already soaked."

"Beautiful." It was a very, very near thing, but he managed to get the word out of a closed throat. "I find knowing that beautiful. Now, ask me any question you wish, so you won't be afraid of me."

"Do you like chocolate?"

It was so unexpected, he smiled. Released her and leaned back. "I don't have a tremendous sweet tooth, but I do like it. Why do you ask?"

"Because you described it as if you really, really like it. Like a woman would."

"No, look forward," he said softly, when she would have turned her head to look at him in his more reclined position against the rail. He studied the small of her back, the line of her shoulders. He imagined her sitting there with her top bare, just the skirt hugging and shifting over the curves of her buttocks, pressed into the seat. Imagined the moisture rubbing even now between her thighs, forming a dark stain on the inside lining of that tasteful skirt. Trickling down the tender pocket of bone between her pussy and thigh to lubricate the crease of the buttock against silky lining.

"You know what excites men, Nicole?"

Her cheek tensed, and he guessed that she smiled. They were both doing a lot of that. "I've been told everything does."

He chuckled. "True enough. But generally, an aroused woman can make our cocks harder than the steel on this boat. A man likes to watch two women together, arousing each other, because their arousal is so internal. So mysterious and yet so incredibly potent. I've no problem believing that women are the strongest wielders of magic, because everything about them is connected to the fertility of the earth. We spill our seed into it, provide it to her, but she *is* Earth, accepting and embracing it.

"When I want to make love to a woman with words or touch..." His voice softened, and he watched her body tense. "What brings me the greatest pleasure is to stir her, stir that deep within-the-earth thing inside her, and somehow, when that happens, I get drawn into that womb, that deep rapturous place as well. Even if it's never consummated in the flesh."

They were approaching the ferry landing at Ballentyne Island, and he lapsed into a companionable silence with her. This early in the season, there were only a scattering of contractors waiting to go off, and a couple of commuting property owners. Less than fifty people lived fulltime on the island, and the remaining hundred homes were investment properties, catering to an upscale clientele who were seeking a quiet getaway at a staggering weekly rental rate. The few stores and shops that supplied their immediate needs were clustered around the marina and its elegant lineup of gleaming yachts and sailboats. The boats waited patiently with quiet metallic pings of rigging like soft bird chatter, until their captains would come take them out to sea and let them spread their wings.

The island was largely undisturbed maritime forest, so the landscaping at the landing transitioned from the whispering fingers of sabal palms, the dark needles of mugo pines and other native species to the more formal beds of lush beds of fall flowers—rust and yellow mums and rainbows of lingering pansies. As she looked over the rail, Nicole saw a moonflower, its white buds tightly closed right now, spilling out of an urn next to the ramp for disembarking.

"It's a beautiful place, as I said." Mark stood and offered her his arm. "Especially when it's quiet."

She rested her fingers in the crook of his elbow, savoring even that light touch, the flex of his biceps beneath her hand. She shouldered her purse. "You like quiet places?"

"Until they're over-discovered, as they always are. As soon as one human finds them, bam, there's a radar signal that goes out. Everyone wants to find a quiet space." He lifted a shoulder. "In the end, I think the only place that forever remains a sanctuary in the 'civilized' world is the bathroom, and then only those required ten minutes of courtesy, where no one will come to find and bother you. Ironic, isn't it, that in order to find a moment of peace in the world, we have to pretend we're--" He bit it off. "That we're relieving ourselves."

Nicole liked that. He believed in being a gentleman around a woman. He didn't take that position that so many men did, that just because women wanted equal time in the workforce and in sports, that they wanted to equally embrace the crudity that came so naturally to the male species. She liked being a woman. Liked being treated like one. She knew to the outside world, what she had with Mark would seem at odds with that idea, but he knew it wasn't. He treated her like a lady, even as he said and did the things he did to her, and that was what counted.

"You know, I have a friend who came back from Iraq, and he does that. Looks for quiet places. Places to heal his soul. Is that what you do, Mark?"

Mark refused to answer that question. "What's your sanctuary, Nicole?"

"You are." She startled him. "You have been, for some time now. Every week, my place to go to feel real, and cherished."

Mark looked at her open, loving face and knew he should be bundling her gorgeous ass onto the next boat and sending her on her way. Instead he was feeling the desire to keep her, make her totally his.

He had told her never to try to find him, and she had disobeyed. He hadn't wanted to see her face-to-face, because he'd known he wouldn't be able to hide how much he wanted her, so much that he felt like he had at last somehow conjured her, and maybe in a way he had. He had never maintained an online relationship as long as he had with "Shy Kitten". He had known he needed to cut her loose, and he couldn't. Not only couldn't he, he had been interacting with no one but her for eight months now. He'd had a choice, every moment, every step of the way. And it had brought them here.

"I've made you angry again."

"No." And he meant it sincerely. Covering her hand with his, he felt the heat shoot down through his vitals as she slid her fingers into the crevices of his, locking their hands together. "I know this is a mistake, Nicole, but I don't know how to tell you to go."

"You're my Master." She leaned forward, rising on her toes until her face was less than a few inches away and all he could think of were her lips, so close to his. "You can tell me to do anything, and I'll obey. Anything."

"Today." He struggled to keep a handle on it, remind them, for both of their sakes. "Just for today."

Her lashes swept her cheeks. "Yes, Master."

In that fashion, they stepped off the boat together, her foot in its shapely black heel with a crisscross of straps on the ankle, his in a brown loafer, comfortably broken in but not shabby. The sun was bright, but had the gentle touch of autumn light. There was something hopeful and wistful about the day, the emotional calling card of the dying summer merging with the harvesting fall.

"You're still angry. I can see it in your face."

"Only with myself. You… I shouldn't have you here, Nicole." But then he put his hand up, squeezed her fingers. "But it's nice to have company today."

"It's where I want to be," she returned, with a careful smile. He was beginning to fall in love with that smile. "It's nice to be invited."

"Wait here, I'll get us a cart. Stand over there by the flagpole, where I can see you." He trailed a finger over the veins in her hand. "I don't want you out of my sight."

She stood watching him, and he turned to consider her, let her see him considering her, as he spoke to the dock assistant. If he had been beside her, he would have told her not to lower her gaze, not to look away self-consciously, but as if he had given the command, she didn't.

Nicole had told him she worked in a bank. When she passed a group of men in the lobby, she probably tended to look away as she hurried by, a primitive instinct he was sure she was unaware of. Just as men tended not to be aware that in packs they stared more boldly at a woman than they did alone. But when a woman belonged to a man, and felt that sense of possession, she did not have that fear that caused her to avert her eyes. She knew she was protected and loved. It disturbed a fierce emotion inside him to see her look at him so honestly, so aware of what they were to each other, something he could not deny, any more than he could keep it for more than a day.

Keep saying that to yourself, Mark. You're sinking faster than the Titanic and you're looking at the mother of all icebergs.

He let his gaze linger appreciatively on her breasts, outlined by the thin shirt, the shape of her bra dimly visible beneath it, the curve of her hip that fit a man's palm, the legs he was certain were shaved smooth and made soft from lotion beneath the sheer hose. He wanted to feel them, wanted to know for sure. He wanted to know if she had kept her pussy shaved as he'd ordered all these months, or if it would show the tenderness that one newly denuded would. He wanted to inhale her. He ached to have her. A million desires he wanted to inflict upon her crammed into his head. One part of him felt like running into the woods, like a wild animal trying to escape his own primitive urge to claim, possess. Did she have any idea how much he'd wanted her all these months? How hard it had been to resist every temptation to meet?

Enough. It was time to get her some different clothes.

He drove his golf cart from the parking area to where she was and beckoned. She came toward him with the grace of an elegant pendulum, marking the short time they had between them with every step of those delicate heels. She arched a brow at his transport.

"Ever see *Chitty Chitty Bang Bang*?" He responded to the expression.

She smiled. "Is it going to fly?"

If it made her keep smiling at him, he'd probably trade his soul to get it to do just that.

If only he had one left to give away.

Chapter Five

She stepped into the cart, settled beside him, putting her purse in the alcove by the steering wheel. "All set."

"Lift off the seat and inch your skirt up so it's at mid-thigh. I want to see your legs. Part your knees slightly, so you can feel the air stroke you. Are you wearing any panties under that?"

His abrupt and blunt shift startled her, he could tell. He experienced a squeezing moment of relief, combined with panic.

Maybe she'll get angry and leave.

Oh, fuck. Maybe she'll get angry and leave.

Then she gave a quick nod, stains of color on her cheeks. She did it, a bit awkwardly, wiggling her hips to help her along, then she settled back on the seat cushion, parted her knees an inch and looked up at him.

"Good," he managed. "I'm going to put my hand here." His palm hovered a moment briefly, and then settled after the warning on the column of her thigh, his fingers caressing her kneecap, insinuating between her knees. Her trembling, evidence of the war between trepidation and trust, made him ache inside for all the things he wanted to do with her, give to her. "Leave your right hand at your side. Put your other hand up on my shoulder to steady you, and so you're not blocking me in any way."

She complied, and her blouse gaped open so he could see the upper curve of milk-white flesh as he had described it. Heat resonated from the dark shadowed tunnel between her thighs, reached out and pulsed against the side of his hand. "You've got a really nice pussy, Nicole," he said in a gentle, warm tone. "I can feel its heat. I'll bet the hose you're wearing are starting to feel a bit tight, because your clit is swelling up, wanting my fingers to stroke it."

"They're...they're lace thigh-highs."

"Lovely. That will make it easier to take your panties off when I command you to do so."

Her thighs contracted against his hand, and a little breath escaped her. "I didn't expect that," she said, easing her knees apart again. "I'm sorry."

"Does it upset you?"

"I don't know. There's something...exciting about a man talking about you in the same way he's thinking about you. I mean...is that the way you think of a woman's...you know? When you look at me, what are you thinking, really?"

She was struggling to keep some sense of balance between them. If he was online, he'd refuse to let her get her footing, but in this case, he thought he could turn her attempt against her, make her realize that keeping control was no longer an option. Perhaps for both of them, though he squelched that thought almost as soon as he had it.

"I think of you in both terms." He nodded toward his notebook. "The esoteric and the primal. The way a man thinks about a woman is much more crude than what I just said to you. If I had been talking to you the way I was thinking, I would have said this." He stopped the cart, turned his upper body to face her.

Since his arm lay along the seat behind her, Nicole felt almost as if he had her in his embrace, his rich amber eyes so close to her face, the warm breath of his husky words caressing her lips. "Pull up your skirt, spread your legs and show me your cunt. The smell of your cream is driving me fucking crazy." He cocked his head, returned to the conversational tone, but his voice stayed rough, his gaze on the pulse she could feel slamming against her throat. "You're a very hot woman, with beautiful tits that are just the right size. They bounce just the way I like them to when you walk, and I want to tear open your blouse and bite and suck on them while you squirm like a cat in heat under my mouth. I like your pussy, and I sometimes call it a cunt, because that word is rougher. There's a guttural pleasure to it. 'I'm eating your cunt.'" He leaned in, brushed his cheek against hers, inhaled her. When she shuddered, he dropped his voice to a whisper. "'I'm fucking your cunt.' There's something satisfying, possessive and animalistic about the word."

Lost in his eyes, in the sound of that voice, she wanted to reach out, dig her fingers into him and burrow. Stay inside that promise of passion until he turned her into a being of pure heat, the fire he roused in her roaring over them both.

He managed a smile, drew back from her slightly. "Pussy puts me in mind of a cat's soft fur, back arching under my touch. They're similar but different, Shy Kitten, and they both have their appeal. Ass is easy. Best word for it, can't think of any improvement for it, though a more poetic word should be used for yours."

She chuckled, startled at the shift, though she desperately needed it, before she turned her emotional response into an outrageously bold physical one. He didn't seem to require her to say anything further, though, so she calmed herself by watching the sun glitter off the water behind him like a framing halo as they left the landing. He followed the curve of the main road that wound around the marina and took them past the few shops, stopping in front of one which looked like a converted Cape Cod home, with three stories and a variety of colorful merchandise in the windows.

"Wait," he said softly when she made to get out. He pocketed the key and came around, offered her his hand as if she were alighting from a carriage. It wasn't necessary, of course. She could put her foot on the pavement and gravity would slide her out of the low-riding golf cart, but Nicole appreciated the symbolism of the gesture, which was far more important than functionality.

She felt her cheeks warm with the blush she couldn't seem to control when he touched her.

"Let's find you something pretty and more casual to wear." When she stood, he kept her hand, and with the pressure of his fingers, kept her still. "I'm thinking, size 7/8 dress, 34-C bra cup and size seven shoes."

"Sometimes I lean toward a 9/10 on the dress, if it's a snug fit," she said. "And it's 34-B, since I lost the weight." She struggled for something intelligent to say as his gaze dropped, studied her there with a warm interest that had her nipples tightening under his regard even more than they already were. "I know of no man on the planet brave enough to guess a woman's clothing sizes. You must be an alien."

He grinned, tightened his grip and drew her after him up the steps to the store entrance. "Just don't pay any attention if I take out my communicator and check in with the mother ship."

The shop had a fluttering assortment of colorful island dresses hung on a thin clothesline tied to the posts of the wraparound porch. Sitting next to them was a basket of wide-brimmed straw hats decorated with scarves that picked up the colors of the dresses. Necklaces strung with beads and uncut gemstones hung like curtains at the windows. Mark guided Nicole into the store, his fingers light on the small of her back, itching to stroke there, fan out and follow the curve of the spine, the tender indentations above the hipbones. Restraint, however, had its rewards. It had taken him a long time to overcome his basic male instinct to grope at the places that immediately appealed to his eye, like the biggest chocolate bar in the window. When he learned to look for more, to sample the fussily arranged truffles, the shavings of sweet white chocolate, the seashell molds swirled with white and dark, he learned to appreciate their form as much as their taste. He had learned how a woman, touched lightly and with restraint, could be roused to an almost fever pitch, whereas a direct manipulation of her nipple or clit before the right time could cause her to flinch. Or worse, steel herself to be still until the discomfort of being rushed passed and her body managed to catch up to the beat of her partner, lubricating itself from force of will, rather than genuine response.

So he kept his hand at her back, just his thumb tracing a wandering line across the silk, and he knew she was aware of that touch, as he could feel the heat of her skin through her clothes.

Inside, the selection of clothing had the whimsy that attracted the vacation shopper, but the quality was higher, and the colors more conservative. "You seem familiar with this place," she observed, as he moved her purposefully through the assorted racks of women's dresses.

He nodded, bent his head close over hers. "I've come in to touch the different fabrics. Remember when I've dressed you online, describing the soft rayon of a dress like this sliding over your stiff nipples, stroking the trembling, generous curves of your flanks, how that fabric would feel against an ass that had been lovingly striped by my flogger?"

He lifted a hanger with a dress done in a blue-green fabric, a muted teal like the color of the Caribbean closer to shore where it became shallow. A tiny row of buttons went all the way from the deep V neckline to the bottom hem, though he suspected it could slide over her head without unfastening them. A matching sash with chimes sewn into the hemmed edges was used to double tie the waist. He picked out a pair of low-heeled slides for her feet.

Nicole stood at his shoulder the entire time, watching his movements. He did not speak to her, but with minute touches on her waist and hip, as he turned and guided her through the store, he told her he was aware of her. By his silence he underlined that he was choosing what he wanted her to wear, and that the choice was his alone.

"Every fold of how this dress lies upon your body, how the color looks against your skin, how the waist, neck and hip lines sculpt the body beneath for me to see, matters." He didn't look away from the dress as he said it, just made the statement and then waited, half turned away from her.

Nicole went with instinct. Her fingers crept under his elbow, touched his shirt, lightly, an indication that she was getting the message and responding to it.

He turned to her, and her hand slid away, poised nervously at her hip, uncertain of where it wanted to be, could be. He took the hand in his, led her back to the dressing room, nodding to the woman reading behind the cashier counter. It was obvious the woman knew him, for she nodded at him. Her eyes lingered speculatively on Nicole, but she gave her a courteous nod as well.

"I want you to change into this." He hung the clothes on a peg in the narrow room, separated from the rest of the small store by a curtain. "We'll get a tote bag to hold the clothes you're wearing. A souvenir of your day on the island."

When his finger touched her face, Nicole looked up at him, trying not to show the jumble of apprehension she was experiencing along with the arousal, but he knew, of course. He knew everything.

"Remember, Nicole, I can release the reins at any time. All you have to do is ask."

This was the knife-edge of how the game was played. Between two face-to-face strangers, it was a different art form, the first steps into a new medium with the same intent, to create a masterpiece on an unspoiled canvas at first attempt. No wonder she felt nervous.

Online, it felt different, more like the canvas had already been practiced on before, by people who came to the game knowing what to expect. Still, it had never been like this, and she wondered if online would ever have the same draw for her again.

She didn't have to worry. Hadn't he told her that, over and over before? A sub only had to concentrate on the commands, on surrendering herself completely to her Master. She could trust him. She had to trust him, even knowing that at day's end it was very likely that he would rip her heart out of her chest, hand it to her and put her politely back on the boat.

"This curtain to the dressing room." He lowered his voice and drew her attention to it. "It doesn't pull across all the way. It has about a one- or two-inch gap at the end. I'm going to stand here and watch you change your clothes."

His voice was steady, calm, in control. She wondered if his actions were to scare her and push her away, or because he couldn't help pushing her toward what she'd sensed he wanted so much from her online. Everything. A total surrender.

He leaned forward, spoke so softly that his voice could only be heard by her. "Your nipples *have* gotten stiff for me, haven't they, Nicole? Prominent enough that I could see them through your bra, though I can't see them through your blouse. Am I right? Tell me."

"Yes," she whispered.

"Then I want to see." He held open the curtain, beckoning her into the dressing room.

She stepped in, and he closed the curtain.

Mark leaned against the wall, crossed his arms. A quick glance from his position told him that, to the lady at the desk, partially obscured by the intervening racks and displays, it would appear as if he was watching the dressing room. Providing comments to his wife or girlfriend through the curtain on her selections. Protecting her from unexpected intrusions or another shopper getting a brief glimpse of her through the narrow opening.

The store employee could not know what a significant moment this was. That this was the first time he was getting to see that lovely flesh. Flesh he had fantasized about, had possessed online, had claimed for his own a hundred times, but had never gotten to see.

Mark was not into humiliation. Public exposure was only useful as a scintillating threat, not as a reality, and he only believed in throwing it in to spice up the mix. D/s was about intimacy, the tethers of control and trust almost invisible except to the Master and the submissive. He suspected Nicole could see the lines as clearly as he could, lines they had woven and forged, ironically, without ever seeing one another. He could have gotten a webcam to see her months ago, bought her one, but he hadn't. The temptation to be with her then would have been too overwhelming. No, better to have the excuse that reality could not be as good as the virtual thing. He hadn't been able to bear knowing what the expressions of her face looked like when she laughed, or seriously considered an issue with a little frown on her face, or was aroused, as she was now.

This moment, this achieving of intimacy while in a public place, was as stirring as caressing a woman's pussy under the table at a restaurant, beneath a tablecloth. Feeling her open to his hand, become slick from his touch so that when he lifted his wineglass or fork he smelled her on his fingers, mingling with the bouquet of the wine or the flavor of his meal. That was a memory worth having. Full awareness through all the senses was what it was all about, and public arenas did provide that opportunity, in a limitless number of settings.

Nicole stood, looking at him. He nodded at her through the crack. "Put on the dress, Nicole. You're beautiful. You've nothing to fear."

She managed a smile, but it was tight, and he did not smile back, just kept his intent gaze upon her, waiting. She agreed to play the game or she backed out. That was the deal, and he was a Dominant. He would make her choose one or the other, not vacillate in the safer territory between.

Her hands lifted, slipped the second button of her blouse.

"Watch me, Nicole," he said, softly. "Keep your eyes on my face."

"I can't." Her head stayed bowed, looking at herself. "It's too hard. I feel too self-conscious."

"It's an order, not a request, Nicole. You don't have a choice, because I didn't give you one. Obey me. I want you to see my face when I look at how beautiful you are. Lift your eyes. Now."

She did, her chin trembling, her hands trembling, but it was not tears in her eyes he saw, but something else. It was a shadow of the protest women made just before they climaxed. As if what was about to roll over them was something they feared, because it was so overwhelming and such a mystery, the place where knowledge did not matter, only sensation.

Her hands slid two more buttons free, and the blouse parted, showing white lace edging the low cups of the shelf bra that barely covered the nipples pushing urgently against the thin fabric. She pulled the shirt free of her skirt, and as her fingers freed the cuff buttons at her wrist, the silk blouse fell off her shoulders, framing her breasts and the lace bra holding them. The movement of her hands, the drawing together of her elbows, gathered her breasts together and lifted them. The slim column of her throat begged for his lips, his teeth, his tongue, and it would be Paradise to ease from there down those fragrant slopes, tasting their fullness.

She slid the blouse from her, the cuffs now open, and he listened to the silk whisper over her bare skin. She reached back to unzip the skirt, lifting her breasts up and forward.

God, she was beautiful. The nipples tight points, the quiver of plump flesh as she reached behind herself. Mark almost groaned when she had to do a wriggle to get the skirt over the flare of her hip and her breasts shimmied with the movement.

She wore matching ivory satin bikinis with a loose tap pant fit, as he had envisioned, so he saw the slope of her mound through the open side. He did not see any hair. He wanted to step in, insert his fingers under that delicate lace tatting hemmed on the fabric along the edge of her thigh and run along the smooth expanse, petting her.

That was way too fast, though. At this rate she was going to give him a hard-on that would cripple him. The snug jeans he was wearing helped hold everything in, but he was sure the seams of the crotch area were starting to feel the strain.

God knows, he was. She started to reach for the dress, her hands empty.

"Stop."

He wanted to look at her like that for a moment longer, in her dark heels, ivory thigh-highs and matching bra and panties, a dark-haired woman with serious eyes and a rapid pulse tapping her throat.

"How do you feel, standing before me like this, Nicole?"

"Like I'm where I should be," she said, in a low voice. "And nervous." She gave a half laugh. Her hands came up, fluttered about, then settled back at her sides.

"I like that you didn't cover yourself with your hands. That pleases me. Why are you nervous?"

She lifted a shoulder, her cheeks flushed in that narrow line of vision he had of her.

"I'm nervous because this is crazy, and exciting, and disturbing, all at once. Because it seems like I want everything, but everything just boils down to one thing." Her gaze rose, held his. "And I'm thinking about what you're thinking about my body, how it looks." Now she looked away. "My thighs, I sit a lot at work—"

"Nicole." He inserted a hand, pulled the curtain out a bit, so she could see him fully. "Look at me."

Her gaze had darted away and about as she spoke, her hands coming up to wring in front of her abdomen. It took her effort, he could see that, but once she had settled, she did look at him.

"You're the most beautiful woman I've ever seen, and if you say one word to deny that, even shake your head, I'll come in there and spank that pretty bottom of yours."

He meant it, and he could tell she knew it. That jolted her a bit, but he wasn't going to smooth it over.

"I'm not anyone's idea of a movie star, not even close." He swept his gaze downward, making it clear he was looking at her crotch in the delicate panties. "But I've made you wet just by standing here, speaking to you. I can make you come with one touch or a word, after I get you aroused enough. Sex isn't about bodies, Nicole, though yours is lovely. And I want you more than any woman I've ever wanted in my entire life."

His palm fairly itched to carry out his desire, and he flexed it, drawing her eye, and her imagination, to the image that was rocketing through his.

He was used to writing it, not speaking. If he became too aware, it would make him self-conscious or stumbling, so he imagined that the words rolling out of his mouth were flowing across a page or screen.

"When I look at you, Nicole, I'm not seeing the things you see. I see a gorgeous woman, with pale skin, delicate ears and neck, in sexy lingerie. I can see the folds of her pussy, the creases of the fabric. She's wearing a bra that makes me want to taste those tits like a tomcat lapping up cream from a cup. I see a generous ass that I want to hold, squeeze, smack and turn it red with the palm of my hand. And your legs...take off the hose. I want to see your bare legs."

He had intended to calm them down, take the sensuality to a slow simmer. So much for that. She was quivering so hard he was concerned her legs might buckle, and he was sweating. But it would be hard for a saint to keep control when that kind of visual feast was laid out before his hungry eyes. The soul he knew and the body he didn't were there before him, and he couldn't control his reaction to seeing them together for the first time.

She bent her head, stepped out of the heels. Out of the shoes, she was several inches shorter than he was. With her head bowed like that, exposing her nape, he was struck by her delicacy, by her trust in a stranger whose words on paper had moved her. She deserved the best of all possible Masters.

His hand reached out to touch the crown of her head, stroke her, steady her and give himself the gift of her softness. Then he stopped, drew back before he made the contact or she saw the attempt. No. He couldn't go to tenderness. He wasn't strong enough for that. She had said she would be his for the day, no strings, no commitment at the end. He had closed the deal, and though he knew she wanted more, hoped for more, he knew it had to stay within those terms. He wouldn't plant false hope with his weakness. He'd been weak enough already.

"Finish putting on the dress, and then come out here. Take off the bra, but you can leave on the panties." He wanted her nipples rubbing against the soft cotton, wanted to see them outlined, their movements etched by the shift and ripple of the fabric. "Tell me you understand."

She raised her head, looked at him with uncertain eyes. "I guess. Mark..." Her arms crossed in front of her, a defensive reaction. "Maybe—"

"Nicole." He reached out before he could stop himself, took her cold and nervous hand in his, and squeezed it. "It's okay. You're safe."

He knew she wasn't. She was realizing just how vulnerable she was making her heart to him, and he'd promised her nothing but today. He knew he could be ruthless, but there were two paths to that ruthlessness, a wrong and a right path. He could put her on the boat, make her go home, never see her or speak to her, in the real or virtual world, again. Or he could make her live up to the terms of the bargain of this day. He had to live with whatever this day, whichever path, made him become.

Then those dark eyes focused on his face, and he saw the fear turn to desire, hope, a wish for something he could never provide. Still he wanted her, with a hard, aching need that didn't just stop at the base of his cock.

"I'm not afraid of this," she said softly. "I just..."

"I spooked you."

"A little," she admitted. "I'm feeling, sort of...naked here." Her mouth curved in a soft smile, and he knew the path he would take. He also knew that there was a fine line between ruthlessness and desperation. He wanted what she was offering, more than any man could resist taking.

"Put on the dress, as I instructed," he said gently. "I'm going to wait out of view, out here." He brought her knuckles to his lips as if she were fully clothed before him, not standing in two scraps of underwear. "You're not spooked by me, as much as you are by yourself. You've never done this before, and it's a lot like the first time you have sex. There's so much you don't know, but that your body craves, so it's natural to be apprehensive. Okay? You need to trust me. I want to keep arousing you, keep bringing you pleasure. You brought me a gift for the day, and I want to enjoy it. When the sun sets, you'll get on that boat, and it will be over. The boat's the gateway back to reality."

Her fingers tightened on his. "And if we don't want to go back?"

"Want has nothing to do with it," he said evenly. "It's just how it is."

She swallowed, lifted her chin, surprising him with that look of barely suppressed defiance. "Maybe it doesn't have to be."

"Don't push it, Nicole. You've disobeyed me once, in a very big way. You don't want to go there again. Take the bargain or leave it, and that means leave here, now. Or come out of this room in the way I've commanded you to."

The darkness was in his voice, in his eyes, and he saw it register with her. In her struggle not to step back from what she saw in his face, something volatile boiled in his gut, stirred by her rebellion. He wanted her to be afraid of him. He didn't want her to be afraid of him. Didn't she understand he couldn't afford her?

He turned and left her, to give her time and space to finish dressing.

Outside, where she couldn't see him and he was blocked from the sales staff person, he took a deep breath and adjusted his jeans to give his erect cock some breathing area. It had diminished somewhat in the course of their last dialogue, but it ached from the strength of the sustained full erection. He wondered if she would leave the bra off. In a way, if she didn't, that would tell him she had decided to quit, game over. He had gone a little overboard there, and he'd hate to lose the opportunity, but it would be a good lesson for the future.

Fuck the future. He wanted her now, wanted her not to run, felt like his whole world might stand on whether or not she walked out of that dressing room with her breasts loose and moving generously with her every movement under the bodice of her dress. He was male. It was hard not to let hormones take over. She deserved a good Master. He repeated it to himself. She deserved a Master who could reduce her whole world to shuddering, mindless climaxes.

He was that Master. He could bring her to that.

Today. Only today.

Today was all that mattered. He'd been down the path of his own destruction once before and nearly hadn't survived it. Might not have, if it hadn't been for the woman in the dressing room, who had no idea the lifeline her presence in his life each week had provided through that computer screen.

Unfortunately, he could only have her in the virtual world. For her wellbeing and his sanity, it was best to impose an hourglass timer on their time together in this reality, and make every grain of sand that fell count.

Letting her go at the end of the day wasn't going to be the hardest thing he'd ever had to endure. But it was going to be a damn close second.

Chapter Six

The curtain rustled behind him and she stepped out, holding the tote bag he'd bought her for her mainland clothes. The soft dress was a perfect fit, the shoulder seams aligned, the deep vee neckline showing a curve of breast in her profile, an unrestrained breast with a nipple shaped and visible under the gauzy cloth.

He wanted to go, force her against the wall, pull aside the neckline and suckle her there and now, until she screamed his name. She was his. All his.

Damn it, that's why he didn't want to do this face-to-face. Couldn't afford it. If it had been any other woman… But she had been his from the first moment he had met her online, had felt it through the computer as strongly as any real world connection. Hence, the actual physical contact was going to turn him into a raving lunatic.

Fine, he would be a lunatic. He had an hourglass, and it ran out with the last ferry off the island. For that amount of time, he would do everything he wanted to do with her. She had signed up for it. She wanted it.

She wants more than that, and you know it. And even if the lunatic didn't, the civilized man cared too much to take her so deep into the water and then leave her to drown. However, the dark, desperate being inside of him knew only want, not consideration, and he knew how well the civilized man did in matches against that being that operated only on primitive instinct.

Nicole, why did you have to break the rules?

Her breasts bobbed gently with her steps as she came to him, stopped before him. "I'm ready for whatever will please you next," she said softly. "Master."

Mark caught her hand in his. "Good," he said roughly. "Good." Her lips were full, cheeks flushed, and her eyes shy, but her carriage was proud. She was brave. Braver than him.

He paid the shopkeeper and led her back outside to the cart. She let him lead her, just a step ahead, responding to the pressure of his fingers. He felt her watching his hard profile, his unsmiling mouth.

"Are you hungry?"

She nodded.

"Snack or meal?"

"Snack," she said resolutely.

"Hmm. But you tend to need something every couple of hours. Your blood sugar gets low."

Nicole sat back in the cart seat. "How do you know that?"

"You told me once, when I asked you if you had any medical issues." He put the cart in forward motion, sliding his arm across the back of her seat so she would feel the press of it against her shoulder blades.

"Is that so I don't fall out?" she asked.

Mark nodded, wry humor tugging at the corner of his serious mouth. "That, and I can't keep my hands off of you."

She flushed with warm pleasure, like a schoolgirl getting her first note from a boy she liked.

"You don't have to," she said.

He slowed the cart at the intersection and turned his head to look at her. "If I start, Nicole, I'm not going to stop. That's why I set the limit, but even with that limit, you may be asking for more than you bargained for. Everything stops at sundown, and you get back on that boat, and we go back to what we were."

"Then I hope the sun never sets again," she returned, matching his gaze. "And I told you I'd give you more. I didn't set the bargain as a line in the sand. You did."

He muttered an oath, swung into the fresh market parking area. "Stay here."

Nicole watched him stride into the market, his shoulders tense. Lord, but the man had a fine, fine ass, and she blessed the good fortune that had him wearing a pair of jeans today so she could get the full benefit of it. She was somewhat intimidated to find he was so handsome. One part of her mind told her that, to the image-obsessed world, his features would only rate as "pleasing" or "attractive", enhanced by the well-toned body. But she saw the explosive sexual male energy beneath that and it made him potent to her senses.

The setting was perfect for their day together, and she determined she would treat it as a good omen. The little market that served the needs of the small number of residents and early tourist weekday crowd had the appearance of a coastal cottage, with basic staples and a deli inside, a winery and open-air carts with fresh produce out front. Mark stopped at a cart with fresh peaches and picked out several, running his hands over the fruit, testing their freshness, and holding them up to check for blemishes. He was thorough, always seeking quality. She knew that about him, knew his thoroughness had brought her incoherent pleasure numerous times. Apparently that attention to detail was part of the rest of his life as well.

He didn't want her here. That was obvious, as obvious as his desire for her. She wasn't a forward or aggressive person, so pushing forward when he so clearly wanted to push her away was difficult, so difficult that when he was out of sight in the market she reached into her purse, took out her aspirin, swallowed them dry to alleviate the dull ache at her temples. Took several deep breaths. Reminded herself why she had come, trusted the Fates who had given her the courage to get this far to get her all the way to the end...or the beginning.

She closed her eyes, letting the early morning sun coming in on her side of the cart heat her skin, the breeze off the river ruffle her bangs, play between her fingers, ripple the dress across her thighs. She was a sensual creature, designed for pleasure, destined for it. Meant for his pleasure.

When she opened her eyes and saw him coming toward her, she let that show in her face, in her hungry appraisal of his wide shoulders, the movement of the body beneath the faded shirt, that wonderful interplay of movement between a man's waist, hips and thighs as he walked.

He noticed, she knew he did, because a muscle flexed in his jaw when he sat down beside her, rocking the vehicle slightly with his greater size. Fried food hit her nostrils and her lips curved up. "What did you get us?"

He situated the two iced teas in the cup holders and maneuvered the cart out from in front of the market and about two hundred yards down the road, where there was a wildflower field still showing a scattering of posies. "Hushpuppies, made fresh. And a few snacks if you get hungry later." He tipped the bag toward her. "Including chocolate."

She moved her head strategically over the bag, so when she raised her attention, their faces were inches apart. "Everything I want in life is in this cart, it seems."

He glanced toward the back. "I don't see Russell Crowe or Liam Neeson back here. Or a little cottage on a mountaintop in Greece."

She grinned, even though her heart did a little jump. "You must have a photographic memory. Aren't most men supposed to catch about one sentence out of every ten a woman speaks?"

He looked down at her, but still neither of them had moved. His breath was warm on her cheeks, the bridge of her nose.

"I remember everything you said to me, Nicole."

She got her wish. He leaned down and placed his mouth over hers.

So simple. So earth-shattering. It was like the roar of the ocean in her mind, everything gone, only the laws of nature and their music filling her senses as his lips, his mouth, pressed onto hers. His hand came up, his fingers settling in a collar on her throat, holding her still as he changed his slant. He rubbed across her lips, catching one in his teeth, tugging her mouth open so he could taste her inside. She opened gladly for him, her fingers curled tightly around the base of the store bag, a discordant crumpling noise that barely registered in her awareness.

She made a noise of pure need in the back of her throat as he caressed her teeth with his tongue, stroked the inside of her mouth. Deliberately restricting her breathing, his hand tightened on her throat, reinforcing his claim, demonstrating his ability to deny or deprive her, as much as to be generous. As he was doing with this kiss, giving her everything and too little at once, explaining the spiral of need that spread through her and took over all her senses. It roused a hunger in her that quickly went to ravenous as he held her still and in check, just giving her morsels. She felt his own desire roar over her as well, but when she lunged against his touch, his strength, his warning growl kept her in place, trembling with a need too powerful to be answered by a kiss, only incited beyond bearing.

"Please," she whispered, begging for more of what she sensed was being held just beyond her reach.

His hand rose from her throat, his knuckles grazing her cheek. "You look a little pale." He cleared his throat. "We'll go eat over there."

She nodded, putting her fingers to her lips, on the impression he had left there, savoring it. "Our first true kiss," she observed, when she was sure her voice wouldn't break, much.

He didn't want to pursue it, she could tell, though he seemed to be as affected as she was. She saw how aroused he was when he got out of the cart. When he came around, offered her his hand, she deliberately let her gaze linger there, slide like the heat of damp palms up from his crotch to his face, ignoring the fist of tension in her stomach that told her that wasn't her way. Maybe it was his. Maybe being more aggressive would push him past his damnable reserve, his insistence on keeping her at arm's length. His expression went cool, but his eyes were flaming.

"If a quick fuck's what you're wanting, we can take it into those trees over there and you can make the next ferry. You'll be home in time to watch Oprah."

Nicole stopped in the motion of putting her hand in his. The cruelty of the words struck her in the chest, taking her breath in a far different way than that wonderful kiss and dominant touch had done.

She swallowed, sat back. "I won't let you drive me away, Mark. You can ask me to leave, but you won't make me run. And meanness isn't your way."

"How the hell do you know?" His fingers curled into a frustrated fist at his side. "You don't really know anything about me, Nicole."

"That's not true," she said steadily, though her insides quaked at the fury in his face, the barely leashed violence she felt vibrate from him, so suddenly roused she felt uncomfortably like she was dealing with a split personality. "You've been who you really are with me, I know it, and you won't make me not believe that. What you're showing me now are just shields, one of a thousand layers. The same type of layers we all use to get through the workday, traffic, the post office. And through the things that scare us." She stared at him, saw her words pass through him like a blade between the ribs, and she felt the pain resonate through her as if she had been stabbed by the same accusation. "On the Internet, once you get past the bullshit, description and preliminaries, it was just you and me. You just said so yourself. It was real. We're real to each other."

She slid out the other side, leaving him standing there. Nicole blinked back the tears furiously so he wouldn't see them. Mortified when he caught up to her and turned her around, she tried to avert her face. He gripped her chin in an implacable hand and held her still. She kept blinking until she had her emotions under control, watched him study her struggle without a word, his face unreadable.

"All right now?" he asked at last.

She didn't know if she hated him or loved him beyond all reason, and she suspected that it was not entirely contradictory to do both. She nodded, a short jerk.

"Don't be who you're not, Nicole. Not for me, not for anyone."

He loosed her face and stepped ahead of her, took her hand and led her single file down the path toward one of the tables. He bent his elbow back behind him to make it easier for their fingers to stay linked, which put their clasped hands close to the small of his back, just above the waistband of his jeans. It made it even simpler for her to hook her loose two fingers into the top of it, to tighten the connection, and she saw his shoulders tense slightly at the more intimate contact, but she didn't take her hand away.

Nicole noted there was a bronze plaque at the entrance to the picnic area, announcing that this area was part of the island's beautification program. A glazed picture showed what the area before them had looked like in its full glory in the spring, wall-to-wall blossoms of so many varieties and colors that they merged into an impressionistic painting.

The current reality of a warm fall showed remnants of that glory. Several varieties of flowers she didn't know, in purple, red and yellow, whites. Nodding in the light breeze, arranged in random individual spots or in clusters.

The three discreetly spaced picnic tables in the field were accessible by paths marked by stepping stones in whimsical shapes. The long body of an alligator, broken into pieces as if the gaps were under green water. The backs of turtles, the grinning faces of raccoons.

Did he know how hard it was for her, trying to determine what was displeasing to him and what was simply his denial of what they both knew lay between them? This level of aggression was not comfortable to her, not as a Southern woman, and especially not as a sexual submissive. A woman in love did what she had to do, and that was that. But she took his advice to heart, for he had always advised her to be true to herself. She would go for what she wanted, but she wouldn't lose her soul or identity doing it. Unless the price of her soul was to merge with his.

That resolved, she curled her fingers more tightly in the grasp of his, caressing the line of his skin through the thin shirt just under the waistband. Wondered what it would feel like bare beneath her palm, her lips, that small of his back, the beginning swell of his buttocks.

He straightened his arm, bringing her around him at the picnic table, which slid her fingers from that place. Firmly, he enclosed all her fingers in one hand.

She wasn't prepared when he shoved her hips against the edge of the picnic table, the backs of her knees against the rough wood of the bench. He trapped her head between his strong palms and this time kissed her with hard urgency, bending her back so she had to grip his waist to keep from falling. Forcing open her mouth with his, he brought his heat and need into her, one hand sliding down to band around her back, his palm taking a firm clamp over her buttocks. His fingers curved into the fabric and flesh, into the crease in between as he brought her pubic bone and the sensitive clit just beneath it up against his cock with brutal intent. She gasped into his mouth, clinging to his shirt at his waist, her grip slipping to the belt loops of his jeans to keep her knees from giving way completely. Her breasts pressed against his chest, her nipples sensitive through the thin fabric of her dress to any movement of his body against hers. When his leg shifted, forcing between her thighs, it toppled her full weight back against the table so she was half sitting on it. His touch curled between her ass and the wood, and she cried out as he brought the length of his thigh solidly against her.

"Just for today," he muttered. She wondered if he spoke to her, or himself, or whatever demons he fought, seeking a truce, a compromise. "Only for today."

She'd agree to anything, even if it shattered her. Cursing her lack of pride, she knew she wanted any amount of time he would give her.

He lifted his head at last, took her jaw in his strong blunt fingers, gave it a little squeeze. "Start behaving, or I won't share any of these hushpuppies with you."

She blinked, and when he feathered his knuckles across her cheek, she turned her head into that touch, closed her eyes. His other palm lay briefly along the other side of her face. She felt his forehead against hers, a soft breath from his mouth across her lips. Heard an even softer, "I'm sorry."

She nodded, not opening her eyes until he lowered his touch, squeezed her hands. When she did open them, he turned away, guiding her onto the bench.

He took the seat across from her. The benches and tables were small, so their knees bumped, and he gallantly spread his so hers were within the vee of his legs. Nicole looked around the field of scattered, late-blooming flowers, absorbed the quiet that an island devoid of engine traffic had.

"Do you know what these wildflowers are?"

He arranged her sweetened iced tea in front of her, pulled the paper container of hushpuppies out and put it between them. "The flowers that look somewhat like small red and yellow sunflowers, that's gaillardia. The plush stuff is purple blazing star, and those delicate pinkish looking flowers are lady's slippers."

She raised her brows, amazed that he knew the answer to a question she had just posed out of the befuddlement of her aroused mind to cover her confusion. "And what about the white star-looking flowers? I like those best."

"Those are Atamasco lilies. Delicate, aren't they?" He leaned back, fished in his pocket and removed a folded knife. He stretched from the bench down to the ground, carefully cut one bloom and brought it back up to the table. "Give me your hand."

Bemused, she did, and watched as he used the stem to create a woven ring that fit snugly around her middle finger, the tiny new white flower the gemstone and setting.

"We didn't kill it, did we?"

He smiled, easing some of the past few minutes of tension. "No. See, it grows in a cluster. It will sprout up another bloom in no time. It's not usual for these to have lasted as long as they have, though. Typically they have a short stint in early spring, but the landscaping company has been trying some different ways of forcing them into multiple bloomings to last throughout Indian summer."

"They're beautiful. I think if you lived here, you'd never want to leave."

"People spoil things that are best left as they are. That's our nature. They can't leave well enough alone." The anger was back in his tone.

Nicole stared at him, then slowly laid her palms flat on the table, leaned forward so her face was close to his.

"Then how about you lay me over your lap and spank me for being such a bad, bad girl? Get it out of your system."

Silence stretched out between them. The way she was leaned forward, so determinedly, shelved her breasts on the edge of the table, pushing the curves up against the neckline. It drew his eyes to their fullness, the shape of the nipples loose and unbound beneath the cloth. He suspected she'd laid her hands down flat so he wouldn't see her fingers shake. He wondered if she was aware her knee was quivering so much that he felt it through his pants leg where it pressed to the inside of his.

The desire in him flared hot and hard and before she could blink, he had her wrist in a grip she couldn't break. It startled her, and in her eyes he saw desire flutter close to a knife-edge of feminine panic.

"Pull the stick out of my ass and use it to beat yours?" He said it softly, a barely leashed snarl.

"Couldn't have said it better myself."

"Didn't I tell you to behave? Don't push me, Nicole."

"Then stop playing Jekyll and Hyde with me." She reached up with one hand, touched his face with trembling fingers. "Master."

It was that quiver that made Mark ease off, rein back the reaction she'd roused with only a couple of sentences. Her actions at the cart had angered him, because the lewd look had been calculated, unnatural to her. Her behavior now was still not a complement to her nature, but there was a difference. Eighteen months of learning who she was had taught him the difference.

His kitten had made herself live and be successful in a world of wolves. She was a successful loan officer in a prestigious bank, a manager of her division. She had done it, not with calculated deceit, but by forcing herself to draw on a reservoir of resolve and determination she cultivated in place of the natural aggression she lacked. She had a nervous stomach before every department meeting. Often woke up with a sense of dread at the responsibilities she embraced and that grew exponentially every day that she succeeded at her job and increased the confidence of her superiors in her.

Inside that successful businesswoman, he knew she was still the kitten, looking for someone with whom she could be herself, who accepted her whether or not she made the bottom line. She'd found it with him online, and now, in reality, he was the bastard, making her push her own boundaries. She had come here because she believed that dreams could come true. For him that wasn't possible, but there was no need to take that out on her.

Nonetheless, everything he channeled online was close to exploding and consuming her in one bite. And she looked to be the tastiest bite any man could ever want. She didn't understand he wanted to get down to the marrow of who she was and hold it in his hand, naked and vulnerable. Hold that power, cherish it, cherish her, but at the same time own her, heart, body and soul.

"What if I'm all Hyde in this reality?"

"You're my Master," she said simply. "I want you as you are." She tossed her words back to him. "You told me not to change who I am for anyone, not even you. How could I not offer the same to you?"

He had no response to that, but before he could fashion one, she continued.

"How about this?" She firmed that delicate chin, gave him a look out of eyes that he could drown in. "You said you'd give me today. All right, I'll stop pushing it. But no-holds-barred. No sniping or underhanded comments, from either of us. And then, at the end of today, if you've got the balls, you push me back onto the boat and that's the end of it, on all levels. How's that for pushing you?"

She had read his mind, it seemed. "All or nothing."

"All or nothing. I'll have today to carry me through the rest of it...if..." She couldn't finish it, and his heart ached, screaming, pounding against the cage it was locked into, as she visibly reined back her emotions. "Are you willing or not?"

He considered her, and the beast lunged within him. "I think you've set enough terms for one day, don't you, Nicole?"

She studied him another long moment, then she cast her eyes down. "Yes, Master," she whispered, relief in her tone, and pain as well.

He reached out, laid his hand on the side of her face, his thumb along the bridge of her nose, caressing there, over one lowered eyelid. She stayed still beneath his touch, accepting it, and him. Reluctantly, he withdrew.

"First, a peach." He took it out of the bag, withdrew his knife to cut it in half. "You need some fruit juice."

"You're good at taking care of people. Of women."

"Yeah. I've got a hell of a nurturing side," he said dryly.

"You do," she responded. "You've been taking care of me for over eighteen months. That's an odd knife," she added, before he could respond to that remarkable statement.

"It's a rigging knife," he said. "For sailing." He showed it to her, keeping it in his hand, not liking the idea of her holding the sharpened blade so close to those slender fingers, as ridiculous as the thought was. She was a grown woman, after all. But it didn't change his desire to protect her. "The straight edge here is kept very sharp, to cut lines quickly if you have to, though you hope that doesn't happen, because good line costs money. This curved spike is to loosen knots. But they can both serve a variety of purposes." He took up the fruit again, held it up for her inspection. "Like feeding a beautiful woman."

He bit the sharpened edge into the soft flesh, completed the circumference of the fruit, split it away from the pit carefully. Perfectly ripe, it relinquished its hold with a succulent noise. He laid down one half and extended the other, flat in his palm. "Eat from my hand, Nicole. Every bite."

Those slender shoulders, so resolute in her defiance of him, eased a fraction, but in contrast the tension in her upper body increased, creating an odd stillness to her as she leaned forward. She raised her hands, and he was about to admonish her not to use them when she set her fingers, like the tiny claws of a bird, on either side of his palm and wrist. She held onto him that way as she brought her mouth down to the cup of his hand and caught an edge of the peach in her mouth. The juices surged forth from the ripe fruit as she bit in, and her tongue came out to lick her lips at the corners of her mouth to prevent as much from getting on her chin or cheeks.

She took her time as he had taught her. She maintained contact with his flesh with her hands and mouth, the latter touching him often, kissing his palm as she bit, sucked, licked. The Dominant in him roared at the restraints he placed upon it, demanding the right to claim her, since she was so obviously demonstrating her devotion, prolonging his pleasure by not rushing his command. The tip of her tongue slid along the lifeline of his palm as she took up a drop of juice that had rolled down the peach side and landed there, and he stifled a growl of sheer need. Even the pose, the clinging to his palm, relying on his steadiness to keep her plate still, underscored her willingness to submit to him, let him feed her, provide her nourishment on whatever level he chose.

He was reading a lot into one action, he knew, but when she looked up at him shyly, her mouth wet and sticky, her eyes soft, he wanted everything she offered and knew she would give it to him readily, no matter the fears he saw in her eyes. For some subs, there was only one Master. She'd never accepted another, never fully loved a man until now. He saw it in her face, couldn't deny it when it so courageously faced him, a man unable to accept the gift he'd wanted and sought for his entire life, it seemed.

She began to sit back, but he caught the collar of her dress in one hand, leaned forward. "Cross your arms under your breasts," he said quietly. "Hold them close together, so you push your breasts closer together, and up against your neckline. And don't move, in any way, until I order you to do otherwise."

He took two pieces of chipped ice from his cup. Placing them in his mouth, he washed the tea off of them before he lowered his head beneath her jawline. Despite his order, she had to raise her chin to give him access. Those beautiful breasts got closer to his face as she drew in a deep, shuddering breath. He dropped the ice, maneuvered the chips with his tongue to position them securely in the valley between her breasts, against the heat of her skin. When he drew back and raised his head, she was staring at him with wide, aroused eyes. He placed his lips over the tender area to the right of her mouth, the corner, and began to methodically work his way around her mouth, cleaning her with his own. Tiny nibbles and licks on her fragrant, sticky skin, a little suction here and there to take away the juice, a tiny vein left behind by the peach, a piece of its flesh adhered to her upper lip.

Her breath was coming in rapid little puffs, caught somewhere between barely breathing and not breathing fast enough. His fingers slid across her sternum, letting go of the one side of her collar to insert themselves in under the other side, just the tips of his fingers stroking the curve of one breast as he cozened her mouth.

When he drew back, releasing her, she stayed in place, her eyes half closed. "Stay there, just like that," he reminded her. He took up his napkin, dipped it into the tiny pool of half melted ice in that crevice between her breasts. When it had absorbed the moisture, he washed her face with it, removing the stickiness his mouth could not remove, taking care of her, seeing to her comfort.

As he finished, she turned her head, disobeying him, catching his knuckle with the brush of her lips. As subs got deeper into their obeisance, it was typical for them to offer such spontaneous acts of devotion, and it tightened the muscles in his lower abdomen and hardened his cock at once, so his voice came out rougher than he intended.

"Now the hushpuppies," he said. "You'll take them from my hand. Anything you eat or drink today will be from my hand. You understand?"

"Yes, Master. I... Could you kiss me some more?" she blurted out.

She looked immediately appalled by her forwardness, but he shook his head. "Don't," he said. "Don't guard a single thought or word from me. I want you to speak every desire the moment you have it, unless I've specifically commanded you not to speak. You don't have to restrain yourself in any way, Nicole. Remember, I provide all the restraints to your actions. Nothing you feel is wrong." A smile touched his lips. "And I didn't kiss you. That was washing. I think we'll wait on any more kissing." *Or I'll lose all control and just fuck you half to death right here.* At her frustrated look, he shook his head, gentled his tone, even as he kept it steady, implacable.

"I said you could voice your every desire. I didn't say I would grant it. As your Master..." He ignored the surge of lust through him at saying it for the first time to her, face-to-face. "I decide when I grant your pleasures and when I make you anticipate them. Bite into this hushpuppy. I want you to feel its heat, its fullness, the sensual experience of eating it here, in this meadow of wildflowers. The sun on your body, your dress flowing around you. Being fed from the fingertips of the Master who is captivated completely by you."

Captured was more like it, but there was no sense in giving that to her. He could not offer her the same honesty that he was demanding from her, but he could at least try to make sure she didn't carry away a single thought of shame or regret for her actions. Not if he could help it. He would let her know in all ways how much he was going to forever treasure this day with her.

Chapter Seven

After they finished the peach and part of the hushpuppies, he took her several miles down the paved cart path that followed the coastline all the way around the eight-mile circumference of the island, parking at an access that was remote from the rental cottage section of the island. The beach was theirs, past season for there to be exercising tourists making the trek this far along the beach from those weekly rental units, and there were no private homes built along this stretch of the beach, though the realty markers suggested that would not be the case forever. He often came here to write and to think. Before long, the "over-discovered" phenomenon would force him to find another place.

"You spend a lot of time alone, don't you?" she asked. He shouldered the strap of a portable beach chair he had apparently rented with the cart and offered his hand as they mounted the staircase of the access that would take them up and over the dune.

"Why would you say that?"

"You're not uncomfortable with silence. That's unusual. I like it," she admitted. "It makes it nice. Gives you time to think about...enjoying the moment, a person's company. I guess, under that definition, silence would be the biggest compliment of all. It says you want to savor being with someone."

He nodded, his hand in a secure hold on hers, and thought she had the prettiest fingers of any woman he'd ever seen. The nails were manicured, for by his order she now went every other week to have them done. That in itself was appealing, that she had followed his will, the connection between them stronger than geography or proximity. There were uncomfortable issues involved in that, issues she'd come here to confront in a manner he could not permit, so he let go of that thought and focused on the fingers, tipped by those lovely nails. Not too long, but with graceful rounded tips that added the illusion of length to her fingers and enhanced the elegance of their movements. Her palms and cuticles were soft, unblemished. As he raised her hand to his lips, tasting, he smelled a feminine scent, some type of moisturizer or soothing cream to make her more beautiful and appealing than she already was.

She flushed slightly as he took her hand to his lips, just for that light brush of contact, and that told him something about her as well.

"You haven't dated much. Since your husband died."

"Some." She lifted a shoulder. "But they weren't...like you. A Master. They were nice, pleasant. But not..."

The capricious sea breeze caught the light skirt. She caught it with one hand and freed her other to catch the other side, trying to maintain her modesty.

"No." He caught both of her hands, held them away from her. "I want the wind to expose you to me, Nicole." His eyes gleamed with sensual intent. "In fact, turn away from me, bend over and take off your shoes with your hands, rather than sliding them off."

She nodded, turned slowly, her gaze covering the beach, as she couldn't stop the natural inclination to make sure no one was watching.

As he suspected, when she bent to remove the sandals, the wind currents coming up under the stairs and decking swirled beneath the gossamer fabric, lifted it as beautifully as if he had taken the hem in his hands and lifted it himself. Better, even, for his hands had only a certain area span, whereas the breeze could lift up the entire skirt evenly. It floated up around her hips, showing just a glimpse of the pale lower curves of her buttocks, bare where the silky panties rode up as she bent over.

She straightened rather hastily and turned, the shoes held in her hand by the straps.

"Leave them here. You won't need them on the beach. You don't have anything to be modest about, Nicole. You have a beautiful body, a delicious ass." He took her hand, started down the stairs. "So," he said casually. "If you haven't dated much, then you've never been spanked by a man."

Her eyes widened and she came to a stop on the stair. "Not...since I was seven. My Uncle John, for touching his rifle without permission when we were visiting the farm at Thanksgiving."

Mark grinned, reached back up, since he was one stair ahead of her, and tucked a tendril behind her ear. She had the largest eyes, and his suggestion had made them wider. Her lips were parted, moistening nervously, her pupils dilated. Signs of apprehension, yes. Also signs of excitement.

He touched her chin. "Don't rush my view again, and you won't have to find out what it feels like to get one in your thirties, from me."

"But..."

He stopped as her hand, still caught in his, tugged him to a halt by the simple fact she wasn't moving. She looked at him with those big eyes, and he knew what she was going to say a second before she said it, so his pulse was roaring in his ears, surrounding the words in stereo.

"I think maybe I need a lesson to remind me, Master. Not to rush."

"So you might," he said after a pause.

There was an observatory deck with a bench at the top of the access, so he took both her wrists in one hand, turned her and led her back up the stairs, to that point. There wasn't anyone close enough to see what they were doing, but he knew that she would still feel more vulnerable and exposed there. Indeed, she looked like she wasn't sure if she had spoken too hastily.

Tough. She was his, she needed a spanking. He kept his mundane life and the Internet play separate for a reason, so he could nurse the belief that his Dom persona was only roused in the anonymity in the digital world. In the mundane world, he was supposed to be a quiet, analytical man. Nicole had stepped out of the computer screen into his life and was challenging him. All his Master instincts, honed to a razor edge, had leaped to the forefront of his personality.

Be careful. No matter how long they had interacted on the Internet, this was all new to her. True physical Domination, where the woman was his as long as he desired the interaction to last, where his power of suggestion over her was total and brooked no disobedience. He was about to find out if she could take it.

He sat down on the bench, put down the chair and let go of her hand as she stood before him uncertainly. "Lay yourself over my lap," he commanded. "And take your dress up to your waist. Hold it there so I can see your bottom."

She awkwardly obeyed, half kneeling to lay herself over his knees. He caught her by the waist and slid her forward, so her feet lost purchase on the deck, flailing, and her hands grabbed at the calves of his jeans.

"Your skirt, Nicole. Lift it out of my way and hold onto it, so your hands are restrained from moving."

She reached back, which put her cheek against his leg with no anchor to hold her up, and found the fabric at the hem of her dress. He held her waist securely now, not inhibiting her in her task, watching her legs tremble as the fabric went up, inch after inch under her moving fingers, until it slid up over her ass. A flirty wind picked up the edge and flipped it forward to her waist, giving him a momentary unencumbered view, then she was gathering more of it in her hands and she had all of it clutched in her fingers, just above the crease between the cheeks, covered by the panties. He could see the pale flesh of her backside, the faint pink tinge of her milk and cream skin where the loose ruffles of the leg openings revealed it.

He made his decision. "A true spanking is done on a bare ass," he observed. He gripped the elastic waistband, pulled on her panties and jerked them to her thighs. Holding her in place with a flat palm against her back, he bent, took them down her legs, tugged them around her ankles and off her feet.

"Part your thighs for me," he said, straightening, his voice gruff. "As much as you can."

In her position, that was about a foot, and he immediately smelled the musk of her arousal.

"You're wet for me again, aren't you? Tell me, Nicole."

"Yes." Her hands tightened. "I'm scared, Mark. Master."

"Of what? You're so perfect."

"I don't know. Of this. Don't stop it or send me away for saying so. The way it feels to me. Like I want you to start and never stop. I've...fantasized, but some fantasies, you feel like it's not possible that you could trust someone to make it a reality in the right way." She pressed her cheek against his calf, looked up at him.

"We agreed to trust each other for this one day, didn't we, though?" He wanted to touch her, but he held back, watching, fascinated, as the wind rippled the hem of the dress over her flesh in a featherlight caress, watched just the fact she was exposed arouse her, making the curves of that delightful ass quiver under his regard.

"We did." She pressed her face harder against his leg, and he felt the surprise of her lips brush him. "I do trust you, Mark. Please do what you've always wanted to do as a Master. Anything. I'll obey you."

He nodded. He touched her first, cupping his palm and laying it lightly upon the curve of one buttock. She shivered at his touch through her whole body, her grip tightening on her skirt. Mark caressed her skin, tracing the crease of her ass with his blunt fingertips. She was soft and firm both, and he bent his head, inhaled the scent of a vanilla lotion, a skin softener. Good. That would make her skin tender, easy to turn even more pink.

"Five strokes," he said softly. "To remind you that your body exists, at least for today, for my pleasure."

Whack!

It made a marvelous, raw sound out in the ocean breeze, the strike of his palm against bare flesh. The curves of her generous bottom rippled as her thigh muscles squeezed taut in reaction, but she kept her legs open as he had commanded, though they jerked.

He put a little more force behind the second strike, seeing what she could take. He was strong, he knew, strong enough to make her feel the impact.

"Tell me if it's too much, Nicole."

"I want more, Master."

Following instinct, not daring to think it over more than a second, he slid his hands between her legs, palmed her pussy and found it dampened his skin. He wanted to probe her with his fingers, but he chose not to do so. For now.

"So it seems," he murmured, giving her time to release the reactionary stiffening she had done against the unexpected touch. He slid his hand free, brought down his hand for the third blow, then the fourth. Then the final.

The red marks of his fingers were upon her, and he stared at that, ran his hand over them, over her. He felt her breath rising and falling rapidly against his thigh, knew it was excitement, knew she could feel his cock, hard against her lower abdomen.

When the last stroke fell, she was trembling all over, and her hips were making a slight, rhythmic rub against his thighs, which pressed her mound against him, her desire roused enough that that small movement had escaped the notice of her self-conscious restraint.

She began to release the fabric and he laid his hand over hers, tightening his grip in reproof. "What was the lesson, Nicole?"

"My body exists for your pleasure. Forgive me, Master."

"Forgiven." He'd forgive her anything she did to him, ever, just for the gift of this moment. He studied the beauty of her reddened bottom laid out before him, her struggle to keep the skirt in her tight fists, stay vulnerable to him.

"You know," he remarked quietly. "I've always wondered about a woman's responsiveness just to suggestion. A man needs some type of tactile stimulation, his hand on his cock as a woman talks to him dirty. But a woman, I don't know. I think it's time for another experiment. I wonder what would happen if I just sit here, studying the lovely color of your ass, the suggestion of your wet pussy between your spread thighs?" He increased the pressure of his hand on her back, letting her feel that he did in fact have the strength to hold her there as long as he wished. "If I kept you on your stomach over my lap, how long would it take you to come?

"I'm going to do just that. Just sit here and look at you, Nicole," he decided. "At how helpless and beautiful you are draped over my lap, your legs spread wide so I can touch your pussy as I wish. I bet your nipples are full and stiff, leaned forward the way you are. Would you like me to feel them and see?"

"Yes," she whispered. Her hips pressed down, and he felt the pubic bone push against his leg as her hips made a sinuous circle.

"Good. I'm not going to, because I want your desire and need to be driven only by my voice."

She made a mewl of frustration, and he shifted his leg, which rubbed her, a movement that could be mistaken for a casual brush versus deliberate manipulation. It put his thigh muscle against her clit, which he knew should be prominent and swollen just below that bone.

He made himself be perfectly still for a few more minutes, knowing she would not make even those involuntary movements if she became conscious of her movements in contrast to his stillness. She was a lady, his Nicole. He reinforced the lesson of her obedience, caressed her ass, just studied her body without speaking, watching how the weight of his silent regard roused her further, until her desire overcame her self-consciousness. Her buttocks began to tighten and release reflexively, tiny movements, as if he was stroking her inside with his cock.

"How do you masturbate yourself when I don't command it, Nicole? Do you have toys other than what I sent you? I remember the first toy I sent you." His hand caressed the small of her back, his fingers tracing down the line between her buttocks, making her shiver. "I remember the wonderful gift you gave me in return for it."

* * * * *

Fourteen Months Earlier

In their short time together online, the Master had given her so much. She wanted to give back to him.

She slid the CD into the burner, positioned the microphone on the night table beside her bed, and sat back against the pillows. The ready light went on.

"I'm in my bed, Master." She cleared her throat, spoke self-consciously. "Thinking of you, the way I am all the time, it seems. I have the toy you sent me." She caressed the vibrator, with its clitoral stimulator and eight-inch shaft, the broad head. "I wish it was you, but I'm imagining your hands are wrapped around it, your voice whispering roughly to me to spread my thighs as you ease it in, so gentle, but so relentlessly at once."

She spoke out loud hesitantly in the stillness of her room, but as she slid it in, her body's eager response gave her the courage to continue. "I didn't have to lubricate it, because just thinking of you makes me wet, as you've trained me to be. I want to read to you. I want you to hear my voice change as the vibrator sinks deep into my pussy, let you hear as I get more and more…" She took a deep breath. "Closer to climax. I'm going to hold out until I reach the end, as I'm sure you would make me do.

"It's—" she expelled a moan, "—going in, sliding in so easy, and I've put the stimulator against my clit. I can barely sit still, my legs are shaking already. I imagine you're telling me to start it at mid-setting. You could start it low, but you don't want this to be easy for me, you want it to be as difficult as possible, because you know you enjoy watching me get aroused to the point of begging for release."

She knew that about him, knew he would smile when he heard her voice on the CD say so. Would he pass his fingers over the top of the player, as if he could stroke her voice, stroke her?

She knew he would. Somehow she just knew he would. She didn't have to see him to know so much about him.

Picking up the book she had chosen, she went to the page she had marked. She'd used the card he'd sent with his gifts as her bookmark, a blank card with a beautiful portrait on the front of a slim fairy winging through a garden of flowers. The handwritten words inside were just as magical to her senses. *You move through my dreams, bringing fragrance and life to them, like this lovely lady. I do not have to see you to know you are there, bringing beauty to my life.*

She began to read, her voice catching on the first syllables. Just the movement of her jaw, the intake of air into her lungs, increased her awareness of the vibrator's stimulation to her pussy. She'd never used a vibrator before, and the sensation was powerful, her inner muscles clenching in rapid response. And she wasn't allowed to rush a single word.

The song of songs, which is Solomon's.

Let him kiss me with the kisses of his mouth: for thy love is better than wine.

Because of the savour of thy good ointments thy name is as ointment poured forth,

therefore do the virgins love thee.

Her voice shuddered like her legs. "I'm wearing a short satin gown," she interrupted herself. "It's a dark green color. I've pushed the spaghetti straps off my shoulders and so the bodice is just barely covering my breasts...okay, sorry." She corrected herself. "It just tumbled to my waist, so I guess you'll be looking at my breasts as I read. My nipples are already full and hard, but they'd be soft beneath your touch."

I have compared thee, O my love, to a company of horses in Pharaoh's chariots. ...A bundle of myrrh is my wellbeloved unto me; he shall lie all night betwixt my breasts. My beloved is unto me as a cluster of camphire in the vineyards of En-gedi. Behold, thou art fair, my love; behold, thou art fair; thou hast doves' eyes.

"My hips are pressing into the mattress now," she gasped. "I can't help myself. I imagine you'd tell me to be perfectly still, but oh, Master, it's so difficult. I never realized these...make you...would make me so excited, so quickly. I want to come for you so much. But I've got to read to the end."

She couldn't listen to the disc when it was over, she knew. She'd be too embarrassed, think she sounded awkward or foolish.

Her fingers clenched on the pages. The vibrator pulsed deep within the womb, every hum of the stimulator like a lick of sensation against her, and that was entirely the wrong image to evoke to maintain control, as she imagined his sensual mouth on her.

You rushed that last section, he would tell her. Read it over.

And so she did, before she proceeded to the next.

His cheeks are as a bed of spices, as sweet flowers: his lips like lilies, dropping sweet smelling myrrh. His hands are as gold rings set with the beryl: his belly is as bright ivory overlaid with sapphires. His legs are as pillars of marble, set upon sockets of fine gold: his countenance is as Lebanon, excellent as the cedars. His mouth is most sweet: yea, he is altogether lovely. This is my beloved, and this is my friend, O daughters of Jerusalem.

Her voice was a broken rasp, a plea for release, but she held her cadence, even as flashes of color framed her vision, like lightning heralding a storm.

...And the roof of thy mouth like the best wine for my beloved, that goeth down sweetly, causing the lips of those that are asleep to speak. I am my beloved's, and his desire is toward me.

The book fell from her hand onto the coverlet and she gasped out the last stanza from memory.

Set me as a seal upon thine heart, as a seal upon thine arm: for love is strong as death; jealousy is cruel as the grave: the coals thereof are coals of fire, which hath a most vehement flame. Many waters cannot quench love, neither can the floods drown it: if a man would give all the substance of his house for love, it would utterly be contemned.

...Make haste, my beloved, and be thou like to a roe or to a young hart upon the mountains of spices.

She gave herself to the orgasm, sliding down on the bed, her legs rising, spreading out for him, her fingers latching onto the vibrator to hold it tighter against herself as the climax roared over her. Giving full throat to her cries, she wanted him to hear her panic and desire, all for him. Her back arched and she displayed herself to him, her breasts, her wet, pulsing cunt eagerly pulling on the vibrator. She wanted to wrap the trembling columns of her thighs around his body, hold onto him, take him into herself, even as she gave all of herself to him.

Then it flowed away, the storm retreating, becoming soft rumbles of distant thunder in her mind, her body weak and exhausted, the fingers of one hand caressing the cover of the book of poems, the other easing the vibrator out of her quivering body.

As she'd promised herself, she didn't listen to what she had recorded. She wrapped it up, sprayed some of her vanilla scent perfume into the envelope, onto the simple note. She did not have his gift for words. She pressed the soft burgundy lipstick imprint of her mouth next to the short message.

For you, Master.

* * * * *

Present Day

"No. I don't have any toys other than what you sent me."

Mark could tell by her flush she was remembering using the toy. He knew he remembered every moment of the CD she had sent to him as a return gift. Just recalling it made him grateful for the coolness of the ocean breeze, bringing him the calming scents of salt and moist sand.

"I...I was too worried about somebody knowing I bought them with my credit card, or seeing me going into a store like that," she confessed.

"But do you bring yourself to orgasm at home? Pleasure yourself without toys?"

"Yes."

"Tell me how. I want to hear the details while the wind strokes your pussy the way my fingers are itching to do."

Her voice was breathy, and he felt the tension of her stomach muscles as the pressing against his leg continued, became more insistent.

"I...I turn off the lights and put my cat out of the room because...I don't want her to see me."

She was so sweet and charmingly shy, and he could tell she thought he wasn't noticing those minute movements of her body. She was probably rationalizing them to herself. *Just small motions, just to relieve some of the pressure.* In the meantime her body was taking over, raising up the rotations of her hips, so instead of sinuous circles, it was becoming a slightly more oblong movement, closer to the way her pussy would want to be penetrated and stroked. His cock ached at the sight, but he wanted to see how it would go, if it would take her by surprise, her body's goal out of her rational control.

"And then what?"

"I touch myself under the covers. I spread my thighs out, imagine that you're holding them apart, telling me to hold them apart, while you touch me. Lick me. Every movement of my fingers is a movement of your tongue, and as my hips start lifting, pressing down…" She paused.

"Honesty, Nicole." He said quietly, his heart pounding in his own chest at the easy admission that it was him she fantasized about when she masturbated. "Give it all to me. Feel that?" He touched one light finger to her inner thigh, traced the moisture there, so close to her center she let out a whimper. "Keep going. Give it all to me. And spread your thighs out wider."

She struggled, because it was an awkward move in her current position, but she managed it, her legs spread out so far for him that the points of her toes barely grazed the decking, which meant gravity pushed her clit down more firmly against his leg and the breeze could whisper in the cleft of her ass, caressing her anus, adding to the stimulation, he knew.

"I…imagine another man, a friend of yours. I imagine he's under me, and I'm lying with my back on his chest and stomach. Each time I press my hips down in the mattress, it's really that second man holding my hips, his cock in my…in my bottom."

"He's ass-fucking you," Mark said. "While I eat your cunt. Have you ever had anal sex, Nicole?"

"No…I don't know if I'd want to. It's just so…I don't know. Thinking about it is arousing. It's so…"

"Submissive. To have your ass fucked. In a way the other isn't, because the other is more accepted. It's indicating that there's no part of you that you'll deny me."

"Yes," she whispered. "Mark…"

Her hips were jerking now, tiny movements, and he saw the wave of response ripple through her legs, her look of wide-eyed surprise as the orgasm took her unexpectedly, a small but intense wave that shot through her so she could not control her motions further. He tightened his grip on her back so she wouldn't hurt herself as she ground herself against him, her legs convulsing in small movements, her hands gripping his pants legs, her mouth fastening on him, teeth biting through denim to his calf.

He watched, fascinated, the quivering cheeks, the flush red color of the petals of her sex as she raised her ass high in the air and pumped it against his leg, a pure female animal, attracting a male to her by a wanton display of the delights she had to offer.

As she started to come off the crest of the orgasm, he caught her on an upward rise, sliding his hand beneath her belly, and curved the palm of his hand over her exposed mound, laying his fingers against her rippling clit, holding her in the air.

She gasped and cried out, working herself awkwardly and furiously against his touch, as the climax that had been on a downward slope experienced another tidal surge at the welcome stimulus. He moved his fingers very little, though he wanted to plunge them deep in her heat, but he contented himself with her wetness against his palm, the full firmness of her clit, distended with desire, and watching her helpless struggles, hearing her beg him with her weak cries.

His own breath was ragged, and he knew if she rubbed against him in just the right way at this moment, he would likely explode, the instant reaction as much a psychological reaction to her as the physical stimulation she was providing.

She was perfect, as he had said. If she was his for more than one day, he would buy her an elegant bracelet and anklet, make her wear them to bed as her only pajamas, and clip them with a leash of ribbon to the bed posts at night to remind her she belonged to him. That silky skin would be his to touch and warm by curling his body up behind and around hers, and he would shave her pussy every day himself, keep it smooth and soft with lotions perfumed like gardenias and other exotic blooms that reminded him of the clit and petals of her gateway visible to his gaze.

She preferred to sleep on her right side. Without the benefit of sight, they had asked one another so many questions, in order to create images. Of how they moved, where they preferred to spend their time in their respective houses, the rituals they performed to prepare for work, for bed. What they did when they weren't together. Wanting to imagine her in her daily routine, he had grilled her on her likes and dislikes, and allowed her the same privilege to a certain extent about him. They likely knew more about one another than most couples who lived together.

When he had her thus tethered, curled on her side, he would slide against her at night while she slept, insert his hand between her thighs, lift the top one up to give him access and slide deep into her warm cunt. He'd fuck her slow and easy from behind, hold her tight against him with a hand around that delicate throat, the other pressed low on her stomach, his fingers just grazing the top of her mound, so he'd feel every sinuous roll of her body along the length of his.

But she wasn't his, and he was getting carried away. There was the here and now, and that was where his focus needed to be.

Mark lifted her to her feet carefully, steadying her with a hand at her elbow. "I'm going to take you down to the water now." He watched her blink, try to get herself oriented. "I want to lay you down in the sand, without any clothes on at all. I'm going to sit and watch you, and write. And after a time, I'm going to ask you to touch yourself, and get yourself very aroused. But I'm not going to let you come. Then I'm going to dry you off, and we're going to go explore more of the island. Do you understand? Will you obey me?"

"I...I..." She was shuddering.

He stood, uncurled her fingers to get her to let go of the last handfuls of her skirt, something she had not realized she was still doing. He smoothed the fabric down over her hips and wrapped his arms around her.

"Lean on me, baby," he said softly. "It's all right."

Her arms came around him and latched on, taking the steady strength of his own body into hers, so he could almost feel it spreading out into her, as if what he offered had the power of the warm afternoon sunlight, mellowing and relaxing her both.

"Sshh…" He stroked her face. "You're wonderful. Take a deep breath."

Her breasts rose where they were pressed up against his chest, and he used that moment to change his position, slide his arms around her and lift her off her feet.

At his last engineering consulting project, the employees there had nicknamed him "Bear" for his burly strength. He'd earned it not only on the job, but in impromptu football skirmishes during breaks on the fourteen-hour shifts they'd had to pull to get the plant up and running. Still, he had never picked up a woman in a Clark Gable kind of way before, and he found he liked it. She was a nice armful. He took the stairs down to the sand, humbled and pleased both when she slid her arms up around his neck, and molded the curved side of her body against his.

The sun was turning the surf to blue violet, its foam to soft cream. It was still early enough in the day that there was a softness to the sun's haze on the water, casting a pink light on the sand with its rise. He wanted to watch her walk in the water. See the movement of her body, the dip of her head, the focus of her eyes as she placed her feet. The way the water rolled down her pale calves.

He took her to a flat expanse at the water's edge and lowered her bare feet gently to the sand. As he did, it put his chin at the level of her breast, and he brushed the bare curve revealed by the neckline with his lips, just a brief touch. He straightened, keeping his hand at her elbow.

"Okay?" he asked.

She nodded and lifted her gaze to him.

"Take your clothes off for me," he said. "All of them."

His instincts told him not to loosen the reins, nor draw them tight at this point, but to keep them steady, let her feel that he held them in a way that was gentle, but firm, not to be denied. Teaching her to trust and obey at once.

She reached for the hem, drew the dress up, up. He watched it rise and expose her knees, then her thighs, then her pussy. The shadows in the dressing room had kept him from knowing for sure, but now he did. She had shaved it smooth, as he had told her was his preference. Then her hips, the curve of her waist, the soft rise of her belly.

He reached forward, took the dress in his own hands. "Raise your arms over your head."

Her hands were shaking, the reaction of a new sub, he knew, her teeth chattering with it. If she let go of the light fabric, even in the relatively mild breeze, it could be carried into the water.

Raising her arms, she stood open to him. He lifted the garment over her head and took it all the way free, careful not to snag her earrings, those tiny cat paws and the delicate silver dangles beneath them.

He left her to retrieve her panties and the beach chair from the top of the stairs where he had left them. On his way down, he spotted a child's abandoned sand bucket beneath the stairs and took that along with him as well. The whole time he kept his gaze on her, standing completely naked by the water's edge. Though her posture showed her nervousness at his lack of proximity, she was beautiful, a pale Venus, with the shallow indentation of her navel, her breasts, the curve of her hips and buttocks, the white thighs. He tucked the panties in his pocket and came back to her. Opening the chair, he laid her dress over it, and dropped the bucket next to the chair.

Then he faced her. Her arms twitched, showing her indecision as to where to put her hands, though he was sure she was fighting the instinctive desire to put them over herself.

"Put them at your sides, palms flat against the outside of your thighs," he said. It was a difficult, self-conscious position to assume, almost worse than lacing the fingers behind the head, but he kept his voice soothing. Relentless, undeniable, and knew she could not refuse him, for he could smell her submission like a predator could smell a mate on the wind. There was an even calm in him, derived from the same source as the power of the sea. The power of nature's truth, of Dominant and submissive, the features that guided life only in the wild, supposedly. But people like him and Nicole knew better.

She had wonderful breasts, small, firm, the nipples tilted upward. He loved the shapes of her, the hourglass nip of her waist, the flare of hip, the body of a mature woman. A well cared for woman. His woman. Manicured, pedicured, waxed and shaved by his command.

Mark reached toward her, but instead of caressing her as he knew she expected him to do, he took her hand, slid his touch up to her elbow. "Down," he said.

He lowered her to her knees in the sand, and then, with gentle pressure, kept easing her back so she knew he wanted her reclining.

She was within the tide line, and so the shallow water washed in to her thighs as she took the position he desired. Nicole tensed at the cold, gooseflesh rising upon her skin and her nipples drawing tight. The water and the day were just warm enough for swimming, so he knew it was just the initial shock of the water's temperature.

"Lay yourself back on your elbows," he instructed. "And I want you to stay that way for me, let me look at you while the water caresses and explores all those places I want to caress and explore. And I want your mind to focus on how it's touching you. How it feels to have the water, wind, sun and earth touching you, loving you. Close your eyes, and trust that I won't let anything bad happen to you."

She nodded and obeyed, the simple acceptance enough to make him want to push her down on the sand with his body, spread those beautiful legs wide and take her, bond with her, make her his in a way that thumbed its nose at the civilized world of protection and precautions. Take her as a conqueror would, staking his claim with his seed, the imprint of his body on hers, the feel of her pussy clutching his cock. Accepting him in the simple, miraculous way she had just accepted his words. He wanted to feel her body writhing beneath his.

He sat down in the beach chair, already reaching for the notebook, though he kept one eye on her. She tilted her head slightly, keeping track of his movements even with her eyes closed, but otherwise lay the way he had directed. The surf rolled over her thighs, foam pooling in the trough between the juncture of her legs and hips, across her belly, into the shallow thimble of her navel, and receded again, leaving her skin slick with the sheen of water, breaking into beads that rolled down her fair skin.

He read it out loud to her. Her lips parted, her tongue coming out to stroke them, a rewetting gesture that he was sure would taste like the salt-laden wind.

"Don't say anything," he said. "Just feel. Nothing is required of you, Nicole, except you sit quietly, letting me see your lovely body and feel what I'm saying to you."

She inclined her head. Her breasts were lifted up from the angle of her elbows pressed into the sand. As the water came up higher this time and caressed her ribs, she arched her upper body and her throat, like a cat enjoying the sun.

As he watched her and continued to write, he could tell the moment that she lost her self-consciousness, a sense of separate consciousness at all, and simply became a part of the natural world around them. In the quiet, writing in his chair like this, the creative process opened him to the currents of energy that stroked her, so he felt part of the same. Caught in a dreamlike plane, watching her, he thought she looked as a mermaid might. Sunning herself on an isolated beach, her movements a sensual dance, a response to the embrace of the elements that caressed her.

Ribbons of tide came in one after the other, sliding over her, around her, infused with the warm light of the sun and its heat, illuminating her skin. The perfect interplay of light and shadow arrested every curve, long length of limb, the pale gold of her flesh, the generous bottom lip she caught in her teeth, revealing her arousal.

He kept a subtle check on their surroundings, ready to cover her with the towel packed in the knapsack attached to the back of the folding chair if he saw the distant figures of any other beach walkers or someone cresting the dune at the beach access. Her privacy was his to safeguard, entrusted to him. The first rule of being a Master. Always take care of your slave, put her wellbeing before anything else. But the rest of his consciousness was absorbed in her, the beautiful lines of her body, the fullness of her breasts, that arched throat, the soft mouth. He didn't want to do anything but stay like this, and now he understood the paintings of sultans, sitting on a dais, simply gazing upon their harem. Many men might wonder what that sultan was doing just sitting there. Why he didn't rise, *nay* leap to his feet, lunge to take his tactile fill of the sensuous beauty before him? But Mark understood the pleasure of power. The power of lust raised by the simple ability to sit, look as long as he liked, knowing that what was before him was his. His to take or not to take, her will subordinate to his own, waiting for him to pleasure her.

"Nicole," he said at last. "Open your eyes and touch yourself for me."

Chapter Eight

She turned her head toward him, met his direct, steady gaze. Her hand lifted toward her right breast.

"No." He arrested her in mid-motion with the command. "Your breasts are lovely, but it's your pussy I want you to touch. Lay back in the sand, spread your pretty thighs, and rouse yourself for me. You're not permitted to come, but I want you to tell me when you're so close you can't touch yourself a second longer without disobeying me."

She was worrying that lip between her teeth again, and she glanced out to sea, where a trawler was trundling back down the channel, headed out to the ocean.

"They can't see you," he said. "Unless the captain's in there with binoculars. In which case, he'd just see something so fine and amazing that he'll spend the day hoping to pull in a mermaid just like mine."

She smiled at the compliment, eased back, laying her body full against the warm, wet sand. The water was coming in just past her hips, so there was no danger of her getting her mouth or face doused. There was just the caress of the water on her flank and limb, coming in, going out, a slow rhythm that was suggestive of a rhythm he'd like to be making upon her. But when she slid her fingers across her thighs, parted them further and arched a little as the water's incoming rush struck her clit directly, he thought this experience was worth waiting for that moment to come.

Her fingers followed the surf, and she tentatively stroked her clit, a shiver going through her skin.

"Pinch yourself," he murmured, his voice like the rumble of the ocean, a command from Neptune. "Roll your clit under your knuckles like I would do. Touch yourself the way you'd like me to touch you."

Her fingers settled on herself like the light touch of a moth, and that was in fact how her fingers moved on herself, a delicate fluttering, a perfect capture of her clit between those two knuckles, the pressure increasing so she arched in response, drawing in her breath. The pads of her fingers sought lower, providing a caressing sensation on the opening to her pussy. She moaned as the surf struck her fingers again, providing an extra burst of sensation. The water splashed up, across her belly, sheeted her in glass, and then slid away, leaving drops like jewels on her skin illuminated by the sun.

Mark touched himself, his hard cock jumping eagerly at the sensation of his own hand, but he moved away from it after just a moment, continued to let his reaction grow just from watching her. At this rate he wouldn't be able to walk himself, let alone help her up from the sand.

He wondered if any of the great romantic artists like Michelangelo ever sketched a lover pleasing themselves. Perhaps he did, the sketch given in love and appreciative passion to the lover, burned at the death of the picture's subject, the sacred, secret moment caught forever only in the mind of the departed and the artist. He supposed that was what he was doing, scribbling down a portrait of her in words, a picture he could keep because no one would ever know the identity of the miracle he'd discovered on a morning ferry ride, no matter if the papers were ever found. Somehow, putting them to paper, giving them voice, meant they were now part of a larger, collective consciousness, never to be lost, inspiring and guiding other lovers in dreams or random, pleasant thoughts. His commands even at this moment might be guided by such a memory, inspired by someone else's imagination and openness to such an experience.

"Master," she gasped. Her hips were rising and falling with her movements, her body squirming sinuously in the sand.

"Yes, Nicole."

"I'm very…close."

"Go thirty more seconds without coming, and then you will stop. I'll tell you when. And don't change anything you're doing. I don't want you to make it easy on yourself."

"I'm not sure…if I can…"

"You can," he said sternly, sharpening his tone. "Because you can only come when I command it."

Her hand jerked as it played on herself. He rose, toeing off his shoes, and circled so he stood above her. He stopped between her spread thighs, took his one foot and gently slid it along her calf, up to her thigh, and pressed, nudging her legs further apart. Her clit was swollen and glistening beneath her touch, her mouth open, drawing air, her breasts quivering and high.

"Arch yourself for me. Offer yourself to me," he said, his voice rough and hard even to his own ears, but power and lust surged through him as she instantly obeyed, her eyes focused on him, desiring to please, hungry to be pleasured. His. She was his. To enjoy. To pleasure. To cherish.

He was losing his mind. He glanced at his watch.

"Thirty seconds." He knelt down over her body, laying his hand on her thigh to slide up and touch her fingers. As he did, his thumb slipped, inadvertently brushing her clit.

Her eyes widened. "Oh no…" she managed.

It was the final straw on a body on sensory overload.

Mark held her hand out of the way and laid his other on her, two fingers sliding deep into her wetness as his thumb pressed down on her clit, massaging it, taking the strangled orgasm to a full roaring throttle scream of release. Her free hand clutched his forearm, an anchor, her face working, body thrashing in the water like a sleek fish, caught above where it could breathe, every muscle fighting the inevitable.

"Mark, Master…" His name was a chant on her lips, her fingers clutching and releasing on his arm in the same rhythm with which he was gently working her, his body tight as a drum against a need that was building to epic proportions.

"It's all right," he said softly, over and over, though he didn't know if he was easing her or saying it as a warning admonition to his own body to hold back.

Nicole's mouth and eyes were soft with wonder at her own responsiveness as the climax washed away, leaving her shuddering. He'd missed that so much, watching a woman's glory in her own intense response to sensual stimulus, the shock in her eyes when she rediscovered something that had been there all along.

"You didn't believe you were a true submissive, did you?" He posed the question, aching so hard for her that he thought he could live on just a broken whisper from those moist lips.

"No." Nicole managed, stared up into his eyes.

"Even after the bathroom?" His eyes crinkled attractively, the sun outlining his body as he crouched above her, strong, powerful and aroused, making her ache to have his weight on her, his body stretching hers, filling her.

"Even then."

* * * * *

Ten Months Earlier

You will do something for me, now that you've proven you can follow my commands so well. When do you go to lunch at work?

Twelve-thirty.

At twelve-thirty on our Thursday, next week, you'll go into the ladies' room. You'll close yourself in a stall, step out of your panties and rub your pussy until you climax, and you will think of me.

What if someone...hears me?

I leave it to you to find ways to be quiet. Perhaps you will use your panties as a gag in your mouth, as I would, so you can taste your own arousal. You'll already be soaked throughout the morning, thinking of my order, worrying and being stimulated at once by the idea. Is your hand on yourself now?

Nicole snatched her hand from herself guiltily. No...I mean, yes, it was. I didn't...I wasn't even aware... She cursed her fumbling fingers and his requirement that she not backspace or edit in any way.

That you were responding to the desire of your Master to see you as a creature of pure pleasure? I will reduce you to pure sensation, Nicole, until you will be on the verge of orgasm just at the thought of sitting down at the keyboard one night a week. You please me, sweet, shy pussycat. You please me very much. But from now on, you will touch yourself when I order it, and no time in between. If you disobey, you will admit to me what you have done so I can administer punishment.

* * * * *

The ladies' bathroom at work had soft pink walls, vanity lighting over the mirror and framed prints of pastoral scenes. Her office building was a typical corporate America environment, tasteful and comfortable for employees and customers alike. They even put fresh flowers on the bathroom counters every few days.

Nicole nodded to the two ladies coming out. Sarah Collins and Etta Madison. Etta had worked at the bank's corporate office for over thirty years, and Nicole wondered at the lines on her face, a map of the paths her life had or had not taken. Etta had children and a couple of grandchildren, but lately Nicole sensed in those quiet blue eyes the wish that there had been something more. She was happy with her life, of that Nicole had no doubt, but she wondered how many people's lives lived up to their genuine expectations. Not just the castle-and-cloud dreams of childhood that one outgrew, but the deep longings of the heart. Had Etta herself lived up to her own expectations? In their minds, they were all princesses or heroes, fighting oppression, striking down evil, traveling to exotic places, falling in love with handsome, caring people. But the reality was a thirty-year banking job, the joys and trials of building a marriage that might or might not have turned out to be with a soulmate, a family to raise, retirement planning.

Nicole wondered if there was room for a person to want and have both. If she reached for it, grasped it with both hands, she would take the risk that she wouldn't have a hand left to raise in her own defense when she reached out too far to grasp that next pinnacle and missed. There was no safety net, no one to catch her at the bottom. Or would there be, if she was brave enough?

She worried about there being security cameras in the restroom, but then realized that wasn't allowed for privacy reasons. She'd checked on the Internet about it, and then checked the bathroom walls carefully as well, just in case. There might still be one behind the mirror, but it wouldn't be in the stall, and it wouldn't have sound.

Regardless, her palms were damp, her lips pressed together nervously as she chose the stall at the far end, slid the latch in place. She eased off her panties as he had commanded, being careful not to snag them on her high heels. The cool air touched her. Putting down the commode lid, she sat on the smooth surface. She wore thigh-high stockings, and as she touched the inside of her thigh, feeling the lace, it was not hard to imagine it was his hand there, pushing her knees wider apart, demanding that she inch that skirt back, show herself to him.

Start exactly at 12:30, no matter what. She all but heard the command spoken aloud in the room, silent except for the piped-in music of the local soft rock station.

Voices. Nicole froze as Jessica and Tina, clerks in the accounting area, filed in, chattering about the clubs they intended to trawl this Friday.

Right at 12:30.

She slid her hand over her leg and touched herself. Her satin smooth pussy lips were still new to her even after these handful of months, sensitive to the slightest brush of her fingertips, and she drew in a breath, holding it as Jessica and Tina continued to talk, several stalls down.

You obey your Master's Will. His Will is all that matters. Show me your pleasure. You belong to me.

"I belong to you," she whispered, a bare breath of sound.

She made light strokes over herself, and a response from her body infiltrated the unease of her mind, the needs of her flesh obeying his will, taking her protesting mind along, pulling it out of civilized constraints into a more primitive world. Her thighs spread wider, and her heels tapped lightly on the tile as she adjusted her stance. Her feet strained to their toes as her hips rocked forward against her touch. She tugged on her clit, dipped into the wetness growing inside her pussy. Bringing fingertips wet with that moisture back to her clit, she rubbed it more.

Jessica and Tina were washing their hands, then drying. And then it was just her again, her and the music. She was listening to a Sade song, and the sensual tones of the jazz singer guided her on, made the sinuous writhing of her body have a rhythm, like a dancer performing for her sheik's pleasure.

She saw herself in her mind's eye, the skirt rucked up to her thighs, lips sensually swollen as she bit down on them to hold back her gasps of pleasure, her legs spread wide. Instead of being appalled by the image, she felt wanton, desirable. She wished he was here, watching her, commanding her to work herself harder, make herself come for *His* pleasure. It roused a peculiar sense of power in her, perversely brought to life by serving his commands. She felt almost…beautiful.

Her fingers were moist, and she could smell herself. Self-consciousness was gone, overwhelmed by her own body's response.

Think of me. Of my commands, of pleasing me…

Of pleasing herself through His Will. She bit down on a moan as a hard, pre-orgasmic ripple rolled through her lower belly, tightening her thighs.

Let yourself go for me.

Her fingers worked herself furiously, no caution now that she was alone, and she let herself take a deep gasp of air. The echo picked up the sound, like the whisper of a tide rolling onto wet soft sand, over the feet, rushing back out, rushing in, rushing over her fingers.

The climax took her, and her hand jerked on herself, her heels skittering over the tiles as she convulsed. She caught onto the metal handicapped bar on the side of the stall and her body arched up. Her buttocks slid forward, slapping against the surface of the lid as she pumped her hips up, meeting his strokes deep within her, his body pushing her thighs wider as he drove into her in her mind.

For that was what she truly wanted. His hands on her, his mouth, his cock deep within her, his body shoving her thighs apart with every stroke, taking her...just taking her.

She laid her temple against the cool tile of the wall, her fingers pressed against her throbbing center. As she gulped in deep, slow draughts of air, several more ladies came in to perform their after-lunch freshening ritual. She pressed the panties bundled in her fist against her lips to muffle the sound of her heavy breathing and tasted the damp arousal she had carried around most of the morning, just as he predicted.

She had no more rituals, no routine to rely upon. She embraced the idea of being a creature of sensation, guided by His Will, trusting that straying outside the traditional boundaries she'd always followed would not lead her to destruction. Her soul was in danger of being destroyed within them, so she felt she had nothing to lose.

She inhaled her scent.

I obeyed you, Master. I surrendered to your desires, to discover my own again.

Chapter Nine

He was right. She loved to play online, had grown to love it with him, an online Master she knew was considered one of the strongest around. But until this moment in the surf, with him above her commanding her, she hadn't believed she was a "real-life" submissive. And that persistent concern had made her worry, even up to the moment she stepped on the boat, that he might not be a "real-life" Dom. The short time they'd spent together had dispelled that notion, but she was still astounded by how strongly the Master and sub dynamic in both of them had roused and locked them together. Nicole didn't know if he was as surprised as she was or not, but she knew it had startled her, how easy it was to submit to his will in person. Not easy, but irresistible. Her body knew who her Master was, in emotional or actual reality, and he was everything and more that her heart had hoped he was.

She found his moments of quiet reserve, his struggle against his own desires, as sexy as she had the flares of Mastery, unable to be suppressed. Now, at this moment, the latter was in full flame as he stood above her, looking down at her naked body. He offered his hand to her, taking both of hers in his one palm and drawing her to her feet.

He bid her stand there while he retrieved the sand bucket. Her knees shook, and she had to force herself not to cross her arms over her body, hug herself for support. She stood, open to his gaze as he returned to her, his eyes taking in every aspect of her bare body, including the wobbly legs.

He slid his hand under her elbow, even as he bent to fill the bucket with the water rushing around her calves. "You grab on if you need to." He glanced up at her with those serious eyes. "I'm going to rinse you."

She'd like to grab onto him with both hands. He had such a nice body, the muscles under the front of his shirt making her want to touch his chest, his stomach. That burliness that was comforting and overwhelming at once, the fact he was taller than she was, though not tall overall. Those strong, blunt hands giving her reassurance that they could overpower her, or hold her close as he wished. Or as she wished.

He had toed off his shoes, but otherwise did not worry about his clothes as he dipped the bucket into the water, the cuffs of his jeans getting wet as he drew up sea water.

Controlling the flow, he poured it over her shoulders, using his hand to follow the track and help rub sand off her shoulders, her back. Her body quivered as he caressed the small of her back, took his palm over her flanks, making sure every grain slid away before the flow of water. His touch was gentle where moments before, on the access deck, it had been stern. She savored both sensations and wondered at herself, wondered if it was the Mastery or the man, or both, or if they were so integrated into each other it was a moot question.

"Nicole." He drew up another bucket. "I need you to hold your buttocks apart for me." A corner of his mouth curved. "Unless you prefer the discomfort."

His teasing changed the direction of her thoughts, though not her desire. Still, she hesitated. It was one thing to do what they'd done together, another to expose a part of herself that she'd barely explored on her own, let alone allowed someone else to do so. But he was right. Writhing around on the sand in the throes of passion had resulted in less than erotic placement of the sand, and she didn't care to suffer that kind of discomfort for the remainder of her day.

She reached back, very aware of how his gaze followed the movement and how it jutted out her breasts for his attention. Slowly, she spread herself apart for him.

She had overlooked how thorough he'd been above her waist. His fingertips grazed over the top of her left buttock, just above her hand, and then he widened her by overlapping his thumb over two of her fingers, pulling her open further, and poured the water down the channel, against her anus.

It was an unusual sensation, one that made her heart pound harder and her legs buckle more, especially as he exerted more pressure with his hand. Responding to that pressure, she leaned forward. It canted her ass to a more accessible angle, leaving her helpless as she held her cheeks apart. His fingers followed the water down, stroked her opening, rubbing gently around the rim, loosening the grit that had gotten lodged in the tender crevices. She let out an uncertain noise between pleasure and apprehension, and her hips rocked up as he caressed her more firmly, this time eliciting a direct response as her pussy rippled in an aftershock. She gasped and lost her balance, grabbing onto his waist at the left side of his hip, her fingertips curling into his waistband. He didn't object, his fingers inserted deep between the cheeks now, massaging her opening, making her whimper further because it felt so good.

He slid his fingers from between her buttocks only when he encountered no more grainy evidence of sand, and then made sure her legs were clean with one more bucket of water before he allowed her to straighten up.

She was taken over, completely under the will of another, but it wasn't the negative lack of control one felt in a bad job or failing marriage. This was a good spiraling, a sensation between the wildest ride at the amusement park, and the quiet humility and tranquility experienced when confronted by something far greater than one's self, like the ocean before her. Or the depths of his brown eyes.

Laying a towel around her shoulders, he began to rub her dry, his hands firm and sure on the contours of her body, the back of her damp hair.

She held his shoulder while he dried her feet, her calves, sliding the towel up between her legs to apply rubbing pressure there while she clung to him and he watched her face, every change as he stroked her.

"I loved watching you come," he said, his eyes and voice intent. She realized then that part of the reason his words had such an impact on her was how little he actually spoke. It was as if he weighed and measured everything carefully before talking, so when it came out, it was pure truth, unadorned, everything unnecessary or extraneous taken away from it, strengthening the impact of it. She gave the gift back to him.

"I love watching you watch me." A foolish smile curved her mouth at the inane comment, but he tsked at her embarrassment.

"I understand what you mean. You know what my ideal is, Nicole?"

She shook her head.

"You near me, all the time. Your body naked, wearing nothing but a tiny clitoral stimulator." His hand shifted down, caressed her. "I would control it by remote. You'd go everywhere with me, and whenever I wanted to watch you come, I'd turn it on. Wouldn't matter where we were. A restaurant. Home. My job. You'd be mine to play with, wherever I wished, to give you total pleasure all the time. You'd only take food and water from my hand. Like a hand-fed exotic bird, trained only to accept the touch of her Master, nourishment from his fingertips. Lift your arms."

She did, but it was difficult, for she was weighted down by the sensual picture his words had painted, the decadence of it delivered in such a quiet, matter-of-fact way, in odd contrast with the vibrancy of his amber eyes. He was doing in words what he had been doing on the page and the screen. Stimulating her, creating images in the air between them, lending them power by the fact she could tell he meant it, that he would truly enjoy having her pleasure at his command if the real world they lived in permitted it.

Mark wished more than that. He wished he could just bury himself in her, make her his forever by doing so. Instead, he enjoyed rubbing the towel down the underside of her arms, into the soft, delicate pocket of her armpit, along the sides of her breasts, watching her twitch. Nicole was shivering, but it wasn't cold causing that quiver through her body. She was such a petite thing, making him feel clumsy and protective at once.

Something pumped through him at her vulnerability. Something confusing, exhilarating and dark at once. He wasn't sure what he should do with it, though he knew what he wanted to do with it.

"Why did you disobey me, Nicole, and come looking for me?" His voice was harsh, reflecting the shift of his mood, thinking about what he couldn't have, what she was tempting him beyond bearing to ignore.

"Should I—" She made a desperate gesture toward her clothes.

"No." On that, he was firm. "You're my slave, aren't you? Then you stand naked before me and answer my questions until I will it otherwise. Why, Nicole?" he repeated.

She almost laced her hands before her, but remembered halfway there, made herself put her hands to her sides. He could feel the desire to cross her arms, make some motion to protect herself, as strongly as if she were doing it in truth.

She lifted a defensive shoulder. "I've dated, I'm attractive, I'm...but you make me feel...more. Closer to something I want to have but don't really understand. I know the difference between emotion and sex and when you'd...be with me online, sometimes it was just the desire to see you, touch you, be near you. It was overwhelming. I didn't...I couldn't *not* look for you."

The breeze strengthened and a ripple of gooseflesh went across her skin, tightening her nipples.

He wanted to touch them, roll them in his fingers, see her dark eyes go darker. See her catch her full lip between her teeth again. But he didn't. He stayed still, his gaze on her face, demanding full honesty from her for breaching the rule he'd set, to keep her or any woman from getting this close to him again.

"How did you find me?"

"Do you remember when you decided to have us meet online two nights a week, instead of just one? On Tuesdays you said we would share dinner on opposite sides of the screen, and just talk. I started gathering pieces of things you said. That you were an engineer, that you did independent consulting. You lived in the South, on the coast, you took a ferry several times a week just to think-tank with yourself on projects."

She swallowed, her color high, even as the gooseflesh continued to stand out on her chilly body. "I started visiting other sites, engineer member lists, chat areas. You said you liked woodworking, all types, and you liked the Do-It-Yourself TV network, so I started visiting their discussion groups. Everything you said, I tried to connect the dots. I narrowed it down to six people." She took a deep breath, faced his unreadable expression. "It was then I hired a detective. He took a picture of all six of you, got all your addresses. The minute I looked at your picture and he told me you went out on a boat several times a week, I knew I'd found you. But I was still nervous about those first few moments, until I saw what you were writing."

"And is that all you dug up about me?" His eyes demanded an answer, and she couldn't lie. Not with him looking like that.

"No. He did a search of public records on your name, found your divorce. I paid him to get a transcript of the trial through his connections."

"Jesus Christ, Nicole."

She reached out for him but he backed away, his eyes cold.

"As soon as I read it, I understood why you didn't want us to meet—"

"Understood?" Suddenly she was on her toes, her upper arms held in his hard hands, her body and mind off balance, his face close to hers. Female instinct instantly recognized the threat of a predator. A furious male predator who could take her in a moment, run her to ground and rip her open with a swipe.

"There's nothing you could have *read* that would make you understand what it's like to have someone you thought you know turn into a vicious monster, slit you open from neck to groin and yank everything out for the whole world to see. You *don't* understand, Nicole."

"I wanted to." Her voice shook like her body before his anger. "I want to."

"Two years learning to suppress everything," he rasped. "And now you want to call it out, make yourself a target for all my rage and need. Is that it?"

Fighting past her fear, gripping her courage with mental fists, she raised her physical ones, as much as his hold would allow, to show him her open palms.

"Yes. *Yes.*" She brushed his ribs with her fingertips. "Take me, Master. Let all your pain pour into me."

"And if I forced you to your hands and knees, fucked you like a bitch in heat here on the sand, shoved your face into it with the pounding of my cock, and didn't care if I was hurting you? If I was goaded on by your cries of pain and distress…if I fucked you in the ass instead of the cunt, only wanting to humiliate you, force you to acknowledge you're mine no matter what I am—" He stopped, squeezed his eyes shut.

"I'm not her," Nicole said, her voice breaking. "And you're not the type of man who could do that, even to her."

"How do you know that? There were times in that courtroom, if I could have stopped time, I would have walked over to her table, past her smug attorney, and snapped her neck with my bare hands."

He released her so abruptly she stumbled, and when she recovered he was three strides away, his back to her, his shoulders heaving with his emotions. The hatred vibrating from him slammed down a force field that kept her from taking a step toward him. Having felt the tight reins of his control online for months, seeing the cool restraint in him for the past few hours, in vivid contrast to the blast of heat coming from him now,

Nicole realized the depths of his soul had been drilled further down than most men. He *had* learned to suppress it. From what she had read of that transcript, he had to bury it, or become the raving beast he just described. There had been no one to take his pain. No one in his life to offer him love and acceptance when he had needed it most. He was strong, a very strong man, and he had borne it. But the cost was this isolation, and she could not bear for him to be lonely.

"Maybe I don't understand." She barely managed words past the constriction in her throat. "But I knew the moment I read it, that this was what had hurt you, what kept you from being with anyone. I wanted to know. I wanted every piece of information I could get to get close to you. You wanted me to be honest, I'm being honest with you. I wanted you to know that I know everything. So you'd believe I'd accept you. *You*."

He did not move, did not turn toward her or give her anything. Her courage broke, along with her nerves. She spun away, snatched up her dress, intending to put it on and run, run from his anger. Her bravado had reached its limit, and she couldn't bear his rejection.

She let out a short, startled scream as his hands caught her waist, turned her. Her hands jerked up defensively but ended up lying on his chest, curled in his shirt as she stared into his eyes. They were filled with pain, the terrible fury of a moment ago swallowed by the ache of regret.

"I *am* a monster," he said quietly, and she could almost see the threads of his restraint reweaving themselves before her, reining back all that simmering emotion. "Here." He pressed away her tears with the towel, hiding her face in the soft terrycloth. "I never want to make you cry, Nicole. Never."

It was a whisper, those words spoken against her hair. She lifted her face and he had his lips on hers.

Mark hadn't planned it, but he had to kiss her, and then there was just her. His Nicole, the parting of her lips beneath the sudden all-encompassing demand that surged through him, made him deepen it, take his hands to a more secure grip around her bare back, tugging the dress away from between them. She clung to it only a moment before she let the protection go, submitting to his desires, brave, foolish creature that she was.

He touched the nape of her neck, bringing the full glory of her unclothed body against his clothed one, the first time he'd had the erotic sensation in anything other than his mind.

"Lift your arms for me again," he ordered, reluctantly lifting his head.

Nicole did, hesitantly. Picking up the towel, he shook it out and wrapped it around her, knotted and tucked it in at her breasts, his fingers pressing the plump top curves. She watched him shrug out of his button-down shirt, revealing a black T-shirt beneath it. He threaded her hands through the teal shirt, rolling down the sleeves to cover her arms, and adjusted the fabric up to her shoulders.

"To keep you warm until you fully dry," he told her. "Come sit with me."

He took a seat in the beach chair, put a second folded towel on the expanse of sand between his feet and brought her down to kneel there before him. "Put your hand on either of my knees," he instructed. "So I can see all of you. And tell me *when* you made this decision to start looking for me." He touched her mouth. "I promise that I won't get angry again. That was wrong."

She lifted a shoulder. "You've a right to be angry. It did sound sort of criminal."

"It *is* criminal. Online identity is supposed to be guarded, particularly on the BDSM sites." He dispelled her tension with the raw tenderness and trace of humor in his face. "But you found me. You strike me as a good girl, most of the time." He flicked her under her chin, the look he gave her creating a pulse of reaction from between her legs. "So I'm sure you didn't do anything too awful. Let's...let's stay away from the rest for awhile, all right?"

"I'm not afraid of you, Master."

He studied her. "You should be, Nicole. Because I'm the bastard who's going to take everything you offer today, and then some." His wolf's eyes sent a shiver down her spine. "And then give you nothing but a ferry ticket back to the mainland."

She nodded, blinking hard, and he cupped her face in his hand, took her forehead back to his chest a moment, held her there firmly. "No tears, Kitten. You'll destroy me with your tears. You've told me how you found me. Tell me when you decided to do this."

"The night...the night you told me your name. When you told me your first name."

"The night you had a nightmare and were afraid."

Chapter Ten
Six Months Earlier

It was three in the morning. He wouldn't be at their message link, as he would be when they played together twice a week. Nicole rejected the word in her mind even as she thought it. "Play" suggested children on a playground, a game easily deserted or dropped at the call to dinner or something more interesting, not the overpowering flood of emotions and physical aftermath that she took away from every one of their sessions together, even the dinners. She'd stopped thinking about whether he had sessions with anyone else. She couldn't bear to consider it. He made her feel so special every time they were "together", more special than any man had ever made her feel in person. She didn't know if that was pathetic, or if it was no different than the roll of the dice with the meeting of two people, in any reality.

I wish you were here.

She logged in and typed it as if he was there, though she knew when she logged off, the message would be erased and he'd never know she'd sought him at the most hopeless hour of the night. But she supposed visiting their chat room was the equivalent of wearing a lover's clothes when he was away, savoring the closest essence of him she could, taking comfort in the impression of his presence.

If you were here, I could tell you how lonely and afraid I am. I had a nightmare, and I'm so cold. I wish I had something... She took her thought and put it on the screen. ...Like your shirt, to keep around me at night, so it won't be so lonely here.

How can you be lonely when I'm here to warm you? What are you afraid of, love?

He was there. Her fingers froze in shock, caught blurting out her feelings without calculation, exposing her needs in raw form. But he'd taught her some things about submitting these past months. One of those things was that true surrender meant no games, no guarding of words. A submissive was to be completely open and forthright with her Master, no artifice. But even so, this was new territory, somehow even more frightening than the sexual areas they had explored in detail, or the casual intimacies of their dinner where they skirted around the details of the lives they lived apart, walking a line between concealing identities and drawing a truthful picture of who they each were.

She'd come, just from his words on the screen. Followed his direction with toys he'd sent to her and ordered her to use. Worn provocative lingerie under her work clothes so he could think of her during the day wearing them. But this was more personal somehow than even that.

Are you refusing to answer your Master? Don't be afraid, Kitten.

No. **she typed.** I just...I thought you wouldn't be there, but I wanted to be close to you.

Tell me about your nightmare.

I've been having dreams like it for a while. It doesn't sound that scary, and in real life, it wouldn't be, but in the dream, it is.

Go on. I'm here. What are you wearing? The truth.

I always tell you the truth, Master. **Though she typed it in reluctantly.** A flannel nightgown. It's comforting. *Not as comforting as your arms would be around me.*

It starts out dark. Everything's dark. It's raining and I'm walking on the street. I'm not wearing anything...and it's cold, but no one notices me. Which you would think would be a good thing, since I'm walking down the street naked, but it isn't. That's not the really scary thing, though. The scary thing is that the sun comes out, but it's still raining

```
wherever I am, and I'm still wet and cold. The
dream seems to go on forever and ever, and I'm
so tired, I just can't stop walking. I know
somehow if I stop, something worse will happen.
Yet the more I walk, the more frightened I'm
getting, until I'm almost choked with it.
```

She stopped, because her fingers were stumbling on the keyboard, making her miss keystrokes, creating typos.

```
Turn on your audio.
```

He had bought her voice recognition software and a wireless headset so she would not be bound to the keyboard when he wished it. The computer would type the oral comments and responses as they emitted through the machine. The first time she had heard his voice, a soft, deceptively mild Southern drawl, she had wanted to hear him speak forever. She'd bought a recording feature almost immediately, not telling him she had done so. Not because he might insist on paying for it, but because she was afraid he'd forbid her to buy it. Now she went to sleep to the sound of that voice, wished she could take it into her dreams to stave off her nightmares.

"I've done it," she said, and watched the words appear on her screen as they went through the microphone on the headset she slipped over her ears.

"Wrap your arms around yourself," he said, the computer voice loud in the quiet room at this dead hour of the night. She turned it down a few notches. "Close your eyes."

She did.

"Take your hand… Is it warm?"

"No."

"Then first put it between your thighs to warm it. I'll wait."

"Okay."

"Put your hand against your face. Spread your fingers out, so you're cupping your jaw, your fingers on your cheek. Stroke your jaw, then slide down to your throat, then come back up.

This is my hand touching you, comforting you. Lie down on the floor, on your right side, as if you're in your bed."

She slid out of the chair and eased down to the floor.

"Bend one arm at the elbow, wrap it around your waist, fingers beneath your hip and the floor. Put your other hand to your temple. Stroke your hair. Slow, firm strokes, as I do them. Are your eyes closed?"

"Yes."

"Yes, what?"

"Yes, Master." She took comfort in the reminder, clinging to it like a child's blanket.

"I'm behind you, my thighs pressed under your thighs, my back to your back. That luscious ass of yours is cradled up against me. Against my cock. It's soft now, not because I don't desire you with every breath, but because this moment is about so much more than that. I'm here, and I'm with you. Keep stroking. Are you feeling me? Be truthful."

"Not as much as I want to, but yes," she whispered, wishing it was real, but willed enough by his voice that she could pretend it was, believe it was.

"Good. You keep doing that, love. Keep doing that."

"Master?"

"Yes, Kitten?"

"Will you...may I ask what your first name is?"

There was a long silence, and she waited, holding herself with the imagined pressure of his arm through the tactile sensation of her own at her waist, her fingers becoming his strong ones, stroking her hair without ceasing.

"Mark."

* * * * *

Present Day

"You wouldn't let me tell you my name, but a week later, you sent me two gifts." Nicole lifted her gaze. "You sent me…your collar, and one of your flannel shirts. Your note said, *'To remind you I'm with you. Always.'* I put the shirt to my face and inhaled your scent for the very first time. It was there, even under the laundry detergent. My first physical taste of you, something your hands had touched, that your body had touched. And I knew why animals are able to mate for life just from inhaling a scent. I knew I was yours, Mark.

"I wanted to put on the collar the next time we were together, but you told me to wear it just like the shirt, when I needed to feel you with me. After that, you never spoke of those two things again, and you forbade me to talk about them." *Because he knew he'd crossed over a line when he sent them, and he was afraid to encourage her further.* He'd never said that, but Nicole knew that was the reason, especially now, seeing the struggle in his face.

Mark shook his head. "You deserve better, Nicole, than a reclusive engineer that spends all his time in his head."

"Thinking about things like this." She reached over his knee, closed her hand on the notebook, laid on the top of the bag. "Wanting to do them, wanting to share those thoughts and actions with somebody, but maybe afraid to do so because he's tried before and it worked out badly. Horribly."

"That would be predictable, clichéd dysfunctionality," he said lightly, but there was a tense set to his jaw, and she knew she was pushing him again.

Nicole shifted her touch to his hand on his thigh. "Predictable doesn't mean trivial. Hundreds of people get murdered every day, and I don't think they stand in line at the Pearly Gates and say, 'Well, I was murdered, but that's boring, you don't want to hear about that'."

That startled a smile out of him. "You have such an odd mind."

"So do you, if you haven't noticed. I wanted to meet you, you remember? I asked a dozen times."

"I told you that reality is overrated," he recalled.

"And I wondered who had hurt you so much, though I wasn't brave enough to ask it again after that last time, the time you left me during our dinner, because I pushed too hard and I was afraid you wouldn't come back."

She didn't know he'd had no choice. That at that point their two nights a week had become the only thing in his life that meant something, the source point that was raising him from the dead. Bringing color back into his life, spilling over from those two days into the rest of the week, bringing interest back to his world, so that a man who had been reduced to seeing the world in lackluster tones of black and white started seeing it as vibrant, sensual life again, open with possibilities. It was about that time Mark learned his heart had been broken, not shattered. That it was possible for a shy woman with a generous heart to mend it, if not completely heal it. And because of that terrifying revelation, he'd almost walked away when she gave him the opening, not willing to risk having it destroyed again.

* * * * *

Four Months Earlier

On the Tuesdays when they had dinner together, he had a standing order for her to lay out her meal, then undress and sit naked while they talked over the computer voice feature.

"I've remodeled the house, painted the rooms, made them brighter," she said. "Added some eccentric touches. I've been ordering prints online I like and then I change the room around the picture. I have one room I've done in just black and white erotic artwork. My master bathroom."

"You're remaking yourself."

"No... I think I'm rediscovering myself, or discovering who I became when I wasn't paying attention. In fact, I know I am. I had settled, and I'm realizing life is too precious to settle for what isn't true to myself, my nature. I don't know why we let fear stop us from figuring out who we are."

"Fear of losing what we have?"

"But what if what we have isn't who we are, then what have we lost?" She played with her fork, shifted on the chair, enjoyed the heightened sensation against her skin, the alertness of her mind, the way he stimulated her on all levels with these dinners. But she had something more she wanted to say. Something she'd been thinking of telling him all week, that she'd never told anyone.

She'd initially convinced her mind that she was telling him because, despite their intimacy, their online situation provided a level of anonymity that encouraged confidences. But she knew it wasn't that. It was because she was reaching the point that she'd tell him anything, give him all of herself, because that's what he'd demanded from her from the first. She was starting to trust him enough to tell him the things she feared in herself.

"My husband died, Master. I was married to him for eight years. I loved him, but…this is going to sound awful. There was this moment about six months after he died that I woke up in the morning, you know that moment when you're not censoring or suppressing thoughts? I had this overpowering sense of relief, not that he was dead, definitely not that, but that I had a second chance to find what I really wanted, not to settle for something."

"You can lose everything of importance in asserting your individuality, Shy Kitten. Just remember that. Enlightened philosophy doesn't play well with human barbarity. Man has an infinite capacity to destroy or exile what he fears."

Nicole laid down her fork. "Is that why you've never suggested that we meet, face-to-face?"

There was a long moment, and she waited, the heated air of the room brushing her skin in the silence.

"Yes."

"Then I'm sorry," she said softly. "For I would accept you just as you are." *I already do*, she thought.

"That's good, because I have three arms, a pimpled face, and I weigh three hundred pounds."

She blinked, then chuckled. "Tell me you have chronic body odor and I'll be in love with you forever."

"Smartass wench." Then he paused, and his voice came through to her far more seriously. "Be careful, Kitten. It's easy to turn what we have into more than it is."

She stared at those words on the screen, managed to wonder how anything said in such a caressing tone could be so painful. Before her hurt feelings could give her mind room to fashion a reply, he was speaking again, the words rolling across the screen and through the speakers.

"Don't be upset. You need to understand what I mean by that. This is a powerful, emotional game, but it's still a game. The way gladiators in the ring are a game, not the way Monopoly is a game. Everything is centered on an intense, focused moment, everything is poured into that, everything is laid raw. But it doesn't exist in the same realm as paying your bills, going to work, doing the laundry. That's a different, real magic of its own."

"But there are those who have brought the two together, who marry after being part of the D/s scene together."

"It can happen, but it usually doesn't. Not this way. And that's not what you're seeking with me."

Not what you're seeking with me. She noted the omission of his own desires, almost let his presumption of her wants and desires pass. Then decided, no, she wouldn't.

"If what we're doing has no connection to the real world, then how do you know what I want?"

"Please don't take this down that road, Kitten. We don't know each other, not really."

When he instructed her how to set up a post office box that would hide her location and identity from him, he had been teaching her first and foremost to protect herself. But she wondered, in this case, if that was whom he was really protecting. She was both gratified by his chivalry and frustrated as well, because it kept him at arm's length from her.

"Master…have you ever…would you ever consider us, meeting? Ever?"

Nicole made herself be silent, resist the urge to rush into the void. *Take it back, before you make him angry. No. I won't.* She firmed her chin, her fingers curling up into balls. She didn't want to take it back.

"No, Kitten. We can't do that. Not ever. It's better this way."

"But…" She stopped, mulling over persuasive words she didn't know how to string together to convey what she felt. Didn't he feel the way she did? She knew he did. It wasn't just about sex anymore. For heaven's sake, he was the one who had suggested the additional day, to eat dinner together like this, exchange conversation, talk about who they were, what they liked to do. He insisted they stay carefully away from certain specific topics, she knew, but as time progressed, he had let certain things slip about his profession, his location. Clues to a treasure map that she was beginning to be willing to take the many risks involved in following. She'd accept the consequences of unburying the treasure and facing the ghosts that might guard it. Let him deny her to her face, reject her in the flesh. Reject her flesh.

"I know you care about me. And we've known each other for over a year now. I feel more complete with you than—"

"Don't go there, Kitten."

"—anyone."

The beauty of computer communication. Despite his attempt to talk over her, she had the final word, blinking on the screen for him to see, defying him.

"Anyone," she whispered. He was gone, the connection shut down. For the first time since they'd known each other, he'd cut her off, left the field of play without a good night.

`Good night, Master.` She typed it, even knowing he was no longer there.

* * * * *

He didn't log in on Thursday, or the Tuesday after. She ached for him, but she wouldn't go to the site where she had found him, knowing she couldn't bear it if he was chatting in one of the groups, had any kind of presence there this week, a bald statement of his rejection of her company.

She left the speakers on, stroked the screen as if it were him, wandered listlessly around the house, cursed men and their primitive fear of commitment, even as her heart told her it was more than that. Masters were not like most men. This Master definitely wasn't. He was afraid of the face-to-face meeting for another reason. Was he deformed? Handicapped? Fat? She couldn't care less. It was his mind, the words that had seduced her from the beginning.

She'd been married to beauty, her husband a handsome man with a generous heart, a good friend. They'd loved each other, but had never been lovers.

If her Master was a beast, she loved him, not in spite of that, but as the whole package. No matter whether he felt the beast was in his mind or his outer form.

She had one secret from him, other than her recording software. She'd started organizing pieces of information about him, trying to pinpoint exactly who he was, where he lived. She told herself it was just curiosity, but she knew she was deceiving herself. She hadn't taken the final necessary step, hiring a private investigator, but the page in the phone book was marked, several names underlined.

Their times together were like phone calls from prison, from a man who'd put himself in the cell and locked the door. He'd told her that he had no pets. He didn't want anything in his life to take care of or — translation — to hurt him again.

He didn't say that, but she heard it. Nicole knew she might be losing her mind, fabricating the missing puzzle pieces to form a whole man that might not exist. She knew what people said about online relationships, that they were fantasy relationships, all the weaknesses hidden away, but she knew her Master was honest with her. What he couldn't talk about, he wouldn't. What he could tell her was the truth. And being her Master, he demanded truth from her.

"Kitten?"

Her cat yowled indignantly as she spun around, nearly trampling the poor Siamese. With that unerring knowledge cats had of where their human might try to step next, he'd stretched his body across the threshold to her home office. She snatched him up, gave him a hard, joyous and apologetic hug, dumped him on the lounger, and slid into her desk chair like Willie Mays stealing home.

She snapped on the microphone feature. "I'm here, Master."

"I'm sorry we fought."

And with those four simple words, she knew. He needed her as much as she needed him. Because if he didn't, she knew he wouldn't have come back. Whatever wounds he nursed were painful enough that his mind wanted him to remain isolated, but his heart was demanding that he reach out, embrace the normal human desire to connect. To love.

She looked toward the phone book, sitting on the top of her desk. At the tab she'd placed in it, marking the private investigators' page.

To hell with the pain or consequences.

"I'm glad you came back," she whispered, her hands beginning to tremble.

"I'm not the treasure you're looking for, Kitten. The treasure you deserve. I don't want to keep you from finding your heart's desire."

You didn't. I've found him. I'm going to find him.

"You won't," she said.

Chapter Eleven
Present Day

"Nicole, I just don't know if I have it in me to trust someone again. And love isn't true unless there's trust, and complete acceptance."

"I'm yours to love when you're ready to love me, Master. I'm here. I'm yours, in a way she never was. I trust you, and accept you. You're in every part of me, you see everything that I am."

"No. You're a beautiful mystery that would take years to unravel."

But he reached out, cupped her cheek, let her press her lips to his palm. "There were nights I wanted you so much I felt I could hear you breathing next to me. I imagined curling around you, your ass nested in the crook of my thighs, pressed against my cock, my arm around your waist, holding your breast in my palm. Playing with it while you slept, until you got roused and wet in your dreams, and I could slide my cock into your slick pussy from behind, fuck you soft and slow. Listen to you come awake, roll against me like a cat, mewl your pleasure, helpless little cries until I slid my touch down, played with your clit and made you come around me."

"And I thought that was just my dream." She bit his palm.

"I'm only good for sex, Nicole. I'm not what you need as a man. I couldn't overcome what I am to stand for the first woman I loved."

"And she couldn't overcome who she was to stand by you. You loved each other, but you just weren't meant to be, Mark. It happens, as it happened with me and my husband."

He turned away, retrieved her dress. "Lift your arms again," he instructed. He pulled the towel away, dropped the dress back over her, caressed her when he rearranged the skirt over her hips, traced her lips with his fingers while she stood still under his touch, barely breathing.

He saw her eyes stray to the place on the sand she had lain and come for him, and color rose to her cheeks, embarrassment making her shy again. He'd been with her over a year and knew she had a core of steel, but a shy, submissive soul. No matter how much he tried, he couldn't keep his heart hardened against her. Somehow, through the pain and trials of her life, she had managed to keep her enthusiastic innocence, her belief that enough determination could win her that which she most desired. He wished he didn't have to be the person to destroy that belief.

Taking both of her hands, he lifted them to his lips, kissed the top of each one, feeling the soft skin under the brush of his mouth, the quiver of response.

The power of it rolled over him, her reaction to nothing more than a situation, a suggestion, the heat of his body pressing on hers.

Online, he'd pushed women to climax before with such tactics, hints and suggestions. But this was different. So different. He brought her closer and felt the warm tension of her body against his thighs, her ass squirming under his hand, her hair and delicate nape on the back of her skull.

"What do you need, Nicole? Right at this moment."

"Tell me something no one else knows about you. A deep, dark secret."

He smiled. "I have the complete set of Partridge Family albums. And I listen to them still."

He loved watching the light come back into her eyes. The tiny smile that became a giggle. "You made that up."

"I did not. Want me to sing some lyrics for you?"

"I think I would have been less worried if I knew you were a mass murderer."

"Well, *that* you could respect."

She choked on a chuckle, and he squeezed her hands. "I can't get involved with a woman without wanting to dominate her. That's my secret, and you're the only one in my life who not only knows that, but knows what it truly means."

"Have you ever…with anyone else, in real life?"

He shook his head. "I've had relationships, but I could tell it wasn't for them. They'd go to a certain point, and then, if I became less than subtle about it, beyond just a suggestion, they'd spook or get turned off." He shrugged. "I found women whose company I enjoyed, who I came close to being in love with, but as soon as I figured out that about them, I knew they weren't for me. I've been there before." A shadow crossed his expression. "I can't ever go that way again."

He slipped the bag with their belongings back over his shoulder, along with the strap of the beach chair. Fishing in the paper bag, he retrieved a leftover hushpuppy, extending it to her. When he shook his head as she made to take it from his fingers, Nicole stopped, lowering her hand. She opened her mouth and accepted his placement of it between her lips, savoring that contact before she bit down on the breaded food, her lips closing on his fingertips.

"What about you, Kitten? Has there been anyone else in your life?"

She chewed, a woman with manners, with her moist lips closed, and waited until she'd swallowed to answer him. Mark wasn't sure he wanted to hear her reply.

"Not since my husband." She surprised him. She hesitated, and he watched her think over her response. "I guess… I didn't want to go that way again, either, unless I was sure. He was different before we were married. I wanted a partner, someone who would want to take care of me the way I wanted to take care of him. Someone who, if I came home with a migraine, could put me to bed and take care of things. Who could handle working out a problem on a bill with the waiter. Someone who would occasionally order for me in a restaurant because he knew what I liked, or wanted me to try something different. Or someone who would tell me to wait in the car while he ran in to get the carton of milk at the convenience store, because it was raining and he didn't want me to get wet. It sounds stupid, inane, really, but—"

"You wanted someone who would take the lead without asking."

"It... Deep inside, I think it made me feel unsafe that he never did, you know? I didn't pay much attention to it when we were dating, but after we got married, it was like, 'well, that's done', and I started to feel more and more like a surrogate mother, all wrapped up and confused with being a wife. I wondered, what if I couldn't handle things anymore? Could he handle it? Could he take care of me if I really needed him to?" She lowered her voice. "You always made me feel safe, even when it was only your voice and your words in the room with me, or even when you were just in my mind. I knew from the beginning you're the type of man who takes care of a woman. Who doesn't let the fact she wants to take care of you make you forget that you're supposed to take care of her, too." Her gaze went to his hands, to the food he had offered. "Not all women need that, and I guess I don't, because I've done well enough on my own. Better than well enough. But it's something I've always wanted, still want."

She looked up at him, her heart plainly in her eyes, and he could not face it, not when he wanted to take what she was offering so much.

"It's time to go somewhere else," he said at last. "And let you do that thing all women desire to do the most."

"And that would be?"

He forced a smile. "Shopping, of course."

* * * * *

The intensity of their time on the beach lingered between them. It was not uncomfortable or awkward. It couldn't be, not when Mark insisted on keeping her hand in the grip of his, resting loosely on his thigh. But by mutual accord, they chose a bit of silence to fill the time between the beach and their arrival at a little cluster of clapboard buildings at the edge of the maritime forest. The buildings were backed up to the beach where the old lighthouse used to be, its foundation stones forming the center of the cul-de-sac around which several carts were parked.

"What is this?" she asked.

"Ballentyne has a strong preservation group that protects the loggerhead turtle nests and the fragile maritime forest environment. Just beyond those dunes is the point of the island. That's one of the largest nesting areas for loggerheads on the southern coast of the United States."

"Have you seen them come in? The mothers?"

He nodded. "I volunteer every year to be a nest protector. It's something else, to see all of the hatchlings trying to make for the ocean, coming out of the shell ready to swim, to live, without a mother's protection.

"They've got an education center, and this gift shop funds the society. It isn't your usual tourist gift shop," he said. When they parked, this time she knew to wait until he came around, took her hand.

She did his bidding so easily, so naturally, that Mark could not resist tightening his grip on hers, hard, for just a moment, to watch her eyes lift to gaze upon his face. He bent, brushed her cheekbone with his lips. "I think you'll like it here."

"You're here," she said simply. An answer in itself, and she leaned on the strength of his arm to slide out of the cart.

He tucked her hand into the crook of his arm to ascend the wooden boardwalk, and they stepped into a shop filled with nature's colors and artistic arrangements of merchandise that related to the Ballentyne environment. The music of the ocean waves and cries of seagulls played through a CD player on the shelf behind the cashier. "I love that smell," Nicole said, shutting her eyes. "Cedar, sunshine, the beach, all rolled into one." She opened her eyes and they immediately lit up.

"Oh, look at this." She kept his hand, but moved to the full range of their linked arms to tap the head of a little wooden turtle sitting on the top of the jewelry counter. It bobbed on a spring. There was a whole basket of them, next to the display turtle, all painted different colors. Mark knew about her love of whimsy, but it was enchanting to experience it directly, see it in the delight on her face. She ignored the expensive silver jewelry in the glass case.

"I need to warn you." She slanted a sober glance up at him. "I have a problem with dustcatchers. I try to attend all the Dustcatcher Anonymous meetings, but so many of them coincide with the flea market sales, I just lose my willpower."

He grinned, took her elbow. "Then you have to pick just one."

She looked down at all the colors and wistful faces. "Oh, God. This is like being at the pound. You choose."

He laughed, picked up a lavender one with deep blue and green shell markings. "This one, then, because it has pretty colors, like you."

"I'll have something to look at and remember today." She took it in her hand, let it sit on her palm, the little head bobbing. Her mouth softened into a sad smile, her eyes watching it move as if all of the hope and innocence that she had lost in the journey to adulthood were represented in that little toy.

Mark moved in closer, his body touching hers, his lips against her ear. "I'll give you plenty of things to help you remember today, Kitten. Every time you touch your own body, you'll remember it."

She shivered against him, and he covered it with a curved arm around her shoulders, giving the cashier a nod as they moved down the counter, still looking into the baskets of items too small to trust in other parts of the store due to shoplifters. Dropping his hand to her waist, Mark stroked her hipbone, his palm brushing the top of one buttock.

"Friendship rings." She chuckled over her new discovery in the next basket. "Let me see your hand."

Bemused by her childlike exuberance, he let his hand be seized. She held up several different rings, trying them out, until she exclaimed and picked up one in black. The plastic resin was fashioned to look like carved onyx. This ring had a bear's silhouette carved in the top setting, and the band looked like two overlapping feathers that met at the base, a bold Native American design that was quite handsome, despite the cheapness of the bauble.

"This is the one." She looked up at him, eyes sparkling. "This one will fit, because it's you."

"You may be disappointed, Kitten. I have fat fingers, and these are made for teenagers to give to their sweethearts."

Her fingers passed over his ring finger, the sensitive flesh where his wedding ring used to rest, and suddenly he saw the light in her eyes become tender, the chin tighten in resolve. "It will fit," she said softly, and slid it over the tip of his finger. She used the hand which still bore the flower ring he'd made her, though the petals had suffered some from their time in the surf. "And they're not fat. They're a man's hands, strong and sturdy."

It did fit, halting briefly over the knuckle as it should before it slid onto the base of his finger in a snug, perfect fit on that whitened band of pigment that lingered as a reminder of promises made and broken. When Nicole stroked over it, he felt the difference of the cool material and the brush of her fingertips on his heated skin.

She let him go at last so he could hand over payment to the lady behind the cash register. He closed his fingers over the ring. Over the feeling of being wanted. Nicole had not said any vows. It was simply a blink of a moment, but it was there, an offering to him, a promise, if he was brave enough to believe in promises again.

"Look at that," she said. The large ficus tree in the corner next to the cash register was covered with silk butterflies, their wire legs clasping the branches as their wings slowly fanned up and down, so lifelike they looked like butterflies in truth. Mark wondered how Nicole got through a whole store when she shopped, since she seemed to be attracted to everything. He suppressed a chuckle and followed her the one step to the tree.

"There are over two hundred species represented," the volunteer told them. "Aren't they wonderful? I want to take them all home. Pick one up on your finger."

Nicole worked the wire legs free from the branch and perched the little creature on her index finger, a charmed smile on her face as the wings continued to move, brushing her knuckles.

"The kids love to hook them on their hands, their shoulders, their clothes."

"But how do they work?"

"Heat," Mark said, studying the bush. "Look at the vent behind them. It's blowing warm air on them. It heats the mechanisms inside them, makes it work."

The woman nodded. "They also respond a certain extent to body heat, so you can play with them a bit on a rainy day. But you can't get them really cold. You get them cold, they grow still." Her middle-aged eyes crinkled. "Butterflies are warm weather creatures, after all."

Mark touched the butterfly on Nicole's finger and then slid his index finger to the inside of hers as he worked the toy gently off its perch onto his. His finger was wider, so when he got it free, she helped, stretching out the curved wires, fitting it over his fingers, her own touching on the underside, on the palm. When she would have drawn away, his hand closed on both of hers, holding her pinioned there, her wrists caught securely in the grip of his one hand.

"Do you like them?" he asked.

She nodded, and he thought the heat generated between their contact should be enough to have that butterfly going double time. As if in response, the wings did increase their rate.

"On summer days, they'll get hot enough to almost fly off your finger," the woman explained. "So don't attach them to anything too light. Aren't they the most delightful things?"

Nicole thought so, so he bought a handful of them, overcoming her laughing objections to make her pick out several colors she liked. He also chose a couple of silly toys, like a rubber frog that hopped. When a ball air pump was goosed, it shot air through a tube into the inflatable legs, which made them kick out.

He wanted to buy her everything in the store that made her smile, but he was enough of a Master of withholding pleasure for the ultimate release that he knew the value of making her choose just a few things, as he had with the turtle.

He realized he was as much under her control as she was under his. A woman could be so many things—lover, goddess, mother...friend. He'd forgotten that could be part of a relationship, but when she had covered the ring on his hand and looked up at him, he had seen that side of her too. The desire to heal, comfort and care for him, as much as he wanted to do it for her.

The confidence that he could be a friend to the woman he loved had been destroyed in the carnage he and his wife had created. But Nicole was raising the idea from the ashes, filling his soul with hope he could not afford.

He brutally reminded himself that, at one time, he had believed in everything that Nicole believed. He knew that love was more dangerous than a crush. Both could spin the illusion that you knew who you were with, that you could trust them. When that realization was exposed as a lie, a crush would only ache. Love could cripple.

Nicole turned, the filtered sunlight from the door haloing her face, and raised on tiptoe. She brushed his jaw with her lips. "Did you say something about chocolate, Mark?" she whispered.

The feel of her against him drove back the shadows for the moment, as he reminded himself he only had to trust her for one day. Just today. He turned her so she was under his arm, and picked up the bag of butterflies, frog and little wooden turtle. "Yes, I did. Let's go outside. There's a swing."

Nicole saw the grimness to his mouth, but before she could speak to soften it, he was moving her out the door. She saw a porch swing over at the education center, where there was room for two, but he didn't take her there. He took her down the steps and a couple hundred yards away, toward the dunes, where there was an area shaded by pines, the sandy ground carpeted and hushed with their needles. A swing was tied to the stout branch of one of them, two long twists of thick rope running twenty feet to the ground to pass through two holes drilled through a flat board, knots tied beneath it to hold the swing safely together, a simple design she'd have seen a hundred years ago or more.

Mark guided her onto it, facing her away from the museum and gift shop, toward the dune ridge just beyond the pines, before he retrieved the chocolate from his knapsack.

"Hmm." He opened up the small block of chocolate, and she saw that the day's increasing heat had melted it in the tin foil. "Depending on how fastidious you are, I think we'll either have to hold off on this, or have you lick it off the wrapper. I still have two hushpuppies if you're hungry —"

Nicole didn't hesitate to analyze or judge, knowing she had nothing to lose other than what he'd told her she'd lose at the end of the day. Which was, in her mind, everything. She reached over, her hand touching and guiding his, and when he slanted her a quizzical look, she slid the tips of his middle and index fingers through it, collecting the chocolate there. Then, her eyes on his, she leaned forward and took both his fingers in her mouth, thinking that there could be nothing better than the taste of him and chocolate together.

She sucked delicately on him, licked between the fingers when he spread them, stretching her mouth, and when he increased the depth, making her clean him from the base of his fingers to the tips, she adjusted, feeling want spread in her belly at the hard flex in his jaw, the tense arousal of his body. He withdrew the digits, glistening from her saliva, and scooped up the rest of the chocolate, easing it slowly in between her lips this time, watching with total male absorption as she took them in without complaint. One hand reached out, the other still grasping the rope of the swing as she caught his waistband to steady herself, give herself an anchor so she could fully savor the taste of him, the movement of his fingers pushing into her mouth. Withdrawing slowly and then pushing in again as he mimicked what she so wished he would do to join with her.

At length, he withdrew his touch completely, carefully folded the wrapper and put it away in the bag. She continued to hold onto his waist until he took her hand and clasped it around the rope of the swing.

"If you swing high enough, you can see the ocean," he told her. "Just over that dune. I want you to go high enough to see it, and I don't want you to do anything to adjust your skirt as you use your legs to take you higher. I'll get you started, and then I just want to watch. Fly for me, Nicole. Show me how beautiful you are."

He moved behind her. Nicole waited for the push, and was startled when he brought his arm around her waist, briefly crushed her in its band just under her breasts as he pressed his jaw to her temple, held her tight against his body behind her. She knew he didn't want her to move her hands, but she did turn her head, nuzzled his face, seeking his lips. When she got too close, he slid away. His hands coursed down her sides to her hips, and then he took the base of the swing on either side, the bitter ends of the ropes, and peddled backwards, taking her up, up, up, until she was at his shoulder height. Then he let her go.

The ground rushed forward and then past, and she was arcing forward, toward the trees. It had been awhile since she'd been in a playground swing, so she yelped in foolish delight as she tried to coordinate her limbs and remember how it was done. She botched it on the first rotation, her awkward pumping setting her at an odd angle, slowing her progress. But then she was back to him, and his strong hands were a delicious caress on her ass, sending her back on a straight path again.

Straighten on the upswing, pump as she came down. Instinct kicked in to guide her, the way it did for the most simple and wonderful acts. Riding a bike, swinging on a swing, loving a good man, riding his cock, giving him pleasure…

As she went up this time, she leaned back, let her head drop so she could see him come rushing back toward her. Her mouth curved in a delighted grin. "If I jump out, will you catch me?" she called out.

"No," came the dry reply. "Because I'll have a heart attack and expire on the spot."

She laughed then, wild and foolish dreams riding higher with her body into the sky to give them voice. "You would catch me," she said, positive of it.

"Nicole, I order you to stay on that swing."

As she went up this time, the air currents from the ocean met her, so the hem of her skirt rippled and then billowed out, almost exposing her before she came back to him again, the wind funneling the fabric around her legs. He couldn't reach her now, so he moved, coming in front of her as he had said he would, watching her go higher and higher.

The light skirt blew up as she flew toward the ocean and she knew he was seeing her bare thighs, the point of her shaved sex fitted between them. She shifted her thighs further apart, just enough that when the skirt raised this time, he could see the petals of her pussy, the satin soft skin she knew by the flame in his gaze he'd not had enough of. His gaze locked with hers as she retreated again, and the world spun by, with him as the only still point.

She remembered something she'd read, that novice sailors were instructed to keep their gaze on a stable horizon point if they started getting seasick, that unpleasant state caused by experiencing the world moving a way the body could not accommodate. She kept her gaze on Mark, choosing him to be the steadying center of her universe, her anchor, certain that by doing so she'd feel the joy of the experience, instead of pain and discomfort.

He had moved directly in front of her now, just beyond the path of her ascension, so she raced down toward him, her extended bare soles several feet from him before she went up, up and there it was, the line of the ocean beyond the dune, the sun glittering on the dark blue waters, sea gulls dotting the sky, their wings tilting as they sought food in the waves. Air blew over her face, pressed the loose bodice against her bare breasts and across her back, a caress from things that had been around millennia more than anything human. The sun, the wind, the timeless motion of the sea. A rhythm of life, rising and falling, the way a lover's body did when buried into the fertile earth of hers. At this moment she had no fear, only hope, more hope than she could contain, so inflated by desperate desire she couldn't doubt herself or him.

"Mark?" she called out as she zoomed down past him, prepared to swoop forward with a pump of her strong legs.

"What?"

"Catch me." And she launched herself just as the swing started to arc over his head again.

She could have warned him that as a child she'd had a sandbox just beyond her swing set, and she'd become expert at judging her distance to her target at launch, but the moment was too spontaneous for explanation. She knew he'd be prepared to catch her, the same way she'd once believed there were dreams bigger than herself that could come true.

The wonder of adulthood was finding out that dreams could come true in a way you didn't expect, marrying reality, and resulting in perfection.

She hit him full body, her arms latching around his shoulders, the impact taking them both down in a manner that would have won the admiration of a professional wrestler. They tumbled and rolled over in the soft sand and bed of pine needles the museum had taken great pains to ensure carpeted this area.

Mark had never greatly appreciated that feature, but when his back hit the ground, he was forced to admit gratitude that he was not hitting a combination of sand and prickly scrub vegetation like what covered most open spaces of the island. Banding his arms around her body to protect her, he came to a rolling halt positioned halfway over her, his knee pressed into the ground between her thighs. She clutched to his shoulders, holding onto his shirt, breathing hard. Her eyes danced with exhilaration and undisguised desire for him. Her breasts pressed against the thin fabric of the dress, the nipples practically begging for his mouth to cover them. His cock grew hard against her thigh, which she slid up against him now, pressing against his crotch, the base of his testicles. Her chin rose, her lips parted, her throat and mouth offered to him, and it was not hard to imagine his collar on that slender column, claiming her for his own, always.

"You caught me," she breathed. "I knew you would."

He propped his elbows on either side of her head, caging her. "What part of 'stay in the swing' didn't you understand? Didn't I tell you to stay put?"

"Yes, you did." Her teeth showed, and he dodged the nip of her fangs on his lips, catching her head in the grip of his hands.

"Be still," he said softly, and lowered his mouth to hers.

He used his thumbs to part her lips, hold her mouth open while he sipped, drew the outline of her with his tongue, nibbled as her breath quickened. A moan escaped from her throat, her body moving toward his.

"Be still, I said." He sharpened his tone, and she subsided, but he could feel the hammer of her heart against his.

Taking his mouth fully over hers, he deepened his penetration, sweeping his tongue in to fondle the roof of her mouth, her tongue, the soft insides of her cheeks. He felt the heat of her breath, captured it as if he were draining her life essence into himself. A vampire interested in only one soul, one particular woman's blood and life.

Perhaps because he'd had to claw his way back from an emotional death, he had learned to experience time in its present form, never counting on tomorrow, never looking back at yesterday for fear of self-destruction. It was a skill that had stood him well today, because looking to a future would give the false illusion of hope. He'd forced himself to be fully immersed in every moment he'd had with her. But his conscience wouldn't let him off the hook that easily, its presence a fist of pain clutched around his heart. He couldn't totally live in the moment because he knew *she* had a future, and dreams she was spinning in it, with him in the center stage. And because he loved her, he wasn't immune to how his actions would impact that.

He lifted his head at last, still holding her head immobile, stroking the fine lines of her profile with his thumbs. "You can't live in a virtual reality, Nicole. This day is no more real than that was."

Her eyes locked with his. "This day, and the past eighteen months, have been the most real my life has ever been. And I think it's the same for you."

"I'm going to throttle you." He rested his forehead on hers a minute, then lifted his gaze to pin her with a stern look. "You took ten years off my life. Flying through the air like a pale blue-green squirrel."

She giggled. "I did see the ocean," she said. "It was beautiful, to see it that way." Reaching up, she closed her hands on his sides, just above his waist. "You know, whether you see it from up there or with your feet on the ground, it's still the same beach, the same reality. Truth is truth, no matter which way you look at it."

They stared at each other for several more moments, and he was conscious of her every breath, the moistness of her lips, the quiver of her body beneath his painfully aroused one. She did not move at all now, but her very life beneath him stroked his nerves, begged for him.

"I can see that I'm going to have to come up with a punishment that will make you mind me better," he said at last, struggling to control his desires. "Or withhold chocolate. It seems to have a bad influence on you."

"That would qualify as cruel and unusual." Her eyes laughed up at him, but her mouth had settled into a quiet curve. Mark stood and lifted her to her feet by taking both of her hands in his and pulling her to her feet. Unable to help himself, he brushed his palm over her hair and down her back, dislodging bits of earth and grass, tiny twigs. She brushed him off as well, shyly moving behind him to clean off his back, her hands lingering on his shoulders, his waist, lightly brushing his hips and buttocks. He tightened his jaw at the spur of hard lust such tentative caresses gave him, a stronger reaction than if she had boldly groped him. Her slender fingers touched his neck, the back of his head, and he could not help tilting toward her touch as it became a stroke through his hair, her hands as entrancing as a maiden stroking a unicorn's forehead, lulling him to submit to her desire.

This Master could easily become the slave to the submissive. She fascinated him on all levels, and he hungered to care for her, guard her from her nightmares, watch her bring home whimsical things to make a bleak house into a home, rich with color and her laughter and many moods. Even during her angry or irritated moments he wanted to be there, because it was all the shades of color that made life a defined picture.

"Master?" she asked, her voice a gentle touch just beyond his right shoulder.

He saw her outlined in his peripheral vision, a mesh of soft blue-green and the pale outline of her face, the dark cap of sleek hair, long fine limbs.

"I need to go to the restroom. Is there one nearby?"

He turned, drew her to him by her waist, and her hands settled naturally on his chest. "Just over there, by the museum. I'll take you."

He picked up their belongings, waited for her to slide back into her shoes, and then took her back to the museum. The restrooms were a separate building connected to the museum by decking, and he took her to the door. Nodding to a cobbled walk nearby that led through a tree-lined path up to the education center, he said, "I'll wait for you right over there, on that bench."

She slid her hand from his, and disappeared into the restroom. He thought of those bare thighs, her raising her skirt behind those doors, the soft fabric sliding up her legs, her tucking the skirt up above the bountiful shape of her ass. The smooth shape of her clit and labia, a lovely bloom she'd exposed when she swung toward him, the skirt billowing to reveal that, just for him.

He moved slowly to a bench at the end of the stepping-stone and cobble walkway, ambling along, looking at the carved names passing beneath his feet, the husbands and wives side by side.

When he turned, she was there, hesitating at the beginning of the path. There was a dense covering of bright green groundcover and flowers on either side, making it impossible for her to use anything other than the path to get to him. Her face, so joyous a moment before, was now troubled.

He went to her immediately. "What is it, Kitten?"

"It's like stepping on gravestones. Like someone stepping on memories of those you've lost, like my husband."

He didn't want to think about her husband. He was greedy. Though Nicole had told him that he had been given something her husband had never sought from her, he wished he had been the recipient of everything she had ever given to any man. Her time, her presence, her conversation and every mood. All the things she was more than willing to give to him. He had only to ask.

Goddamn it, get over it, let it go, or put her on the boat now. He'd think his subconscious would be weary of this litany by now, but it seemed eager to keep up the self-flagellation. Perhaps he had as much of a masochistic side as a sexually dominant one.

He almost chuckled at himself, relieving his own tension, then he looked at her distressed expression. While they'd not been passionate soulmates, it was obvious Nicole and her husband had cared for one another. They'd been friends, something he and his wife had destroyed the potential for within the first six months of their marriage through rejection and betrayal, something friends did not do to one another.

Perhaps Nicole's husband had never realized the whole world inside his wife he'd never tapped. Shy as she was, it had to be coaxed from her, and the key to the locked door hadn't been in their relationship. He sounded like he'd been a good man, though, and Mark knew the frustration of not being able to fully claim the woman he loved. He found himself grudgingly hoping, as he knew Nicole did more generously, that her husband had died without knowing she'd never given him all of herself.

Unfortunately, women were often far more intuitive than men, and his wife had sensed it almost immediately, early in their marriage.

"No, it's not like stepping on gravestones. Here, slip your shoes off."

She obeyed, trusting him, sliding back out of the sandals, and standing at the start of the path in bare feet.

"Now, take my hand." He extended it and she laid her fingers in the grasp of his.

"Step here." He tugged her onto the first flat turtle-shaped stone. "See, the way it works is the donor buys a stone that represents one of the mother turtles that comes here every year to lay her eggs. So the money contributes to the continuation of life, and the stone donation furthers that, because it keeps a memory alive. I tend to think, if you stand in your bare feet on them, you absorb a little bit of the memory of that person. Like this. Alissa Morris. Died at age seven. Close your eyes." When she did, he brushed a knuckle over her soft cheek, unable to help himself. "See a little girl with dark hair and blue eyes. Hear her laughter. Imagine the first crayon drawing she brought home from school for her mother to put on the fridge. They brought her here once to take the nighttime turtle walk, to see all the hatchlings rush to sea."

"You knew her." Nicole opened her eyes.

"The education coordinator leading the walk that night brought them to the nest I was guarding, and their timing was perfect. The babies started coming out of the ground within a few minutes of them being there. You should have seen her, running around with her parents, trying to drive off the crabs. Trying to give the babies a shot at life. She was so excited at the thought that one of those that made it into the water might become an adult loggerhead that would come back to this very spot and lay her eggs." He shook his head. "She was a child. Innocence and joy personified, everything that's real. After it was over, she was tired, and cranky, and her father carried her back down the beach. I remember the way they disappeared into the darkness, her cheek pressed to his shoulder, her hand curled around his neck."

Mark squatted, still holding to her hand, and placed his free hand, palm down, over the little girl's name, just by Nicole's foot. "She died last year. Recurrence of her leukemia.

"Now, here." He straightened and tugged her forward, balanced her with both hands. "Put one foot on this stone, and one there. You're now connecting Mr. Robert Massie with Mrs.

Elizabeth Massie, husband and wife for thirty-six years. They died within two years of each other."

"Did you know them?"

"No. Them I didn't."

"We all know them," she said after a moment, as if she was reading his mind. "They're in here." She freed her hand, laid it over his heart. "Like everyone we meet, or who passes on. Maybe they become part of a great collective unconsciousness, and guide us with their love and experience." She slid her touch back to his waiting hand and held it again, connected them together in a circle with each other and with the Massies. "So if we stand here long enough, maybe they'll share with us what made thirty-six years possible."

"Lots of road trips apart? A mistress on the side? Or maybe they were simply together long enough that nothing else seemed worth the effort."

She cocked her head, refusing to rise to the bait. "Maybe," she said gently. "Or maybe, if we listen with our hearts instead of our fears, they'll tell us."

"It will pop into our head like a neon sign. 'This was our magic secret.'"

She studied him, her eyes soft with love. "I suspect it's not a spoken message, but something that's like a feeling. A wisdom that transcends words, built on a thousand experiences that made a magic all their own, a spell that took years to weave. And maybe, if your soul is open to it, it's a message you only understand a little bit at a time, as you experience it yourself. A chocolate cake whose richness can only be appreciated one bite at a time."

"Over thirty-six years?"

"Perhaps." She closed her eyes again before he could say anything else. He could have roused her with sarcasm or cynicism, brought her back to him by tugging her off the stones and pulling her close to him. Bring her back to his stark reality, banishing the spiritual moment with a physical one. But for some reason he couldn't put into words, he simply stayed still, holding her hands, watching the serenity of her face, the fragility of it, knowing how easily she bruised beneath the skin. She hadn't let calluses form as he had. She was still willing to be wounded in the quest for her dreams.

He closed off his own worries and shut his eyes, telling himself it was no big deal. He was just joining in for the hell of it, to draw in her scent, her touch through his palms, the feel of her skirt blowing softly against his legs. She tugged, and he stepped closer, onto the two rocks with her, and then she put her bare feet on top of his in the broken-in loafers. Her warmth and life sandwiched his against the memory of the Massies, and her arms slid around his waist, her body leaning into him. When her chin tucked under his, there was no choice but to enclose her in his arms, hold her against him, feel the simple tranquility of her against his body, from knee to throat. The soft ocean breeze whispered promises around them, the bugs humming by, the seagulls and forest birds continuing to call out, pursuing the cycles of life and death.

It was the reality of life he told himself he heard, not the promise of those who had died. They had taken the secrets of their happiness with them, if they had ever had them to begin with.

Mark eased out of her arms, stepped off the stone. He touched her chin. "I think that you're procrastinating on your punishment for that wild stunt, Kitten. It's time to take care of that, before our time runs out."

Chapter Twelve

He thought the emotional withdrawal might hurt her, but she simply nodded and let him take her to the cart to drive on through the forest. He left the ocean and went down the wynds that ran through the forest itself, among the few homes. Veering right on a fork, he left the asphalt roads behind, and bumped them along gravel paths that took them even deeper into the isolation of the maritime forest.

No homes had been built in this area yet, which was why the island government had chosen not to pave the roads. The packed dirt and marl were broken up with patches of grass and potholes of soft gray dust. He brought them to a cul-de-sac, where the maritime forest clustered around it like a sacred circle, the tree branches filtering the space so it was shadow and dim light, bringing it an even more isolated air.

Mark parked the golf cart on the side of the worn-down road before it crossed the line into the filtered circle, and then stepped out. Nicole waited until he came around to get her, but when she put out a hand, thinking he was going to help her from the cart, he pressed her hand, bidding her stay, and squatted to his heels. He kissed her fingers, then laid them in her lap and reached for her foot.

He eased her sandals off her feet, leaving her barefoot again.

"You have beautiful toes, Kitten. Small and well shaped. Soft as silk. I like the burgundy nail polish. I wish I could come with you and watch them do your pedicures. No, don't say anything." He slid his palm down the wide part of the bottom of her foot, slightly damp from nervous perspiration, to the ticklish arch, and cupped the heel. "They're new shoes. I was worried that they're hurting your feet."

"You haven't let me wear them much," she whispered, not sure if he wanted her to respond.

He smiled. "I once read that most women would take a good foot massage and a hot bath over sex. Why do you think that is, Nicole?"

He began to knead the heel, his other hand coming up to curl around the arch to do the same, relaxing the muscles there. Her shoulders eased, her fingers straightening on her knees. If she were a cat, she thought her eyes would narrow to pleased slits and she'd begin to purr.

"It's still." It apparently took her a moment to remember to respond. "Nobody wanting anything from you that you can't fulfill, or that you have to fulfill." Her voice was breathy and soft, brushing the hairs on the nape of his neck like the touch of fingers. "You just lie back, and the water closes around you, soothes you, pleasures you."

"When you feel like that, everything you do or don't do...it's just a natural response to pleasurable stimuli, nothing calculated," he said.

She focused on him. "Yes," she said. "I guess you could say that."

Mark straightened, offered her a hand. "Leave the shoes," he said. "You won't need them."

Nicole smiled at that, and stepped out onto the soft, packed earth and tufts of grass pushing through it to erase the presence of man. Mark led her to the center of the cul-de-sac, where there was a patch of sunlight unlaced by the interlocking arms of the live oaks and fluttering fronds of the tall fan palms and longleaf pines.

Mark knelt in front of her, holding her hands. "Are you afraid, Nicole?"

She managed a half smile, a little shrug that sent a quiver through her breasts beneath the soft drape of the dress.

He tightened his grip on her fingers, just a gentle squeeze. "You don't have to be afraid of me, Nicole. I won't hurt you, not for anything. Any moment, any second you want this to be over, you just say so, and you can go home."

"You've already hurt me," she responded quietly. "And my heart is broken. It wants to go home, as much as my soul wants to stay here as long as you let me, until that last boat comes. I don't want this to be over. Ever." Her gaze shifted to encompass their surroundings, the corners of her mouth turning up. "My only nervousness comes from city girl stuff, you know. It's so…quiet and isolated here."

"I know. But I didn't want to do this where people could see us. And if I can't have your body bare for me now, I'll go insane. Do you know how I'm going to punish you for disobeying me, Nicole?"

She shook her head, her eyes large in her face, silhouetted by the shadowy depths of the forest around them.

"The purpose of a punishment is to teach a lesson. And that lesson is that you're always supposed to obey me. If you don't, I just have to remind you that you exist for my pleasure, and make you helpless to me in all ways."

He released her hands. Moving slowly, his gaze on her face, he placed his fingers on the double-wrapped sash at her waist. It swung and made the chimes speak softly as he worked the knot free.

He rose to his knees and unwrapped the first pass around her waist. "Hold the ends," he said, pressing one into each of her palms. "And don't move. Not even a twitch. Not a blink."

As if the suggestion had caused it, her body chose that moment to make her blink. She blanched, dismayed. Mark grinned at her, making her laugh, and he touched her nose with a finger.

Then he took that same finger down over her chin, her throat, along the line of her sternum. Instead of taking the dress over her head this time, he chose to unbutton the tiny row of buttons all the way down the front, from neckline to hem. He parted the two panels of fabric as if he were opening a curtain. Gazing down at what he was doing, her features showed a combination of arousal, apprehension and anticipation he wished an artist could capture on canvas. The female face had so many expressions, and so many nuances for every one of those expressions, it was like a book that he never wanted to finish reading. The man lucky enough to have Nicole would never have to close the cover and call it done.

The fabric caught on her right nipple and then the tight tip was free, drawing up even further from the touch of the air. The left breast was flushed, as if her heartbeat was increasing the blood flow just beneath the surface. The soft concave plane of her upper abdomen trembled when the muscles contracted beneath it.

He removed two of the butterflies from the bag, one in a rich royal blue and yellow, the other a vibrant orange monarch. Loosening the wiry curl of their feet, he raised the first one to the mauve nipple, already tightening in aroused anticipation of his intentions.

Nicole drew in her breath as his fingers brushed her breast, kneaded its weight in his hand, then pinched her nipple between thumb and forefinger, tightening the butterfly's legs on it so her breast was grazed by its silken wings. The heat surrounding them here in the hushed forest gave the butterfly's wings a gentle beat that brushed the plump curve as he left it free and moved to the other breast and nipple to give them his undivided attention.

Her pussy dampened at his methodical application of the butterflies. She suspected the heat coming off her skin spurred their wing beats as much as the warm air around them. The wings rose and fell almost with her breath, up, down, the tiny feet shifting imperceptibly to the eye with the movement, but her highly sensitized nipple felt the slight increase and release in pressure, so that she was hard-pressed to obey and remain motionless as commanded.

"Not a single movement from here on out, Kitten," he warned again. "Or you'll displease your Master greatly. This is your punishment. I'm going to arouse you so high and hard, withholding your release until I desire it, to make you remember whose Will you serve, always."

"Yes, Master." She stifled a throaty whimper as even the vibration of her vocal cords appeared to impact the clasp of the tiny legs on her distended nipples.

It was music to Mark. Her thighs were shaking again, and from the expression on her face, he suspected it was arousal tempered by trepidation at her own capacity for daring, heretofore unexplored. That knowledge spurred his own desires, the sense of possession that he knew was false. Even so, his mind said it fiercely.

Mine. Mine to claim. To possess. To fuck. To do this with.

This was a first for her, all she was doing today. It overpowered and humbled him, to see the innocence in her face.

Still keeping his movements slow, he took the ends of the sash from her hands. He passed them down between her bare legs, moving closer so he could reach around her to complete his intent. He used tension rather than touch to ensure the lengths of the sash followed the joining slant of hips to thighs, framing but not touching her pussy. He brought the ends of the sash up behind her, making them form a sling that gathered up the bottom of the dress in back, like a bustle that exposed her pretty backside to his gaze.

He crossed the two ends of the sash around the front and then to the back of her waist again, blessing the designer who had made it a double-tied sash that provided him plenty of length left to realize his own design. He pressed the two ends back into her hands. "Nicole, I want you to begin twisting the slack of the sash around each of your wrists, until you have bound yourself as closely as the sash will allow to the crosstie at the back."

She nodded and began to turn her wrists, looping the slack of the sash around her, the delicate bones. As she twisted and looped, the slack diminished, and her wrists were drawn back, lifting and jutting her breasts out from the frame of the pale green fabric.

She could free herself at any time, but the binding made her look helpless, bound for his unlimited explorations. Mark, still kneeling at her waist, could smell her response. As he watched, a drop of that response trickled down her thigh, slowing until it poised, just at mid-thigh.

She had some of the softness to her upper thighs that women who worked in offices had to combat, but he liked the gentle give of her skin beneath his lips as he pressed them there, tasting her salt and slickness. She let out a little moan, her hands flexing on her bindings. He eased his hand in between her legs, out the other side. Fanned his fingers out over the left cheek of her bare ass, and curled them around the small area of sash between her two wrapped wrists, pulling her up and back further, holding her in place.

"Mark...Master," she said, her voice hoarse.

"Nothing required," he said, looking up at the wondrous loose movement of her upturned breasts, the convulsive swallowing in her throat. "Just a natural response to pleasurable stimuli...nothing calculated. Another example of the benefits a Master claims when he kneels before his slave."

Before she could say another word, he bent forward and placed his mouth over her dripping cunt.

The texture of the aroused pink clitoris and labia against his mouth was exactly like that of the inside of a sun-warmed fruit, like the peach they had eaten, just as it was so often described. The tactile experience was sweet, but the taste was not. The taste was something incomparable to sustenance of any kind, unless this was what had been meant by manna from heaven.

He traced the engorged petals of flesh with his tongue, licked with a firm stroke. She moaned again, her head falling back on her shoulders. Steadying her with that hand on the binding and her ass, pressing there so she felt the restraint against her buttocks, he grasped the generous meat of one cheek, his fingertips tickling the heated back entrance and soft feathers of hair around it. She let out a soft, protesting cry at this new stimulus, but he kept his fingers tight there, holding her, forcing her to enjoy his will.

There was a crackle of twigs. She stiffened, and he raised his head. To their right, a doe slipped out of the forest, watching them with mysterious and yet innocent dark eyes. Eyes like Nicole's, he realized.

There was no hunting on the island, and deer had learned a wary curiosity but no fear of the humans who shared the island with them. Nicole was as still as the creature, and Mark recognized that he had control of the next move. He put his lips back onto Nicole's moist pussy and she drew in a breath, startled. He eased his tongue deep into her passage. As Nicole let out a guttural groan, he was aware of the doe, satisfied with their absence of threat, stepping further into the clearing and lowering her head to browse on the grasses there around them.

He withdrew, tongued the clit again, slow, so slow, and Nicole shuddered, hard. It wasn't enough to make her come. He made it too slow, and he kept doing it, the upward, gradual sweep pulling her to the cliff edge, and then withdrawing, leaving her teetering.

Making love to a woman's pussy with one's mouth was an art form. It had to be studied intensely to be understood, to know what areas would be oversensitive to the wrong type of touch, and what areas needed rougher treatment, and at what moment. Mark had put effort into learning. Always an engineer, he had thought at one time some woman could make millions off a "practice pussy" wired with different lights that would go off when a man did it right, before he tested his oral skills on the real thing. The only problem was, every woman was different, and so a man had to experiment. Not necessarily a hardship.

He fucked her with his tongue again, swirling it along the sides of that tight passage, and her knees would have given out if he hadn't been holding her. He made sure his nose caressed her clit as he did it, and he heard the rapid gasp of breath from her throat, a woman straining to release. But not yet. He was the Master. He could keep her this way for hours, until she was mindless with the desire for release, her exhaustion so great she abandoned any rational thought for the writhing need to be fucked.

The doe's head came up and Mark froze, even as Nicole made a noise of warning. A mature stag crashed into the clearing, his rack of antlers as wide as the golf cart's windshield, and the light in his eyes clearly that of a male in the midst of manic rut. He focused on them, on Mark specifically, immediately identifying the male scent.

"Stay still," Mark said quietly. "And if he charges me, run for the cart."

He heard Nicole swallow, felt her shiver, a little convulsive shudder caused by the crash of her arousal into fear from physical threat. Her juices made her thighs glisten and Mark experienced some of that same struggle himself. His cock was rock-hard and he was sure the smell of sex was strong in the air. He hoped the stag didn't decide he was a challenge for the doe's affections.

However, while their presence downwind had startled the stag, he now seemed to be recovering from his shock, his attention shifting to his true intent.

The doe was stepping prettily away from him, her tail raised high, showing what assets she had to offer, making Mark realize he had been giving chase to her before she came into the clearing. Typically, the does preferred to be pursued before they went through this final courtship dance.

The stag snorted ferociously, making a bellowing, blowing noise. *Possession*, was all Mark could think as the powerful animal took a step forward, reared up and was on her, not more than twenty-five feet from where he and Nicole stood, close enough that they saw the impressive equipment ram into the doe's eager opening.

This would be a good time to retreat, but watching the stag madly pumping into the doe, her head reared back, wild eyes rolling, gave him a different idea. Nicole made a sound of shock as he turned his head and went back to the business of eating her pussy.

The smell of the stag was strong, as was their coupling, and it mingled with the smells coming from Nicole's body, the gleam of perspiration on her skin. Her soft cries did not faze the stag. At this point Mark suspected a hunter could walk right up to the intent male and plant a bullet in the noble brow at point blank range. For that matter, he could say the same for himself. Like all males, he and the stag would die with smiles on their faces. Or snouts.

The rhythmic grunts, shifts of hooves in the earth, the smell of animal, forest and woman, all drew around him in a cocoon that tightened his hold on his woman, made the long strokes and deep stabs of his tongue more insistent.

Something featherlight touched his skin, and he saw that in her convulsive grip, tangled in the sash, the flower ring had disintegrated, the woven band tumbling to the ground, its petals picked up and swirled onto his wrist and forearm by the breeze. The flower had come apart the way he wanted her to come apart for him.

Come for me, the tight grasp of his fingers on her ass demanded. He jerked on the binding holding her wrists, bouncing her breasts, stimulating them as he shoved her harder against his mouth, made it a rhythm, sucked with smacks of noisy pleasure on her quivering flesh, snaked his tongue in and out of her, squeezed her ass. Their rhythm matched that of the stag and willing doe. She looked too fragile for the brute clinging to her back, but she held him up, though his powerful thrusts drove her head toward the earth and looked more than capable of bringing her to her knees.

Nicole cried out, the noise of a wild animal, and her clit and labia spasmed against his mouth, that involuntary shudder that orgasm brought. Like a rippling tidal wave that affected the body inside and out, it turned her bucking form into pure energy and sensation. She writhed, tried to break free as it became too much, but he wouldn't let her, taking her higher, trying to shatter her. Her cry escalated to a scream as he milked her response, using his mouth to prolong stimulation to the thousands of nerve endings centered in this one part of her body. The pulsing continued, like the long ripple of a manta ray's wings as it shot through the water. Those wings were carried by elements the manta understood by instinct, mysteries beyond the limiting confines of rational knowledge. Like Nicole's surrender to pleasure, some things were understood only by the soul in its most primitive form, where need and desire had no judgments.

If nothing else, he could give her that, for this moment at least. Take her past worries and fears into the realm of desire and energy. She could look back on this day and know, without question or fear, that he had never wanted to claim a woman more.

Chapter Thirteen

Nicole's scream must have startled the deer, for when Mark surfaced from his absorption in her pleasure, their animal companions were gone, their business completed or taken elsewhere. He knew the stag would mate with the doe several times over the next few days, protecting her and being her companion for that time. But then instinct would drive him on to the next doe and he would abandon her.

He pushed that thought away as he removed the butterflies. He freed her hands, pulled the front of the dress together, tied the sash to hold it rather than redoing the buttons. Nicole's knees were so weak in the aftermath that he simply picked her up, taking her to the golf cart, sliding her into the seat next to him. The day was getting late, and there were only a few hours before the ferry would leave for the last run of the day.

When he put the cart into reverse, keeping his arm around her, she lifted her head heavily from his shoulder. "Where are we going?"

"To my house," he said, and his mouth lifted in a smile that didn't reach his serious eyes. "As you probably know, if your PI was worth his money, I live on Ballentyne Island."

* * * * *

She must have dozed after that surprising statement, for Nicole quite suddenly found herself somewhere she hadn't been only moments ago. Or what seemed like moments ago.

She was on the angled portion of a sectional sofa, curled up on her side. She was facing a panoramic window view of the marshland behind Ballentyne Island and it was late afternoon.

The significance of that struck her and she mentally cursed her weariness that had robbed her of even one moment of consciousness in Mark's company.

She jerked up, and found her mobility had been restricted. A soft nylon rope tied her wrists together in front of her and ran down to her knees. The binding wrapped around them and then traveled to her ankles, likewise held together by clever knots. She was in a comfortable spoon position on her side, but the ropes were taut, so she could not straighten any further out of the S-shape. She was completely naked, the dress lying over a nearby chair.

It was a clear action of ownership. He had unclothed her, tied her up, and now sat directly across from her, watching her with a singular intensity that made her hunger leap back to life in her breasts, her loins and the pit of her stomach, mingling with the apprehension of being so helpless. She was his, and they were completely alone.

"I'm sorry I fell asleep," she said softly.

He shook his head. "You weren't out for long. And I liked watching you. Planning what I'm going to do to you."

Her heart rate increased further at that, but she tried to keep her voice casual. "Pretty good knot work for an engineer."

His grin was quick and potent. "I also sail, remember?" He slid the ottoman out of his way and stood, which forced her to tilt her head to see his face, and underscored the upper hand he had at this point over her. She licked her lips.

"So, may I ask my Master what his plans for his slave are?"

"To make you scream with pleasure, over and over again, until it's captured in the stillest echoes of this house forever."

His face was a little frightening in its determination, and she understood how pleasure could be a threat. She shifted. "What's this under me?"

"You're lying on a light covering of plastic so we won't get any oils on the couch. I've cushioned it by laying a quilt beneath it. It's very soft, one I've had since I was a boy." He reached out to smooth a hand down her bare calf. "You have them wax you, instead of shaving."

She nodded. "You told me it was the best way to stay smooth." Watching his face, she lifted her right top thigh as much as was permitted, just a couple inches in this position, but enough to draw his eyes to what she was trying to reveal. "Especially here. I went every two weeks, as you commanded."

"It's hard for you, isn't it?" he asked quietly. "To be this forward? To respond when your Master is being such a brute."

She closed her eyes, felt his hand touch her face. She wanted to let the dam break, tell him everything she felt and knew. But she was afraid he'd send her away, and if today was all she had, she was going to do what she had to do to cherish every moment until sundown.

"You're holding back on me, Nicole. A slave doesn't do that."

She raised her lashes. "Do you want me to tell you everything in my heart, Mark? Spill it out on the floor so you can sweep it up and throw it away once you toss me back on that boat?"

He thought the depth of the emotions he saw in her eyes would leave a stain over everything around him that he'd never be able to sweep away, even if he wanted to do so.

He didn't blink, but she felt the reach of her emotions bounce against him, resonate back on her as if she had screamed into an empty canyon. "Yes, Nicole. I want you to give me everything. If a man goes off to work, and he's killed in a crash on the way home, how do you think his wife would have lived her life differently with him that day? How would they spend the moments of their morning together, if she'd known what was going to happen, and knew there was nothing she could do to stop it?" He pressed a finger to her lips, made them open so he could touch her tongue, the inside of her mouth. Withdrawing, he took his damp fingers down the line of her throat, to the slope of her breast. "What would you do, Nicole?"

His gaze hardened. "For that's what a Master demands of his sub, every minute, every day, every interaction. Everything, every part of you. Open to me, all mine, in all ways until I release you. Then there are no regrets, no would-have-beens, should-have-beens. Every day is treated as if it's the last day we'll ever see each other."

Tears spilled onto her cheeks, and he bent forward, placed his lips against them and took them into himself, her pain into him. His arm came around her shoulders as he moved toward her mouth and she turned her head, meeting him.

After his carefully chosen words, the slow pace of this caress, she expected the kiss to be gentle, controlled. Instead, at the first contact between their mouths, his arm tightened around her back and his mouth forced hers open, his tongue taking command of hers, leaving her no room to think or breathe. He held nothing back, at least in this exchange. He let her feel how desire raged through him. She moaned, her body clutching inside at the evidence of it, and she wished she could hold him, dig her fingers into him, but she was only able to absorb the shock wave of his need through all her senses, through that one heated point of contact. He bit her tongue, soothed it with firm strokes, and kept such a forceful entry her jaw ached, her throat working to swallow the moisture from their mouths.

It put her in mind of something else, something that grew into an overpowering desire, overriding inhibitions and shyness. Even so, she might not have voiced it, except that he had just demanded that she voice every desire, no matter how vulnerable it left her, teaching her that equity and fairness had nothing to do with the D/s relationship.

When he pulled back, his hand coming forward to lay along her throat, his thumb on her jugular, pressing against the pounding life there, she swept her gaze down, focused on her desire.

"Master," she whispered. "I want to..." She swallowed, kept her eyes down to give her the courage. "I want to suck on your cock."

He tipped up her chin roughly, made her look at him through her embarrassment. "Soon," he promised, his voice harsh. "I'll stretch that pretty mouth of yours soon. But there's something else I'm going to do with you first, so I'll always have it, and your scent with this quilt."

She hated how everything he said seemed to emphasize that they would be saying goodbye soon. Nicole closed her eyes, turned her face away, but he wouldn't let her close herself off. He moved from her lips to her throat, that most sensitive of all her erogenous zones, and sensation shot through her shoulders, her breasts. Before she could call herself a traitor she had arched her neck, offering it to him. His fingers played down her back, to her waist, and gripped her as his teeth scored her.

"Are you mine, Nicole?"

"I hate you," she said brokenly. "You know I am."

"Tell me."

"I'm yours, Master."

"Good." He drew his head back, so she missed him with the not-so-gentle nip of her teeth. Catching her chin in hard fingers, he gave her a little shake to make her behave and rose, his eyes raging with the same turbulent storm she knew he saw in hers. "Stay here."

She didn't have long to wait, for he returned with a tray of items that he turned and placed on the coffee table out of range of her view.

"I'm hungry, Nicole, and I intend to make you my dinner, arousing you so you come so hard you can't think of anything but me. You knew the risks in coming here. I want to take you over, make you my submissive. Since I can't do that beyond today, I plan to be merciless in claiming you in every way, so you'll never forget me, so no man will ever be able to claim you as I've claimed you." He slid his finger over her cheek. "All you have to do is say stop."

She might have done that at this moment, when she felt so stricken by the overwhelming combination of his desire and rejection, but she didn't. Digging up her courage and hope, she looked him in the eye. "I love you, Mark. You may do anything to me that gives you pleasure. I'm all yours, Master, and I have been since the moment we met on a computer screen."

His expression went flat, unreadable, and he reached out, ran a hand along the side of her breast, as if testing her words, not giving her anything emotional. She lay still under his touch, trembling, waiting.

It was a long several moments, and perversely, the more withdrawn his visage, the more intimate his touch became. He fondled her nipples, slid his hand down her belly, fingered her cunt, making her gasp as he touched her as if she were his possession in truth, like a prized sculpture. As if he owed her nothing, expecting total compliance from her.

"I love you, Master," she whispered, refusing to let him distance her from his mind. She'd been inside his mind, she knew she had, and she clung to that man, the man she knew beneath this destructive armor. She knew all the dangers for a woman who believed she could save a man's soul, but she felt so closely entwined with his that she thought her own life might depend on her actions now.

He jerked his hand away with a soft curse. Not looking at her, he took a seat on the ottoman and released the line connecting her wrists, knees and ankles, but left her wrists and crossed ankles bound as he rolled her to her back.

"Spread open for me," he ordered.

Her knees fell open, forming a diamond shape since the ankles were still wrapped together. He picked up a bottle from the tray she could not see and poured some of the contents in his hand. A tangy aroma touched her nostrils as he brought it to her.

He began to rub the oil over her smooth mound, his fingers dipping immediately, decisively into her. No preparation time, as if she were his slave in truth, and he had no need to inform her of his intentions, just to simply do as he wished to her body, because she was bound and open to him.

He was a very commanding Master in person, more so than online where some distance could be established. There was no distance here, nothing but him overpowering her senses, and she suspected that if he was not constrained by his own self-imposed restrictions, he would be Mastering her even more definitively. Was this what he feared? That she couldn't take it? That no woman could take what he wanted?

She gasped as he worked her clit, went deeper into her passageway.

"I'm not sure you needed that," she managed. "As wet as I already am for you, Master."

"You will need to be very, very wet for this," he promised, his look sliding a frisson of anticipation up her spine. She wished she could see what was on that tray.

"You know what I appreciate, Nicole?" He worked his fingers even deeper inside of her and she gasped, squirmed as he unerringly stroked that dense spot of sensual release within her. "You need to answer me."

"What…Master?"

"I appreciate the diversity of a well-made salad."

It startled a chuckle out of her, somewhere between nervous hysteria, arousal and true humor, and saw a flash of the latter in his gaze, steadying her. It warmed her in places that had become cold from the emotional chill with which he had tried to freeze her.

He had let her come behind his formidable shields in the digital world, and so now, despite his intimidation in the real world, he couldn't shut out the truth from her. Or at least one truth. Seeing that flash of reassurance in his gaze, despite his intentions to be aloof from her, it reminded her of what she had sensed for a long time about Mark. Even if she failed and today was the end, he would be there if ever she truly needed a friend or rescuer. He loved her too much not to be. His heart had spoken to hers and told her that a million times over, even as his mind and words denied her what they both knew was true.

Between the many interactions they'd had as Master and slave, man and woman, friendship had planted its roots, and it provided some comfort now where it was most needed. She wondered if he even knew it was there, born during those weekly dinners he had instigated, where they had cultivated a genuine interest in one another.

"It makes me...angry, the way they throw too much lettuce into a bowl, toss in a couple tomatoes and a slice of cucumber, drown it in dressing and then call that cheap, put-together thing a salad." He considered the contents of the tray outside the scope of her vision. "A salad is a mixture of carefully chosen ingredients, prepared in certain ways, arranged and selected not just for taste but for presentation. The marination of the dressing is important. You want each piece of the salad lightly immersed, to bring out its taste, so the taste of that dressing enhances each crevice." His fingers withdrew from her, stroking up the line of her clit. "Draws out the pleasure for the taste buds. And you can put all sorts of surprises into a salad. Seeds and nuts, exotic bits of dried fruit someone hasn't tried before. They bite into it, thinking it's perhaps a pear or pineapple, and discover it's a starfruit or a bit of mango."

He lifted the glass bottle of dressing where she could see it, and Nicole's eyes never left him as he administered more golden oil to his hands, then drizzled it over her body, starting at her sternum, moving down over each breast, circling the tip, then drawing a line to her navel, swinging up to anoint the opposite nipple as if he were making a chain out of the fragrant liquid. He sat the decanter back down on the tray and began to slick her body down, spreading out the dressing, rubbing it onto her breasts, her throat, her belly, her thighs. Leaving no area untouched, he worked it into places like the crease beneath her breasts and into the navel area. His touch was warm, strong, absolute. Confident in the way he touched her, so confident she was not tickled when she normally would be, as if her body was in a curious state, between relaxation and arousal.

"It's a balsamic vinaigrette I'm putting on you now. I've added some olive oil to it because you're going to need it. Turn on your side, Nicole. Away from me."

She did, and his hands replenished with oil and then slid up her back. He surprised her when he buried his hands in her hair, slicking it back in sleek lines from her face, so no expression could be hidden or altered by its frame about her features.

When he massaged the dressing into her back, she couldn't help purring, almost writhing, which caused her thighs to slide easily against one another. The oil made the plastic beneath her a slippery surface, against which no undulation or sinuous writhing met any resistance, her only restriction coming from the bindings he had on her wrists and ankles.

His hands molded her waist, her hips, his thumbs working into the small of her back, down, inserting themselves in between her cheeks.

"Relax, Nicole," he admonished, his fingers lubricating the rim of that secret and dark passageway. She felt his shift as he moved, reached for the bottle again. Holding her cheeks open, he placed the metal tip of the bottle close to his index finger, which prodded at her tight opening, enough so she felt the trickle as he poured a draught of oil directly into her.

"Mark…"

"Easy," he soothed. "Trust me, Nicole."

She was oiled inside and out, the wetness of her own body combining with what he had applied to make her ready for anything. He leaned over her and even greased her lips with the oil, causing her to moisten them, an involuntary reaction, taking some of the taste inside.

"Now that's not going to work, if you keep licking it off," he reproved with a smile that was fueled by the heat of his gaze. "Open up, love. As wide as you can for me. Your mouth," he amended, as she spread her thighs wider, as much as the ankles allowed. She colored from the neck up, but he shook his head, reproving her. "Your willingness to offer your pussy pleases me, Kitten. No shame. Now, your mouth."

She obeyed, and he produced a firm red tomato. With the residue on his hands lubricating it, he inserted it into her mouth, going in slowly, as Nicole widened at his direction as far as she could, her jaw muscles aching. When she thought there was no way it would fit, it abruptly slipped past her teeth and settled onto her tongue, pressing it down and fitting snug against the roof of her mouth, trapping her tongue so she couldn't exercise the ability to speak or the involuntary reaction to lick when he applied oil to her mouth again.

She had felt many things since she stepped on the ferry. Excitement, apprehension. He'd brought her to orgasm. But this was a ritual preparation, as if each action he made was a step toward total submission. His Mastery was taking her, not against her will, but overpowering her will, making everything inside her out of her control. As if she was not the person she'd always thought she was.

Parts of her she thought she had solidly sealed or reinforced in her psyche were starting to loosen and fragment. Like her body was a planet she'd thought was inviolate, until the sun drew close and all of what was cool and collected deep within her began to heat, simmer, boil and then erupt forth, destroying her terra layers until what emerged was a shimmering, shivering pure energy being, responding to his pull on her.

And what made it even more intense, the brimming, explosive energy, was that she saw in his eyes he knew exactly what he was doing to her, what was going on inside her. He knew the emotional turmoil she was in, but had drawn the heat forth anyway, demanding it from her, if only for a day. She had wanted not only to play submissive but to *be* his submissive, and he had taken up her gauntlet. He was showing her what being Mastered by him meant. To give him everything, to prove to him she was his submissive, willing to trust him, even with nothing promised to her beyond sundown. It was an act of devotion, and she had no intention of failing in it. If he turned her away, it would not be because he doubted the commitment of her soul to him. She fiercely believed he deserved that once in his life, even if it destroyed her heart.

"Don't bite into it," he said. His eyes studied her face. The light in his eyes showed he was entranced with her. The room grew exponentially more still and warm to her, like the hush of a church as he made her into the altar for his particular devotions.

"If you have pain or discomfort at any point," he said quietly, "I want you to shake your head, 'no'. I won't take it as a refusal, but that something's wrong. I don't want to hurt you, Nicole. Not a moment of unpleasant pain."

I trust you, she said with her eyes.

"Good." He turned her on her back again and retrieved two radishes from the tray, about the size of large marbles. They were clean, washed and trimmed, so she saw the white flesh at the ends, framed by the dark fuchsia hue of the shiny skin. Mark withdrew his knife and notched one end, creating a cross slit. He reached forward, touched her nipple between thumb and forefinger as if measuring, and then hollowed out the radishes slightly with the sharp curved spike. He deposited the displacement on his tray, and then bent over her.

She quivered at his touch on her breast, his quiet absorption as he worked. She didn't feel ignored; if anything, she felt equally absorbed into his conscious awareness. Even as his attention was on his task, she somehow knew that his senses were highly aware of her awkward breathing through her nose and around the tomato, the slick feel of her body as she made slight movements against herself and the warm plastic cover.

Now she made a gasp in the back of her throat as he pinched her slippery nipple. He pressed on the sides of the radish, opened up the cross slit and then slid it over her nipple. When he released the sides and the tiny red orb clamped down on her, the immediate effect was pressure bordering on pain. She almost shook her head, but he was watching her carefully, and she wanted the experience he was offering to her. So she opened herself up to the pain, took deep breaths through her nose, and the pain merged with an arousing tingle in her whole breast, centered densely on the nipple area. It communicated itself to her wet pussy, made her thighs want to close and tighten on that sensation. But since he wanted her open, she remained so, though even the touch of the close air was stimulating the lips of her weeping sex.

He lifted the other radish and went through the same process with the knife. He could have made the cuts on both radishes at the same time. But by doing them one at a time she had several excruciating moments for the anticipation to build, especially now that she knew what was coming. Watching his hands handle the knife, the spike, the studied expression, his firm jawline. The amber wolf's eyes that did not flick to her, but she knew were registering every twitch, every gasp of arousal as she lay there, writhing in tiny movements, her body glistening with oil, her pussy open to him, her mouth stretched around the shiny red flesh of the tomato.

When he leaned over her, she lifted her head, brushing her temple against his chest, unable to help herself, pressing her nose into his side, wishing she could bury herself in him now.

"Sweet girl," he murmured, and his hand came up to cup the back of her head, hold her there as he slid the other radish into place, the oil and strength of his fingers gripping the sides, allowing him to do it in one maneuver.

The instance of pain followed by release, the proportionate rise of desire. She was going to detonate from all the stimulation.

Her body arched up at the clasp of the firm vegetables and he stroked his knuckles down the slick line of her ribs, caressed across her stomach, grazed his fingertips over her mound.

"I want you on your side again," he said.

She'd left an imprint of the oil on his shirt, and it caught his attention in that moment. With a movement so casual it denied his awareness of how greedy she was for a sight of his uncovered flesh, he removed the black T-shirt, revealing that the chest, shoulders and arms beneath were indeed like that of a wrestler. Dense, compact muscle, a light mat of copper hair over the defined pectorals and sectioned stomach muscles that drew her eyes to his waistband and all she hungered to see beneath it.

"Turn, Nicole," he reminded her softly. He helped her, folding her knees back together and turning her. She grazed his chest and upper abdomen with her bound fingertips as he bent over her. She wanted to caress, dig in, hold handfuls of his firm flesh to her.

A shudder ran through his body at her touch. She realized abruptly that it was the first time he had permitted her a caress, something other than her clinging to him during the spanking, or the contacts he had initiated. The flare in his eyes showed her a maelstrom of emotions tightly compacted behind that stern expression. She moaned around the gag, wanting him desperately.

He eased her to her side, denying her the view of his body. She heard the clink of the bottle, knew whatever he was considering was receiving lubricant. Then he brought it into her view.

A carrot of impressive size, with a peeled and rounded top. It had been thoroughly washed like the radishes, so its orange color gleamed. The top end was far thicker than the bottom, and the bottom had a diameter of two to three inches.

"Some of these larger carrots don't have the same sweetness as the small, but I've found if you peel them, coat them with the dressing, it will sink in and bring out the carrot's flavor. But for you, I've left the skin on the length of it, because I want you to feel the slight abrasion of each rounded ridge as it's inserted into your anus." He passed his fingers over the ridges. "Until we get to the largest one you can take, or this final ring here, which will be wide enough to hold it outside your body. You need to take deep breaths," he said. "And relax. Relax all your muscles for me, Nicole. Show me how much you trust me. Give me everything. Deep breaths. One...let it out. Now, take it in."

The tip went in on her next released breath, and when she drew in slowly, he inserted the next two rings. The long shaft eased in, enabled by all the oil he'd put into her and on the carrot, but it was the first time she'd ever been penetrated in the ass, and it was just as it had been described emotionally. It was a personal submission to him, more personal even than her pussy, and that internal fragmentation she had been experiencing ratcheted up to a landslide, the crumbling of a mountain. A whimper of need came from her throat, her fingers clutching the plastic in spasmodic reaction as he took it deeper and stretched her, going past the strong sphincter muscle like it wasn't there, having made her helpless to this penetration with the lubricant.

When it was lodged so far in her she felt stuffed, immobilized, he stopped. Stopped his forward movement, but not his playing with her. He caressed her ass cheeks, squeezed them around the carrot so she felt every ridge within her, her stretched rim, played with it with his fingers until she was rocking and gasping, struggling not to bite down on the tomato, her eyes tearing.

He rolled her to her back again slowly, and the motion put pressure on the two inches of carrot protruding from her ass. The base was too wide to drive it deeper, but the pressure rocked the stimulus within her. Almost incoherent in her own thoughts, still she put up a token resistance to the turn. She didn't want him to see that in her excitement she had salivated around her mouth. Her eyes tearing had made her nose run, and no amount of sniffling was helping.

"Nicole," he said sternly, when she tried to avert her face, struggling against him. "You will look at me." The turning he did himself, her bound body no match for his strength. "Now," he said sharply, and she turned her face toward him, brought there partially by his hand against her cheek.

He ran his finger down a tear track, touched the side of her runny nose. "You're beautiful to me, and I want you in control of nothing, including your own bodily functions. Every part of you is mine to care for. Now…" He wiped her chin, around her mouth and the corners of her eyes with a wet cloth he had on the tray. He pulled a tissue up from a box on the coffee table, held it to her nose. "Blow," he instructed, more gently.

She did, and felt something deep within her quiver as he cared for her this way, taking care of her at every level, leaving nothing for her to call her own. She shook all over now, and was glad for the warmth the quilt provided beneath the plastic, for it was almost like where he was taking her was putting her in a state akin to traumatic shock.

He set the tissue and washcloth aside and withdrew another object from the tray, one that made her eyes widen and her stomach simultaneously clench with lust and trepidation.

"No salad is complete without a cucumber," he commented, pouring oil over the dark green skin before her eyes.

At its widest part she thought it was three inches in diameter, easily, and it was about eight inches in length.

"Now a man would have difficulty keeping a cock this large and broad fully erect to satisfy his woman," he observed. "But the wonder of nature is, it compensates." He slid forward and she tensed, she couldn't help it.

Mark laid a hand along the side of her throat. "Nicole, look at me."

She pulled her eyes away from the thing, and up to his brown eyes. "All you've got to do is shake your head if it becomes painful. I don't want to cause you distress, remember. But I think you can take this. I know you can, if you trust me."

His faith and confidence were like a balm on her nerves, and she felt the peculiar stillness returning. She nodded, once, and he leaned forward, kissed her nose, then the curve of her lips, stretched over the tomato, robbing her of speech.

"Deep breaths again, and I want you to raise your legs up slightly, pull them back, as if you were going to give birth."

He applied firm pressure to her bound ankles, raising them higher in the air so he could take the cucumber in beneath them, increasing her sense of vulnerability and trepidation. The movement shifted the carrot within her, set off a ripple of response that increased in intensity as he began to insert the firm head of the cucumber.

He was distending every orifice of her body, making her take more than she thought possible, and this last orifice was like the final nail on a sensual crucifixion, her senses now opening to a world they hadn't even known was possible. She could hear her blood running through her body, the pulse points pounding in her wrists, heart, womb. She tilted her hips, undulated, her body's instinct working with him to make full penetration possible.

The smell of the balsamic filled her, pooled in her mouth, and she had to fight the desire again to bite down into the fullness of that tomato, savor the juices its aroma said were waiting just beyond the fragile leash of restraint. It was a fresh garden tomato, bringing her the scent of sunshine and earth. Mark stroked her clit with his thumb as he eased the cucumber in through the diamond of her raised legs. Incredibly, she felt her body opening wider, muscles and bones relaxing in ways she didn't realize they could, responding to his commands, desires which matched her own, the synergy of Master and slave coming together to reach a pinnacle that could not be reached alone.

"It's there, Nicole," he said, husky. "You did it. You accepted me in every part of yourself, as a devoted slave will. I'm very, very pleased with you. Now..." he sat back, unfastened the top button of his jeans, but did not open them to her avid gaze yet. "Bite down on the tomato, Nicole. Take in its juices. Go slowly, very slowly. If you go slow enough, when you're done, I'll reward you with my cock in your mouth."

Her incisors sank into the firm skin, one of the most human-like in texture of all vegetables. As she controlled the descent of her teeth with a trembling jaw, she felt the slow seep of the flavor trickle onto her tongue. She had never been so ravenous for a tomato in all her life, and not just because of the prize that waited for her when she consumed it. Every nerve ending, taste bud and sensory input were on high alert. The feel of the radishes on her nipples, the cucumber and carrot stretching her pussy and ass, the oil that made her body's movements slide sinuously over the light cover, the bite of the ropes into her wrists and ankles, all stimulated her.

And his eyes enhanced it. His intent regard, his nearness, the heat of his body and the desire she could see strong against the crotch of his jeans and in the fist clenched at his right side. The only visible sign, other than his cock, of his desire. He was a cool one, her Master, but she now knew he was a volcano, she was so closely linked to him. She wanted the altar and sacrifice she made before him to call forth an eruption. She wanted him to claim her, immerse her in his fire, let her be consumed by him, as if he were a powerful fire god in truth.

Some of the juice and seeds escaped from the corners of her mouth, but this time she minded his words, and did not avert her face. She kept her aching, fierce eyes upon him and she chewed the pieces, broke them down, swallowed the nectar the fruit had to offer. Running her tongue around her lips to collect as much of it as she could, she experienced the flavor mingled with the heated taste of her own aroused flesh.

"Please, Master," she said, her mouth clear at last. "Let me give you pleasure. Put your cock in my mouth."

"You've done that, Kitten. In ways you can't possibly imagine. Now prove you're mine. Suck me off until I come in your mouth, savor my taste as you have that tomato."

"More," she whispered. "I'll beg if you want me to."

"Beg, then," he said roughly, his hand going to the open button of his jeans.

"Please, Master," she repeated. "I'm begging you. Let me serve your cock, serve you. I need your cock in my mouth. Please…"

With simple, deliberate movements that tightened her lower parts to an excruciating level around the invasive tools he'd used, he shoved his jeans down his hips with his underwear, and showed her his cock.

She saw a well-proportioned shaft, stretched to its full length, the skin pulled taut over its hardness, the small network of veins pulsing on the surface just below the broad head. She swallowed, tasting the flavor of the tomato lingering on her tongue, and wanted the heat of him mixing with it, wanted to taste his come in her mouth.

He stepped closer and turned her ninety degrees, lifting her legs so the backs of her thighs were against the backrest of the couch, her calves along the top edge of the headrest. As he carefully reseated the cucumber and carrot in her passages, she whimpered in sensual distress. The carrot pressed deeper into her as he situated her bottom firmly in the joining angle of the back and seat cushions. The cucumber pushed against her clit in its forced angle provided by the upper cushion. It was not a wide couch, so her neck curved over the front edge of the seat cushions, her head sloped somewhat down toward the floor.

He straddled her face and leaned forward, placing his hands on either side of her knees on the couch.

"Open your mouth to me, the way you'd spread your legs and offer your cunt."

She did, and he thrust home, his thighs rubbing against her temples, the rough hair and heated muscle surrounding her, his testicles pressed against the bridge of her nose as he took himself deep, so deep she gagged, began to cough.

He withdrew, but not all the way, broad head still in her mouth. "Relax your throat, Nicole. Relax it the way you did your pussy muscles, so it could take the cucumber, the way your ass did to take the carrot. The way you take my Will. You can take me deep, I know you can."

I already have, she thought. *So deep in my soul I'll never pull you out. Never want to.*

"Relax," he repeated, his hands rubbing over her calves, sliding down the inside of her thighs so she shuddered. "It's not relaxation like we know. Not like when we say 'sit down and relax'. It's the relaxation of a veteran soldier before battle, that hypnotic state where every part of the body is intensely alert. The consciousness narrows down, and everything in life is about the next few moments, so there's an odd tranquility of sorts that allows the body to relax and do things it can't normally do.

"I'm your Master, Nicole. Your body will accept me in whatever manner I desire to penetrate it, to fuck it. Let your heart and soul overtake your mind. Open up for me."

His voice entranced her, held her as much as the touch of his free hand now on her neck, his knuckles stroking her jugular.

His cock was deep against the inside walls of her throat before she realized he had eased forward again. Her lips pressed almost to the base before he withdrew, then surged forward again. He set the rhythm he wanted and she sucked and licked on him, stimulated by every stroke within the sensitive walls of her mouth and throat. As she would be if he was stroking her cunt in a like manner.

As intense as the physical stimulation was, the psychological far outstripped it. Here in the isolation of his home where it was only them, no one knowing where she was, she was bound, helpless, serving his cock with her mouth. It underscored that she was completely his slave in these moments, and she knew he knew it, was as absorbed in it as she was, so that the act was almost sacred, something known and shared only between the two of them.

She used her tongue on the downward strokes, darting it along his length to give quick licks to the sensitive vein right at the base of his cock, above his testicles, and she spoke her pleasure, making noises of hunger for more at each insistent shove. His thighs trembled, his grip tightening on the couch as he thrust roughly into her, over and over, his thighs slamming into her shoulders, his testicles slapping her face, his musky smell in her nose, and it was all a smothering pain she reveled in.

His cock pulsed and jetted, the come shooting in a hot trail deep down into her, already past the gate of her gag reflex so she swallowed it as a smooth hot stream. She suckled him with her mouth, pressing down with her lips as he bucked in and out, so it was like the clench of her cunt on him. Her tongue flicked wildly all over him, under, over, sucking the broad ridge of the head, crying out her passion as he did his, so stimulated by the moment that she had to give voice to it. Her pussy convulsed around the cucumber as he reached down, clasped it, and put a thumb on her clit.

Now she screamed, and though she'd milked him dry, he kept his still-hard cock in her mouth as he relentlessly worked her through her own orgasm, using his fingers to hold the end of the carrot and move it within her at the same time he pressed up on the cucumber and on her clit, so her body moved against the stimulus like an engine that had been on high idle, waiting for the gas pedal to be pushed. When his hand pushed it, she shot down a racetrack with dangerous curves, a stadium of screaming fans, and heat and haze.

Bound as she was, she had no control of the intensity or the length of the orgasm and so it catapulted her much higher than she'd ever thought she could go. She pushed past the moment when she usually withdrew her touch or lowered the vibrator, where the orgasm passed into an over-stimulated discomfort in its intensity. He took her through that mercilessly, and suddenly that moment was past and she was on a much higher wave, her legs spreading out like butterfly wings in truth, his careful fingers penetrating her everywhere while her mouth stayed trapped around his cock. She screamed and gasped around it, fought through panic and reaction to an area of complete surrender, where her body shuddered down to her bones, rattling her teeth even as he stoked her orgasm into a third wave.

It was a while before she started coming down, in little convulsive jerks and whimpers, intense aftershocks that kept reason and motor control beyond her reach. She hung onto his gaze, the desire she saw, the want and need open and hungry in his expression, and it kept her shuddering, realizing at last the depths of how much he wanted from a woman. And how deep she was willing to draw in herself to give it to him. He believed he didn't have the right to ask it, much less hope that there was one out there willing to give him that much of herself. And yet she was here, and wanting nothing more in life than to do so.

When at last her body lay limp, every muscle worn out, unable to command itself, he slowly eased the cucumber out of her, holding her lips apart to ease the passage. It felt odd to not have it there, to not have his cock in her mouth, now taken from her view because he had refastened his jeans, though he left his shirt off. It was as if he was releasing his claim on her as slowly and deliberately as he had claimed her, no matter that her eyes begged him not to do so.

Next came the carrot, then the radishes. He turned her to her side, then upright, bringing her feet to the floor.

"Lay your head back a few moments until the blood settles," he instructed. He sat next to her, moving the plastic, rolling it up between them so he was sitting on the quilt while her oily body still sat on the plastic. He stroked the slick line of her hair while she simply gazed at him. He sat facing her, settled on one hip, one leg bent onto the couch so he could study her, shelter her with the curve of his body, his elbow propped on the headrest while the other hand touched her face.

"In a moment," he said quietly, "I'll release your wrists and ankles, and you'll go shower. Then I'll take you to the boat."

Chapter Fourteen

She curled her fingers around the ropes holding her wrists, over the knot. "No." Her chin trembled and she lifted it. "No," she repeated.

He sighed, put his forehead against hers. She closed her eyes, pressed hard, mind to mind. "Please, Mark," she whispered.

He shook his head, and with a quickness that was startling and a little frightening, he flipped out the rigging knife, caught up her hands and sliced through the loop on the top of her wrist, the ropes falling away. He bent and did the same to her ankles even as she twisted, tried to get away, and then her arms and legs were both free.

"The shower." He lifted her to her feet by the elbow, with a gentle but firm pressure. "It's down that hallway. You'll find soap and towels there."

Nicole set her jaw, made her decision. She let her legs go out from beneath her, dropping her oiled bottom to the Berber carpet, making him stumble over her. "I'm not showering, and I'm not going," she said, curling her arms in on herself, a maneuver she suspected worked well for porcupines and badgers. "You try and make me, and I'll fight you every step. I won't make this easy for you."

In a very short time, he'd taught her to turn herself over to her emotions, let them lead her in D/s interactions. She made that switch now. She just didn't expect him to do the same, so fast and so dangerously.

She felt the tense cloud of warning around him, drawing closer as he bent down, hard purpose in his expression. "You're going."

He reached to lift her up by the shoulders, and she punched him in the jaw. She'd never hit anyone in her life, but there was nothing to lose in the strike, no calculation, just a desperate effort to win this battle in any way she could.

She had known that he held a part of himself back. She knew it was at least partly pain and fear that kept him from giving her everything he could dish out, but the insecurity that lurked in her woman's heart had also wondered if it was because he did not want her with the all-consuming, violent need she possessed for him.

With the throwing of the gauntlet, it was as if the horse charged the field without the rider, finally pushed beyond the hold of the reins. The need to rise to the challenge and charge into action overwhelmed any restraint and came together in a full tilt of wills she'd unleashed.

He swore, and recovered more quickly than she expected, but then it had been an inexperienced blow, and he was much stronger than she was. He caught her wrist on the next swing, captured her body and swung her up onto his shoulder, holding her relentlessly at the knees and across the waist as she screamed. She used her nails, raked at his bare back with her free hand, sank her teeth into it. He took her down the hallway and she kicked one foot loose, hit the wall. It knocked them both into the opposite wall. Straightening up, she twisted and grabbed at his hair, struck at the side of his head, struggling and wiggling like a greased animal at a fair. It vaguely penetrated her mind that he was letting her do the damage, keeping his hands occupied in a tight hold on her that would protect her from falling as much as he was using his strength to force her to obey his will.

He managed to get them into the small bathroom and dumped her in the tub. She scrambled to get out, clawing past his legs. When he caught her around the upper body, she twisted, striking the side of his head with her elbows, knowing she was hurting him, not caring, not caring at all, because he was hurting her past bearing. When he tried to grab her arm, contain the elbow strikes, she sank her teeth into his fingers.

"Son of a— All right, that's enough."

He tore his hand away, caught her body, and spun her onto her stomach in the tub. Locking her arms behind her back, he pinned her there, stepped into the tub and sat on her, pressing his hips firmly down against her ass, holding her arms as she screamed.

His blood was on her lips, and she snarled like a feral animal as he turned on the shower, blasting them both with cold water. She squealed and squirmed ferociously, but he shoved her back down when she tried to claw her way out. She shrieked her rage at him, kicked and fought while he hung on grimly, not an easy task with her anger and the oil helping fuel her advantage.

Then she caught a glimpse of his face, the anger and frustration both, the raw pain and absolute determination, and she knew she could fight with her fists until he was black and blue. She still wouldn't win the battle. There was no victory to this war, because it wasn't supposed to be a war. By making it one, she had already announced defeat.

He said nothing, letting her wind down to rasping sobs and futile bucks, the occasional kick, while her cheek was pressed hard against the slick side of the tub, her neck at an uncomfortable angle. She was crying, just crying now, because she couldn't do anything else.

She wasn't even aware of when he let go of her arms or eased off of her and turned off the water. Or how long she lay in the uncomfortable position, her legs bent up behind her against the fixture side of the tub, her shoulders raised on the back upward slope so she was bent in an awkward crescent. She felt the ache in her lower back, and the soft stroke of his hand on her hair, soothing her at the same moment. Pleasure and pain, comfort and loss. Was there ever a time it got to be perfect? Never mind the glass being half full or half empty. When did it get to runneth over? What did she have to do not only to find the love of her life, but to get him to admit the same, to make all the stars and gods line up to let her have the man she wanted?

"I never should have come," she said bitterly.

"I know." He pressed his knuckles and thumb to her temple, so she looked up at him through red eyes. His face was shadowed, and he bled where her nails and teeth had caught him. His hair and jeans were soaked from the shower, water drops sliding down his bare chest and sides to drip onto the tile. "But I won't ever regret you did, Nicole. Know that."

Using that strength that had been more than even her fury could shake, he gently turned her to her side. He kept his hand at her waist and the small of her back to shift her upright to a sitting position. Leaving one hand on her, he turned on the water, this time on a warm setting.

"Bath or shower?" he asked, his voice wooden.

She scrubbed her hands over her face, trying to stop the trembling that seemed to be coming from some place deep within her, beyond conscious control. "Just let it run."

Bowing her chin to her shoulder, she averted her countenance, wanting to block him out of her sight. She gasped as he yanked her head back, his hand hard on her nape. He was curved above her suddenly, darkening out everything else as his lips punished her with a brutal kiss, complete with teeth as he nipped her lip sharply. She clung to the wet muscle at his waist, felt the moisture of the shower on his face press against her own cheek before he pulled away. He kept several inches between their faces, and when she raised her lids, she found that cloud of danger pressing in on her from all sides.

"You do that again, and I'll beat your ass to within an inch of your life. Don't ever defy me, Nicole."

"Then don't ever leave me," she said. "And you would never hurt me. Not like that."

He snarled, pushed away from her and stormed out of the bathroom into the hallway. He came to a halt a few paces away, standing there for a moment with his back to her while she laid her hands on the wet side of the tub, where his body had left it damp.

"You..." He shook his head, and when he spoke, she heard the aching pain so clearly beneath the fury that it made her heart stagger beneath the weight of it. "It's not you, Nicole." He gave a harsh, bitter laugh. "Isn't that the cliché no one wants to hear? But it's not. If I could give you what you want, by God, I would. You deserve it. It's me who doesn't."

"I don't want to hurt you," she said, a hitch in her voice. "I'm sorry. I never meant—"

"No, don't." He took a breath, turned and faced her squarely, a well-made man in just a pair of jeans, whose beauty and pain constricted her heart in her chest.

"It's never been you who caused me pain, Nicole. You're the one that saved me from it. Now's the wrong time to tell you that, but there won't be a right time."

He lifted a shoulder. "I understood early on in our marriage that Mandy wasn't a true submissive. We had an honest relationship, a good friendship, and so I told her what I wanted. She said she couldn't give me that, but she was fine with me indulging it in limited ways, with her knowledge and agreement. I'd visit a club once every couple of weeks, just to watch, no actual sex involved, though of course being there was a sexual turn-on. I subscribed to several of the magazines, which I kept carefully away from my son, locked in our gun safe. I'd surf online, do some casual play with others out there like me. People who had vanilla relationships to which they were committed but wanted to indulge their D/s cravings. I'd do it after she went to bed, never in front of her, respecting her as my wife. Even with her consent, though, it felt wrong. All through the marriage, it felt like cheating. And it was lonely, because I wanted her with me, to understand and be part of it. I could always feel her disapproval hammering at me. I thought it was a moral judgment. I missed what it really was until it was too late."

"From the beginning to the very end, you were telling her she wasn't enough."

She didn't gloss it up, didn't condemn, just offered the simple truth. He nodded.

"There are some women who only want part of a man they marry. Mandy's like you." His eyes swept over her body, warming her. "She wanted to be with her soulmate, but she couldn't handle what was in my soul. So I locked those doors to keep her from having to deal with it. The price of that was holding my soul out of her reach.

"She got a better job on the west coast. Maybe she even planned it that way. She wanted to move, and I realized what she really wanted was a way out. It was then I understood, or thought I understood, how much I had hurt her, through consideration of her wishes. When I suggested a divorce and joint custody, instead of being relieved as I expected, she took it as the final insult."

He swallowed, his jaw tight.

"I have a good job, make good money, and I was an attentive, loving parent, a large part of his life. The jury was responding to that, and she needed something better. So she told the lawyer about my sexual preferences. I had destroyed her self-worth through misplaced kindness, and all she had left was vengeance. In her mind, my son was the fair price of it. I needed to keep them in state for joint custody. When you turn love into a vicious weapon, it's worse than hate.

"They collected the Internet site listings, the subscriptions, the club membership information, and grilled me on the stand. They did all the things they've done to gay men wanting to be parents. Made my sexual preferences sound like something that was a danger to a child's wellbeing. My lawyer couldn't defend it. Partially because it's just the way society is, but partly because I could tell he had the same distaste for it that everyone else seemed to have. So I lost him. I lost Kyle." He chuckled dryly, a sound she thought held as much humor as dead leaves rasping over bones. "For a while, I thought I'd lost my soul. Until I met a shy kitten."

Her gaze filled with tears, but he wasn't done.

"I know you read the transcript, but as I said, there isn't a way to describe what it's like to have your son taken from you. To have your wife, the woman who said she'd love and cherish you until death do you part, sit on the stand and paint you as a perverted freak. They convinced the jury that I would endanger my child with my 'twisted' tastes. Hell, she and her attorney nearly had the jury believing I was a child molester that needed to be on a sex offender list. Mandy said she didn't intend it to go that far, but hindsight doesn't mean shit to a jury that's already passed judgment. She couldn't face what I am, who I am, Nicole."

"Maybe she couldn't face that she couldn't be that type of person for you. It was horrible to read," she said softly. "And as horrible as it was to read, I know I didn't, couldn't understand it. I just hurt for you. I cried every time I read it, imagining you sitting in that courtroom by yourself, with no one. Are you allowed to see him at all?" She reached out, couldn't reach him, and he didn't move toward her. She firmed her chin, grasped the edge of the tub. Looked at him and waited.

"I get to go visit him one weekend a month," he said at last. "I can't have him here, but I can get on a plane and fly over 2000 miles to see him every thirty days. Fortunately, he's turned into a geek, like his dad." Now a faint smile did touch his lips. "We email a lot. He talked his mom into a webcam not too long ago. I told her that I'd pay for it, and so now we can talk face-to-face, so to speak, once a week. To a lot of people, that sounds like plenty of time."

"No." She shook her head. "You're his father. You want to see him every day, watch him grow up, and be a part of it."

"I looked into moving there and she flat out told me she'd push to have a complete ban on visitation if I lived any closer than I do now. She wants me on the east coast. And she has the hammer."

"Couldn't you appeal?"

"My attorney was a close friend, and a sharp guy. And a hell of an honest one. He told me it doesn't matter if it's tomorrow or five years. Every time they bring up the magazines and movie collections, the Internet memberships, the jury will side with the mother. He told me to accept what I can't change, 'accept the consequences of my actions'." Mark spat out the words like poison. "'Move on.' As if my son had died."

"Oh, Mark."

He shook his head, clenched his fist on the doorframe. "It's legal for parents to blow cigarette smoke in the faces of their babies, pump kindergartners full of drugs so they don't have to deal with normal hyperactive behavior, but I'm forced away from my son because of sexual proclivities that I'm as discreet as any parent should be around their children. Maybe more. Most kids would have the chance to at least find a Playboy under their dad's mattress. I kept everything related to it locked away from him.

"The rage nearly ate me alive, and that's still in me. It hasn't gone away; I just had to learn how to channel it, put it away. Jesus Christ, she took my son away from me, refused to be my wife, refused to accept who I am."

His eyes had become embers, and Nicole felt it press against the walls of the bathroom, that fury close to the surface. For a shuddering moment, she believed what he had said, that he would have broken his wife's neck if he could have done so. His wife had taken his life, his child from him, and Nicole wondered if she herself wouldn't have felt the same murderous rage. She groped for something to say.

"Why did you say 'was your friend'? About the attorney."

"What? Oh. Stuart. Yeah. After he found out all that about me…well, you know how it works. We used to work out in the gym together, watched football, went out for drinks after work. Suddenly he was busy a lot."

She nodded. Everyone had turned away from him. Had refused to accept him. And yet he had survived it, to stand here before her. She wondered how many years he would have continued on in this isolated bubble of existence, resolved that there was no one with whom he could be his true self, that wonderful Master she'd experienced in person for only a few hours and knew she wanted to keep.

"Please, Master. Let me help."

She said it, despite the raw and frightening thing she saw on his face.

"I wouldn't be gentle, the way you deserve. I do want to dominate and own the woman in my life, Nicole, on so many levels."

"I'm not asking you to be gentle. Keep me here, tie me to your bed as long as you wish. Fuck me..." Her voice trembled audibly but she swallowed it, tightened her jaw muscles. "Fuck me as long and hard, and however you want. My pussy, my ass, my mouth. I'm yours, Master, and I don't have to go anywhere. Not today, tomorrow, or even the next day. Lose yourself in me. Heal yourself in me."

He shook his head. "No."

"But—"

"No," he snapped. His fist hit the door molding, cracking it, dislodging it from the sheetrock. She jumped. He drew a deep breath, closed his eyes. "For a hundred times, *no*, Nicole. You can't live in my reality. I'll chew you up with my bitterness, and I'm not going to do that to you. I love you. I do. Like I've never loved anyone in my whole fucking life." He issued it like a threat, and it hit her low and hard, what she wanted to hear, but in a way she had never anticipated hearing it. "And I can't do that to someone I love as much as I love you."

He continued on in a lifeless tone as she stared at him, tears spilling over her cheeks. "It's more than what Mandy did to me. It's what I did to her. The attorney told me I might have a million-to-one shot at increasing visitation, and fighting for the right to live near Kyle, if I went into counseling. We could try again in a year or two, prove to the court I'd gotten 'help' for my problem. It was the hardest decision of my life, Nicole. I knew if I played the game, pretended to be who I wasn't, I had that flimsy chance of being near him."

He took another steadying breath. "There's this part of you connected to your family, part of you connected to yourself. We all give up a lot of ourselves to be a family. No one denies it. In happy families, there's the agreement that those pieces are filled by a whole new world, a whole new wealth of experiences, a path that recreates who we are. But there are things that you can't give up and still be essentially who you are. We love our children, but we're separate from them and have our own paths to walk as well.

"Even so, I would have done it. But when I looked in Mandy's face, I knew it wouldn't matter, because this never had anything to do with her opinion of me as a father. The poison that became hatred in her, that turned her into a monster, was planted by me. The more I had tried not to impose my interests on her, the deeper it became, because every time we made love, she felt me holding back that part of myself from her. I couldn't love her the way she deserved to be loved. Do I think it was a crime worth having my son taken from me? Hell, no. But it was a crime. There was nothing I could do about it, in the end. I fought and fought and fought, and I was defeated by what I was. What I am," he corrected himself with a snarl. "What I can't deny in myself."

"Something that many men have," she protested. "Not all at the same level, and sometimes in ways they don't understand, no more than women understand why they respond to it. But they have it. It's not an aberration, Mark." When he would have turned away from her words, she pushed on. "And so you closed yourself off to everything. That's why you wouldn't meet with me. Was I the only one you were playing with, Mark? How many of us were you using to assuage your loneliness?"

"I wasn't playing," he snapped. "What does it matter, anyway?"

She studied him. "It's only been me," she said slowly. "For some time." And despite the awful pain of this moment, she felt joy unfurl low in her stomach under the intensity of his gaze.

"You kept me sane, and alive."

"But not entirely. Not until you accept me in all parts of your life."

He shook his head. "I can't trust to that level again, Nicole. And love is a sham without trust. I told you that."

"It's not 'again'. You can't trust someone if they don't fully accept who you are." She leaned forward in earnest supplication. "For the first time, accept someone who fully accepts you. If your son was the price of your sins, then you paid your debt. More than any man should be asked to pay."

"You don't understand, Nicole," he said, his face transforming to something tired, bitter. "It was beyond crippling. He's my flesh and bone, my blood, and he was taken from me. For a while, you're in so much pain, you can hardly fucking breathe. You don't have children, you don't know."

"You're right," she said, so moved that the syllables came out disjointed, almost incoherent. He was bruising her with words, but God help her, she didn't care; if it was the last touch she'd ever feel from him, she wanted him to leave permanent marks on her soul, feel the imprint of his barbs forever. "I don't know. But I do know what it is to want something so badly that you'd do things you didn't think you'd ever do to get it. And you're intending to make me understand what it feels like to fight tooth and nail to have it and still be denied it. And what's worse, Mark? To be unable to get what you want because it's imprisoned from you behind legal walls, or to have it here, within your grasp, and have it turn its back on you? Your son still loves you, wants to be with you. You haven't lost that."

Mark shut his eyes. "Nicole, I...I just can't."

"No. You *won't*. Even though everything in this world worked against you, you still made sure you had contact with your son, to make him know how much you care. There's nothing you can't do. Only things you choose not to do."

"All right, *won't* then. If that's what you want to hear."

She flinched as he delivered the cruel words in a near shout. He did it without looking away this time, meeting her gaze with those eyes that could become so cold and ruthless. "I won't trust anyone again, Nicole. I married a woman who loved me, and whether I was the cause of the transformation or she had it in her all along, she turned into a nightmare I didn't even recognize, and it almost destroyed me. We both became monsters. You deserve better. Get dressed. If you're not ready in fifteen minutes, I'm taking you to the ferry as you are."

Chapter Fifteen

He gave her more time than that. He apparently had left the house to cool off, for the house was silent and empty when she emerged from the bathroom after her shower. She found her dress lying on the chair in the living room, but the tray and plastic were gone, the quilt folded up on a chair. She bent and smelled it, and smelled her scent and the scent of the dressing.

She went back to the bathroom and used his hairbrush. He kept it clean, only a few stray hairs caught in it, but she stroked them between her fingertips. He had allowed her to touch him very little today. She suspected that had less to do with his preference as a Dom and more with that tight yoke of control he had over himself. The one she'd slammed face-first into so ignominiously.

Nicole looked through the medicine cabinet, smelled his aftershave. No prescription drugs. He hadn't chosen any of the mood drugs so readily available these days to avoid having to accept or deal with emotions. It didn't surprise her, knowing his discipline.

She put the aftershave in her purse. She could buy the brand from the drugstore, but she wanted the one that he had used, his hand had touched.

She wandered out of the bathroom and down the hall, to his bedroom.

He had the curtains drawn, and it was a quiet sanctuary that smelled and felt like him. Did he ever bring her in here on the headset? Or did he at least bring her in here in his thoughts? Or was she only in the home office, a part of its décor and furniture, but in no way integrated with any other part of the house or his life?

There was a nondescript ocean print on the wall directly in front of her, and some type of detailed engineering drawing framed on the wall facing it. His name was inscribed on the bottom as the designer, something for which he'd perhaps won an award. Dim light came from a large ficus tree in the corner strung with fairy lights. For some reason, she suspected the framed drawing to be a company appreciation gift, carelessly hung to keep it out of the way. The ficus tree was likely the touch of a female relative visiting for the weekend, or perhaps a creative maid service trying to liven up the indifferently decorated atmosphere. The furniture of the room suited him though, the heavy dark sleigh bed and the large armoire she suspected was an entertainment center, since he had a closet. There was a dresser of the same good quality.

On the surface of the dresser was a white flat disk she couldn't readily identify, so she approached to find it was a plaster handprint. *Kyle Age 7* drawn on it in crayon. *I love you, Daddy.* She passed her fingers over the block letters. Next to it was a lopsided woven basket in which she found a few pennies, a half empty pack of gum, a book of matches. A deposit container for his pockets at the end of the day, and from the workmanship, likely another gift from his son at a slightly older age.

There was a picture of the boy, a dog with him, and then a couple shots of what appeared to be Mark's parents and siblings.

She turned and sank down on the sleigh bed, stretching out on the heavy brown striped quilt, on the left side, where she knew he preferred to sleep. On the right-hand side of the spread were a couple of engineering magazines and an espionage novel, confirming it. She flattened her palm on the pillow as if she were somehow holding or touching him, in that silent and dark room.

Lying there, absorbing his resonance in her body, was like taking air into her lungs. Simple, uncomplicated, vital. Even his Master side was direct and unpretentious, clear in its execution and expectations.

She rose, because she wanted to learn more, take in all of him she could before he got back, and because she thought she might be too tempted to bury her nose in his pillow and just stay there. Melding herself to the image of his sleeping body until she could dissolve and become a permanent part of his dreams, as he had of hers.

The flickering light thrown out the door at the end of the hallway told her where his computer and office were. She stepped into a room that had an overstuffed sprung couch, looking like it dated from his college days, and a top-of-the-line desk unit that covered three walls with shelves, file organizers and other ways to manage the rolls of drawings, files and other things that pertained to his professional life.

His screen saver was a kitten that playfully chased a ball of string, an animated design that had caused the flickering light. Nicole passed her fingers over the image, wondering. Some part of her wanted to ransack this office, see if he had kept any scripts of their evening sessions, any CDs of the vocal interactions. The CD she had sent him, where did he keep that? But what if she searched and found more than herself here? Or nothing. Is that what she wanted to know?

"Who are you?"

She yelped, spinning around. She'd been so comfortably absorbed in the heavy silence of the room, the youthful voice struck her between the shoulder blades like a slap.

A web cam screen had come up on the monitor, and she was looking at a younger, gawkier Mark. His son, somewhere close to fifteen now, if she had to guess. A teenaged boy with wire-rimmed glasses, Mark's sensual lips and beautiful long-lashed eyes blinking at her from the computer screen.

"Are you my dad's girlfriend?"

"I...I don't know." She smiled. "I hope to be. I'm trying to get him to agree to it."

The boy digested that unexpected answer, then gave her a critical once-over that amused her. "You're pretty hot. Are you nice?"

"Yes, she is." Mark's hand touched her shoulder and Nicole turned to find him there, standing behind her, his face in shadows.

"Good. You need someone nice, Dad. He spends way too much time alone," the boy informed her. "*The Beauty and the Beast* thing."

"I'll see what I can do about that." Nicole pressed her lips together against another smile. "I'm sorry." She cleared her throat on a cough. "I didn't understand that."

"You know, the old show with Ron Perlman and Linda Hamilton? They run it on that sci-fi channel sometimes. You know. He's 'the Beast', always wandering around the sewers, reading sappy poetry and contemplating on the futility of life? That part's pretty lame. But then, when she's in danger, all of a sudden he throws all that off and becomes primitive action-hero creature, with the fangs and all that. Duality. That's Dad."

"You know, there's such a thing as having too much intelligence. The annoyingly high levels that might get you smacked."

Kyle grinned. "Got to blame that on your genes, Dad. Might as well smack yourself first."

Nicole giggled and the boy's smile grew wider, showing his appreciation of her. "Guess what, Dad?"

Mark gave Nicole a glance, and she slid off to the right, out of view of the web cam. *Take your time*, she mouthed, and settled down on the edge of the cot he obviously kept in this room when he didn't want to face an empty double bed. She imagined him there, listening to her voice. She fingered the headset that had been left on a side table next to the cot. She pictured him with them on, listening only to her voice, her gasps. Lying on the bed stroking his cock, imagining it was her mouth, her fingers on him.

"Mom's going to let me come spend a month with you this summer."

"What?" She saw his face go tense with shock, his attention fixed on the boy in the screen. His mirror image at that age, she'd bet. In the young face, she saw the quiet confidence and exceptional intelligence she had sensed in Mark from the very first. Even more importantly, she could tell the boy knew how much this moment meant to his father and had wanted to tell him right away, at an unscheduled time. She decided she liked Kyle, very much.

"Yep," he said with a casual shrug. "I want to come spend the summer with you, Dad. And I told her it wasn't right of her to keep me from being with you just because she was mad at you for whatever happened with you guys. We actually had kind of a good talk about it. I thought I'd scope out that way for colleges. NC State has a great engineering school, you know. Mrs. Gorsky, she's my guidance counselor, says I'm a shoe-in to qualify for early admission programs in my junior year. NASA needs good engineers as soon as they can get them."

Nicole watched Mark absorb the boy's words. Mandy hadn't destroyed Kyle's love for his father. Nicole was certain that Mark had a lot to do with that; that the proud man she knew had done whatever groveling was necessary to make sure he wasn't driven away, had taken every possible step to stay in the boy's life. With the monthly plane trips, the email, the webcam, his ex-wife had been forced to acknowledge he was as much a part of Kyle's life as she was. Nicole imagined he had likely bought the boy his first computer and every upgrade since. He'd probably swallowed a world of bitterness to make weekly calls to Mandy to find out what Kyle needed from week to week. Enduring her jabs, the derisive comments, knowing that was far less important than letting his son know he loved him, was there for him.

He'd never mentioned much about this side of his world, but she'd pieced parts of that together as she had the rest. Now, the hope, the realization that he had been successful, that his son was still his son, filled the room, swelling from within him. She could feel it like the sun of an early summer morning. While she was not one to be presumptuous, she wanted it to be a sign of Fate that she was here at this exact moment to share the victory with him.

"We'll start doing plane tickets and stuff next week, so we can get the best rates, since you know she'll want you to pay for it." The boy made a comical eye roll.

"Your mother loves you, Kyle."

"Yeah, she does. But she can be such a pain in the ass. Girls really hold a grudge, don't they, Dad?"

Mark smiled, and Nicole's heart tightened. "It's a good thing to remember, son."

"Yeah. I got to go, Dad. I told this girl I'd call her tonight and you know what you told me."

"Never keep a lady waiting."

"That's right." The boy grinned, gave his father a wink that had Nicole stifling another giggle. "You either, Dad. Hope I get to meet her."

"Little weasel." But Mark still had the smile on his face as he turned from the monitor. It was the type of smile she hadn't seen him make before, that dropped ten years off his face and told her how much of him had been shattered by his son's loss, how many years it had drained from him.

He turned toward her in the wheeled office chair, and she smiled back at him. "If you want to do a cartwheel now, I'll pull the breakables out of the way."

He laughed, and her heart lodged into her throat at the rich, warm sound of it, at the smile that stayed on his sensual lips, the heat that grew in his eyes as he brought his chin down and regarded her. There were shadows there too, as the memory of what had taken him away from the house resurrected itself between them.

"You opened your heart and summoned a miracle," she said softly.

"No. You're the miracle, and the cause of the miracle. You're everything."

"I think I do remember that show," she said. "And he's right. Whenever Catherine, Vincent's soulmate, needed him, he would abruptly shed that maudlin persona, and the protector and hero would come surging forth to her side. He was fascinating and dangerous. He was so much more than man or beast, just one face. He's right. That is you."

He considered her, rose and took a step toward her. She tilted her face up, the pulse in her neck quickening. She didn't back away from his expression, which had shifted to something primitive, much like the character she was describing.

"I've said it three times at least, Nicole. You're not listening. You don't know the extent of what I want. What I need. What I'll take. If you give yourself to me, what if I want to share you with others? What if I'm that kind of Master?"

She raised her chin. "You're not. It isn't all about what you said and did to me today, or even online. It was a lot about what you didn't do, didn't say but wanted to." She deliberately laid back on the bed, ran her hand over the covers, an invitation. "You laid here, thinking of me, wanting me, aching for me, while I did the same thing a few hundred miles away. Why would you deny yourself that? Yes, I could hurt you as she did. I think I'd rather slit my own throat than do that, but I understand why she did it.

"If the man I loved couldn't want me with every ounce of who he is, I could grow to hate him as she grew to hate you. Love and hate are so close… I hoped my husband never looked into my eyes and saw what your wife had to see. That the wrong choice had been made. It was nobody's fault, because we all want love. We all take wrong paths to get there." She extended her arm and brushed the side of his leg, a tender caress. "It hurts so badly that we have to make it someone's fault, just like wild animals in pain turning on what's closest to them."

He had flinched at her first words, but as she continued, his eyes got thoughtful, serious, intent on hers. "What do you think I want, Nicole?"

"I know you want a woman who's all yours, Mark. You don't want to share. If anything, I suspect you'll be an overbearing and possessive Master who doesn't even want me to talk to other men." She arched a brow, her lips staying curved. "And I'll have to make sure you know that you're the only man I want.

"I want to be taken over. I crave to be loved totally by a man. I want him to dominate me, possess me, emotionally and physically. I want to be his possession, in the deepest, most profound sense of the word where love is concerned." Her voice broke as he reached down, touched her face. "I want the dream to come true. And I believe you're holding the key to that."

He studied her, and as he did, there was a heat that grew in his eyes that made any further words dry up in her throat. "You know how many nights that I stretched out on this bed, imagining the sound of your voice, the feel of your hands, your mouth on me?"

Since it was so close to what she imagined, Nicole couldn't speak to that, but she found a whisper. "Let me do it for you now, Master. Pleasure you with my mouth, my hands."

"We'll get to that, but first I want your cunt, Nicole. Spread and wet for me. Stand up."

He moved back, just a step as she rose on unsteady legs and obeyed. She hung on a knife edge of hope, uncertain if they'd reached a turning point, if perhaps his son's words had given him the hope needed to make that step, but when he met her eyes, he saw her hope, and gave a slight shake of his head.

She swallowed. They'd had the fight, the struggle, and she couldn't let everything tear loose in her like that again. Not in front of him. Later, when she was alone, she'd fall apart. But she wasn't wasting another moment with him if this was all he could give her.

In a movement she did not anticipate, he set his hands to the collar of her dress and tore it down the front, the gauzy fabric ripping away beneath his strong hands. A shower of tiny buttons clattered to the floor as the dress fell from her shoulders, pooling at her waist, laying her breasts and taut nipples bare to his gaze. He pulled the rest of the dress past her hips, let it drop, and she was standing naked.

"Lie down on the bed," he said, his eyes and mouth a blast of fire and sensual intent. "And spread your legs for your Master."

It was the dream she had lived too many times, never fulfilled, and her eyes filled with tears. She was about to be granted it, perhaps the one and only time in her life. But then, the most special moments only happened once. That's what made them special. Not wanting him to see the tears, she turned to do his bidding, but of course he saw, cupping her face, bringing her back to him so her hip pressed into his thigh, his other hand a light restraint at her waist. He pressed a kiss to her cheekbone, brushing the lashes of her lowered right eyelid with his lips lightly before he lowered her to the bed and then bent over her.

He laid a kiss on her throat, closing his hand on her chin and raising it to give him better access. Then his mouth moved over each breast, one then the other. A trail down her belly, toward her mound.

His slow methodical movements were a ritual, resonating from his mouth through her nerves, communicating to her brain, her heart and soul. He was marking her with his mouth, imprints that would last forever, that had to last forever. A caress that was a brand, as he ensured the path along every vital center was touched by him.

His mouth was on her mound, then on her clit, a soft nibble on her pussy, then down her thighs, until he knelt on the floor at the end of the cot, pressing a hard, long open-mouthed kiss on the tops of her bare feet. Then the soles. When he raised his head, his features were shadowed, the light of the monitor playing off of his face.

"You…you're kneeling…" she said, puzzled, confused and pleasured at once.

"You think it unusual that a Master would bend his knee to his slave to cozen her, care for her? Don't you realize that's part of the pleasure of the Master, knowing he can pamper his sub, treat her to manicures and pedicures, keep her happy and beautiful through his commands and actions, and she must submit to that, as much as to his more difficult commands?" He considered her, his eyes gentle for once. "I think that was the most difficult part of mastering you. You were still punishing yourself for not loving your husband enough, and you didn't think you deserved to be beautiful and cared for." Something she recognized a beat too late as humor crossed his face. "You got over that mental block pretty quickly."

It startled a chuckle out of her, and he gripped her feet, tickling the soles, until she was wiggling around on the bed, laughing, begging him to stop.

When he did, he rose and came to sit beside her, his hip pressed against her side. "And what of you, Master?" She reached up to touch his face. "Don't you deserve to be cared for…loved?"

He drew back from her touch. "Time to go, Kitten. Let's get your real world clothes back on."

Chapter Sixteen

The drive back to the ferry landing had none of the peaceful tranquility of their early silences. Nicole felt the desperation rise in her, but didn't know what to say to change his mind. They passed the new lighthouse, the one built just after the Civil War.

If they had all the time in the world, not just a day, maybe he would have taken her to the top. They would have run up all three hundred stairs, like children, so they were out of breath. Then he would have made love to her from behind, making her look out the window at the breathtaking view of the island, the ocean rolling onto its wide stretches of beach, the brilliant green of the marsh side, the deep mystery of the forests. He would look with her. Seeing the whole world stretched before them, they would know that they were such a small part of it, of so many things happening and changing all the time, that all things were possible for them.

Oh, Nicole. Maybe he's right. Maybe it's time to stop believing in a dream that's not going to come true. Protect your heart.

As he had protected his, so love could not find its way through a single crack, no matter how she beat her fists against his walls and screamed for entry.

He was closed to her now. She picked up his notebook, caressed it with her fingertips, the reality of him she knew.

"It's not real, Nicole," he said shortly, as if reading her mind. "It's like weaving a spell. Like a sorcerer entrancing the fair maiden so she doesn't see what's behind the skillful words and the touches."

"No, it's not like that at all," she responded. "It is a spell, but it's a spell that takes a person inside you, past the surface, and lets them get to know you from the inside. And it's the inside that we really are." She gripped the notebook to her breast, felt it against her beating heart. "If we could turn the inside out, so a man's ability to stick with a woman and care about her was what stood out instead of the size of his biceps, a lot of people would look a lot different. Your writing did that for me. You became the most handsome man in the world to me. You blinded me to illusion, Mark," she said softly. "So I could better see reality. I feel sad for both of us, because I gave you all of who I am today, and we both know the more time we'd spend together, the deeper we'd go, the more we'd find in each other."

"And learn to despise each other. Things that might hurt or drive us away from each other."

"You're driving me away right now," she pointed out. "Sometimes the good and the bad are like water mixing with sand to form the concrete that holds everything together. Your arrogance, your assumption that you're right about every damn thing, would make me want to push you into the river nearly every day."

She almost smiled at his startled look, but her heart was yearning too much for him to make this into a moment of levity. "But imagine a painting where there are no shadows for contrast. What would be interesting about it? Why would it be art? It would just be a cartoon, a virtual reality, not this." Her voice lowered in its urgency. "Not this."

He pulled up to the landing. "You don't know what you're asking."

"You keep saying that, damn it," she snapped. At his sharp look, she took a breath, let it out with a count of ten, conscious of every tick of the clock. The boat would leave in five minutes. "But I do know. I've felt how strong you are, even when you're holding back. *She* wasn't willing to go all the way. Well, I am. Because it's not a game to me, or to you. I know that."

He shut his eyes, closed her out. "You still don't get it, Nicole. I don't know if I can hold it within the threshold of sex, if it wouldn't extend to your everyday life. Outside the door of our home, your career, your life, your decisions are yours. I want you to be and achieve everything you want to be. But when you bring home that project you're working on around the clock, I'll want you working on it at your desk naked, my collar on your throat. When you're hungry, I'll demand you take food only from my fingertips, never lift your own utensils. You'd take water or wine from my mouth."

She trembled at the images. Yes, they made her apprehensive, because she knew he meant them. "You're getting through loud and clear, Mark. I've had half measures. I want it all this time, whatever the risks. I'll take the pleasure with the pain, however you dish it out, because I know you love me, and I trust you."

He shook his head. "A submissive is almost always braver than the Master, because he/she will give it all, take the risk of the plunge, not knowing if the Master will be a true Master, and be there for her."

"And sometimes he turns and claims her," she responded. "Embraces his true nature, and they become far more together than they ever were apart. Just as brave."

"Brave or foolish?"

"Either way, a gift. Don't you remember the story of the king and the fool? It was the fool who understood the pure meaning of love, its most powerful face in the simplest form. The hardest form for a king to trust and accept, and transcend his fears to become far more of a king to his people than he could before. To find Camelot, he has to be as vulnerable to his people as they are to him."

When he would have spoken again, thrown up another defense, she laid a hand on his arm, dug her fingers into his forearm. "Knowing what I know about you, I know how hard it must have been, not to cherish and love the woman you had claimed as your own in the way you wanted to do, in a way that would fulfill her. I know what it must have taken you to maintain your sanity. The strength of character to overcome that. And I think that healing process is continuing. Perhaps if I waited another year or two, you'd be more accepting of me. But

Mark, I can't wait. I won't wait. I need you. I am that person that meshes with you, the yin to your yang, and perhaps it was your pain that drove you to me, that brought us together. Do you know how long I was in a relationship of expectations, expectations I fulfilled until I felt as fragile as an egg with all the insides sucked out of it? So delicate that one more impact would shatter me? You knew how to deal with that. You've filled me again, made me solid and real, who I want to be."

He swore under his breath and pulled away, got out of the cart. It was a moment before he came around to get her, to hand her out. A group of employees went by, their faces curious, picking up on the tension surrounding them.

"Your son wants you to be happy. I want you to be happy, and I know I can make you happy." She knew her face had to be pale, strained, and her hands stayed flat against her sides, not giving him the opportunity to tug her from the cart. Not yet. She had three more minutes. They hadn't even sounded the horn yet.

"Why don't you deserve happiness, Mark? Because the world passed judgment on you, said you didn't deserve it? Because it didn't understand what or who you are? Well I understand what and who you are. I didn't at first, because I didn't know the same thing lay inside of me. I just knew I had to find it, and when I did, I knew it. I knew you. And I know it's nothing anyone needs to be afraid of. You're a true Master, Mark. Through and through, in the blood. Maybe you're just born in the wrong time or dimension, but you're here. I love you." She did reach out now, her fingers touching his forearm. "I love you," she repeated. "And I want you. All you have to do is take me, and I'm yours. Why would you throw that away? To prove that you're not what we all know you are, deny the truth of it, and live your life as a half-life? Life's too short, Mark."

He was a statue in front of her, as if the stone wall he'd built around his heart was expanding to encompass and immobilize all of him, but she kept on. She'd never been good with words, but she put aside her self-consciousness, took a page out of his book and spoke as she might have written to him, a love letter with the potent strength of a farewell, except that she didn't want it to be the end. She was fighting for it to be the beginning. *Two minutes.*

"You and your wife made the wrong choice. It happens every day, two people believing that they're meant for forever, and they discover they weren't. The crime you committed was in marrying a woman you couldn't love completely, with all your heart and soul. You paid for that crime as though it were done maliciously." Her voice stumbled as he laid his hand over hers on his forearm, put his other under her elbow, and began to use his strength to lift her off the seat. "It's time to forgive yourself, and accept the love being offered to you. By me. By your son. By life."

He drew her purse off the back seat, threaded her arm through it, adjusted the strap on her shoulder, and her voice clogged with desperation. From his impassive expression, she didn't know if he was even hearing her.

"And maybe, things happen for reasons. Maybe you had to go through that with each other to be in the right place at the right time for the real thing. I don't want to be reaching, but life's too short to throw away a second shot at the real thing, Mark.

"You remember what I said, that sudden moment of relief about six months after my husband died, taking me by surprise, like a slap in the face? The little girl in me who had believed in true, deep, permanent can't-breathe-without-him love came back out of her playhouse in her princess dress, ready to find him again. The woman in me who had simply loved a good man as a friend and a partner, who gave him a fond and heartfelt farewell, finally let go of the guilt. That woman took that little girl's hand and we both came looking for you."

That stopped him, and he looked down at her, his hands coming to rest on her upper arms as she continued to reach into herself, into the well of her heart, for a flow of words that would never dry up, not as long as it was him and their love at stake.

"The love of your life isn't an either/or proposition. When you find him, it's not about love and hate; it's about who you can't live without, a man who may be both your best friend and your greatest adversary, but never your enemy. Every dinner we had, every moment we had as Master and slave, I felt that grow between us. And if you send me away," her voice trembled, "it will be like the Sistine Chapel. I can always remember what it looked like, felt like, even though I couldn't stay there or take it home. Maybe the knowledge that such beauty and meaning exists in the world will be enough, though I can't reach out, indulge my senses with it every day." She cocked her head, her eyes stinging with tears. "But please don't make me have to live with that."

He stared at her a long moment, and her hope rose in her throat, strangling her, keeping breath from her. If he did not make his decision soon, she knew she would expire right there before him.

Please, Master. Please Mark. Love me. That's all I want. Just love me. The purest and simplest love of fools.

He shifted his gaze to the water, and his hands dropped. There was an odd stillness to his body, as if he thought if he moved too quickly, everything she'd roused between them would simply explode and consume them both.

"You need to get on the boat," he said stiffly.

* * * * *

Throughout his life, he'd learned that the truly awful experiences always felt as if they'd happened only a moment ago. The ones he wished hadn't happened and that he could take back. Time didn't heal all wounds, because around some wounds, time stopped. They were ageless, etched on the dark wall of the soul. With those seven words, he knew he'd just created such a wound, in a heart that didn't deserve a moment's pain, let alone the mortal blow he had just dealt it.

He felt her anguish lance through his own heart. He saw her short nod, saw her turn away, her slender shoulders tense, and her movements stilted. As she walked toward the ramp, she had the gait and body language of a woman so close to tears he knew she was using everything she had to hold it in. She had pride. But she had tossed all of that aside to come here, take the risk, face him, meet him. Show him what they could have, what he would be missing for the rest of his life.

The ferry mate made her stop for a moment at the threshold to make an adjustment on the ramp for the rocking of the boat. In a moment, she'd step across, and be gone forever. He would never see her again. Or talk to her again, for he knew this was a transition. They could never go back to where they were before, and she was strong. He knew she'd cry, have those lonely nightmares, but she'd disconnect her email service before she'd let herself succumb to the desire to reach out to him again, take half of what they could have. Would she reach out to another Master eventually, or pretend that it wasn't in her, settle back into a vanilla relationship, end up a vaguely dissatisfied wife...

No, not her. She'd made her decision. She'd been the half-life route before, hadn't she said as much? She would...

"Oh, Jesus." *Mark, stop thinking like a fucking engineer. Break out of the box. Listen to what she just said to you and stop thinking you know every damn thing. Don't be a coward.*

"Nicole!"

He shouted it, blurted it out with the self-possession of a kid seeing the ice cream truck turning the corner out of the neighborhood.

She stopped in mid-step, so suddenly she lost her balance on the turn, and the ferry mate had to quickly reach out and steady her. Her face was blank, lost in the ache of failure, and hope didn't even have a chance of inserting itself in the moment.

"Come back here. Now."

He made it imperious, a blatant public demand that had several of the female ferry staff exchanging affronted glances.

Get a load of that asshole, thinking he can order a woman around.

If they only knew. She stood there, staring at him, and he inclined his head, his heart in his throat, pounding madly. His fear and desire together choked him so he wasn't capable of any further words.

She took a step back, another step, another, and she was off the ramp. Then abruptly, she abandoned the same civilized veneer. She was the kid who would take off full tilt after that ice cream truck, not caring that she looked silly, with her sneakers pounding on the pavement, running full tilt with arms pumping, knowing that any risk of dignity or pride would be worth that double scoop of chocolate vanilla swirl.

She leaped and he caught her up in his arms, her feet leaving the decking as she wrapped her arms around him, and now the tears did come, wetting her cheeks, the side of his face as he cupped his hand around the back of her head, his arm around her waist, holding her to him. Rocking her, absorbing what it was to hold a woman who wanted all of him. Who wanted to be his, body, heart and soul. His woman. For better or worse.

Chapter Seventeen

At length, he let her down, took her hand. "Are you sure, Nicole?" he asked. His voice, though husky, was a demand, his eyes direct, piercing. "Because I'm not settling again, either. This time I'm getting everything I want from the woman I claim as mine."

She shivered. "I'm here because I didn't want to settle again, either," she reminded him, tightening her grip on his hand, so warm and strong around hers. "I'm yours, and I'm willing to do whatever that means, because I know you love me, Mark. I know you'll take care of me, and let me take care of you. Please make me yours in all ways." She lowered her voice, moved closer. "Please, Master."

He brought her all the way to him, took her lips in a kiss that bruised, his arms banding around her, one hand slipping down to palm and fondle her ass, grabbing and crumpling a handful of her tailored skirt, right there in front of the ferry mates and boarding guests.

Nicole knew he was testing her, knew he might test her for a very long time, because his trust had been so abused. That would be the true challenge of their relationship. He'd accepted her, he'd taken the leap. Now she knew he needed to know how far she'd be willing to take the plunge with him. She suspected that his act here was a very deliberate decision to test her, not his natural inclination, since he'd made a point earlier to tell her he was not the type of Master who enjoyed publicly exposing or sharing his sub.

So she opened her mouth and moaned into his, letting her body relax and be supple, compliant against every angle and curve of him. He pressed her against the erection growing between them, and she subtly shifted so she rubbed against him, giving him the answer she knew he wanted.

He broke free with a gasp and a near growl, framed her face with his hands. "I'm going to take you somewhere and fuck you, Nicole. And I've got a lot of need stored up in me. I *won't* be gentle, just as I said I wouldn't."

"I only want you," she responded, putting her own blazing need in her eyes.

She didn't know where he was taking her when he pushed her into the cart, she just hoped it wasn't far.

As it sped by, Nicole realized she loved this island, with its isolated roads, the thick, quiet forests. While she had an appreciation of nature, she knew it was as much because it was a reflection of Mark's world she was seeing. His nature, the levels of quiet interspersed with the vibrant contrast of life, struggling, surviving, growing, diversifying. Violence and tranquility existing hand in hand. It was as if the island was a mirror of what was in him, and she embraced it as she wished to embrace him.

They bumped down a gravel path, and when they reached the end of that, where a faint deer path started, he grabbed her hand, pulled her from the cart. "Come with me."

They emerged in a small overlook area on one of the island creek tributaries, where a dock for a small boat had been built on the creek edge, surrounded by trees. It was lushly private from the island side, but open to the water and the sweeping view of island marshes, where the sun was starting its descent, giving the sky a late afternoon glow.

"This is on the land behind my house," he said. "Where I keep my boat. Strip, Nicole."

She turned, surprised.

"Now." The command in his voice weakened her knees, and without further hesitation she slid the blouse off her shoulders, let it fall, not looking to see if there were waterfront homes that could see her from their windows. Her mind had made its choice to trust him, and now she gave the reins to him. She unzipped the skirt, kicked it to the side. Took off her bra and panties and stood before him naked.

He dropped her purse at her side, on the deck.

"Kneel in front of me, and give me your collar."

Emotion closed her throat, keeping her from speech. She didn't know how he knew she had brought it, but it didn't matter.

She was unselfconscious in her nakedness now, because she had made her choice and was committed to him, to what he was. She withdrew the second gift he had given her when he sent her the flannel shirt. Kneeling at his feet, she lifted it.

The choker he had sent to her, the collar to let her know he was with her, through every nightmare, every passionate wish.

"Please put it on me, Master," she whispered. "Accept me, as I've accepted you, for everything you are."

"And everything I'm not."

"And everything you're not. All of it. I want all of it."

Mark stared down at her, at her upturned face, the soft mouth. Her steady, determined gaze, full of willingness to try, to open to him, to give to him if he was willing to do the same. How much did he know about her? Less than she knew of him, obviously. But everything pounding in him, inspired by her words, begged him to take the chance, take the leap, stop living in a virtual reality and clasp living, warm flesh to him again with all its risks and promises of heaven.

He took the collar from her hands, held it. "I'm messy. I leave my clothes all over the floor. I can step over the same empty pizza box for a month and never throw it away. My house has all the warmth and charm of an office cubicle."

"You'll pick up the box to make me smile, because I'll do everything to make you happy," she returned. "I'm a nester, and an obsessive neatnik. I alphabetize my spice drawer."

"You're scaring me." But there was a smile struggling against his stern expression. "Do you cook a good breakfast?" he asked bluntly, his eyes lingering on her in a possessive way that felt more natural than anything he'd ever done.

"Do you wash dishes?" she returned, a gleam in her eye.

He grinned, then. "What if it doesn't work out?" That question he delivered in a more serious tone, and her eyes softened on him, loving him. It roused a protectiveness in him, a desire to always see her happy and safe, to give her pleasure and joy, a hungry rush so sudden it almost made him lightheaded.

She lifted her pretty shoulders, drawing his attention to those bare breasts, the nipples tight with her aroused emotions. "Then it doesn't work. Half-living is worse than being dead, I think." A quick smile. "Not ever having been dead, I think that's a guess."

"I've been dead." He lifted the collar in his hands. "And you're right. You were always right, Nicole."

She swallowed, and made herself be still as he lowered the collar to her. It had been perfect for her tastes. He'd had her measure her neck exactly, telling her just how much tension to put on the tape. She'd seen pretty, delicate things on the Internet that she'd liked, but when she received what he'd chosen, it had been nothing like those. It had spoken of what she had learned today, that he was not just a part-time or Internet Dominant. It flowed through his veins, so that in private and even she suspected in subtle ways in public venues, ways that would not be noticed by those who didn't know the language or the gestures, he would be her Master. Now that she'd roused him to the possibility of it, it had surged past any restraint and was here, vibrating between them. Surrounding them.

The collar was a solid band of pewter engraved with flowing Latin script inside. Now at last, she asked what she never had before.

"What does it say, Master?"

Mark turned it over in his hands, but his eyes were all on her. "'Many waters cannot quench love, neither can the floods drown it.' From the Song of Solomon, you'll recall." He brushed her flushed cheek with his fingers. "I wanted it to be in an old language, one created when the lines between the human and the natural worlds were still thin. When the primitive world was as valued and respected as the civilized one."

The collar had a hinge in the back to open in two crescents and then lock around the throat. The border around the outside edge was the stylized etching of a string of cats with elongated bodies. On the front clasp, the tails of three of the cats became three-dimensional, a tiny welded oblong loop wound together to form a tunnel of three links just smaller than the circumference of her pinky. There was the same effect on the back, on either side of the hinge, and on the east and west sides of the collar. The inside with the inscription was a smooth silver inlay.

He held it in both hands and stepped forward, lowering his arms so he aligned the hinge at the back point of her nape, then brought the two halves together in the front. It was snug, as he had intended it to be, pressing just below her voice box. The front lock mechanism just above the cats' tails was diamond-shaped, and the slim cover that slid over it, latching and hiding the key hole, was a cat's eye, the iris a chip of amber.

To the unknowing world, it was a very unusual and expensive choker. But the fit and one-inch width made her feel undeniably like she was collared, a prized possession of the man before her, and her response trickled down her thighs before his shrewd, knowing gaze.

"You've never put it on."

She shook her head. "You never ordered me to, and I wanted you to do it."

"And how does it feel?"

"Tight. A bit uncomfortable. It..." She licked her lips. "It arouses me, Master. I would wear it always, at all times, if it pleases you."

"There will be times I'll remove it to nibble on that neck of yours, but for now, it stays on. Only I will remove it. Stand up, turn away from me, and put your hands on the railing of the dock, face out to the water."

She did, but he bent down, gripping her elbow with gentle fingers to help her to her feet. He didn't let her go immediately. Instead, he fingered the collar, stroked his touch up her throat, gazed down at her body, bare for him except for his claim.

He held her face in one hand, leaned forward until they were close. "Lower your gaze," he murmured. When she did, he brought his lips to her cheekbone, whispered across it while she trembled at the soft kiss. His hand moved to her waist, settled on her hip, his fingers stroking her bare ass, caressed by the breeze off the water.

"In our private lives, I want you to be mine, my slave, my submissive, and let me have you in every way a Master wishes to love and cherish his sub. Can you accept that, not knowing what that might mean, how deep that may go? What if I tell you that life with me means that I'll want you naked except for this collar whenever it's just the two of us? Whether you're checking your email, reading a book, working from home, cooking supper, I'll always demand that you observe the rules and demeanor of a cherished slave inside the walls of our home."

A tiny smile appeared on her lips, her lashes still fanning her cheeks. "I will serve my Master's desire," she murmured. "And ask only that he keep the heat up sufficiently."

It got a smile out of him, and that let loose something stronger. "I love you, Nicole."

Her eyes flew up, startled enough to forget his order, and he pressed his fingertips gently over them, reminding her to look down again.

"And that frightens me so deeply I can't even begin to tell you. I'm afraid my way of loving you will drive you away."

"Do you want me to give up my friends, my career?"

"Of course not."

"Will you beat me, Master, and cause me pain I do not enjoy?"

"Never," he said softly. "How could you think so? I couldn't hurt you any more than I'm capable of raising a hand against my son."

"Will you be there when I'm afraid or sad? Or so happy about something that the first person I want to share it with is you?"

She peeked at him from beneath her lashes. At some point her touch had crept lightly onto the waistband of his jeans and now he felt her small fingers digging in, communicating her tension and need.

"I'll do my best." *Better than my best.* He wanted to be everything she could ever need to be happy.

"Then how could I be afraid of being loved in a way I've always wanted to be loved, but never have been?" He palmed her cheek and she laid the weight of her head in it. "Please take me, Master. Make me yours before I can bear it no longer."

"Very well, then." He turned her, and Nicole noticed those capable fingers had a tremor to them.

"Put both your hands on the rail and bend forward."

The evening shadows were gathering. The branches and hanging vines, the Spanish moss of the trees, formed a curtain of shadows over them.

Mark's hand braced on the rail next to one of hers, and he banded an arm around her waist as he murmured into her ear. "Lift your ass for me, Shy Kitten. Show my cock how eager you are for it. Tell me you're mine. My slave."

"I'm yours, Master," she managed in a rush of breath. "Yours. Your slave."

"To fuck whenever I wish."

"To fuck whenever...you wish."

"To love forever."

She closed her eyes, her throat thick with emotion. "To love forever."

The soft lap of water drew her attention and she raised her lashes to see two kayakers round the bend and float down the creek, not more than a hundred feet away.

The kayakers, while unable to tell their features, would be able to see their silhouettes, enough to know what she and Mark were doing. The first one, a man, passed without seeing them, but the woman in the kayak behind him did. Nicole locked on her eyes, watched the nuances of expression. Curiosity, surprise, shock, followed by a discreet fascination and the first lick of desire, as the woman became aware that they knew of her scrutiny, and yet were continuing to follow what nature drove them to do. She spoke softly to the man, perhaps her husband, and he looked, as she came up next to him, the paddles holding them against the current.

"Lower your body down on the top rail, Nicole," Mark murmured to her. "And hold the lower rail in your hands."

She did as he produced a length of nylon cord similar to what he had used in the house, only a bit rougher. He had brought it in a mesh bag he'd withdrawn from the cart when they left it on the path.

"That was *your* golf cart, not a rental," she realized.

"I was picking it up from the dockmaster. He borrows it sometime when I'm not here for long stretches of time." He lifted the twine. "This is usually in case I see a dog out loose on the island that needs to be returned to his human, so I ask my slave's forgiveness that it isn't soft enough for your beautiful skin."

He threaded it through the tunnel of rings formed by the cat's tails in the front of the collar, looped it around the top rail, drew it taut so her neck was held flat against the wood, her breasts hanging on the inside of the rail. He crossed the two slack ends of the line between her breasts, looped them over her back, did a holding knot, then took the ends up to the back links of the collar. When he took the two ends through the back links and then back to the horizontal tie across her back, he drew it taut, so her head was pulled up by the collar to the extent allowed. He then took the rest down to her wrists, cuffing and tying them to the lower rail so she was completely immobilized, bent over at a ninety degree angle, her ass and pussy accessible to him.

She could do nothing but stare out at the water, the tension of the line at the back of the collar such that she could not lower her head, but must have every expression displayed to the distant kayakers.

"There used to be a practice of pulling carriage horses' heads back. It was a cruel method if abused." He reached forward, fondling her loose breasts. She gasped, writhing, rubbing her ass wantonly against the front of his jeans. "But done correctly, it is very pleasing."

"Master, please—"

"Please what, Nicole? You know I like hearing you beg. Say what your mind is thinking, let it pass those pretty, ladylike lips that sucked so hard on my cock earlier."

"Please...fuck me."

"Fuck your what?"

Nicole moistened her lips, and he could feel her struggle, her apprehension about the kayakers, who could not hear but could see her, though they did not have the lovely view he did, of the heat and liquid desire running down her legs.

"Fuck my pussy, please. My cunt...please. It needs your cock fucking it."

"Nothing's going to stop me from doing exactly that," he said, and he took down his jeans. She moaned at just the sound of it and moved back against him the little slack he had permitted, seeking him in her eagerness. He gave her bottom a sharp slap with the flat of his hand, leaving a print.

"Be still. You will be absolutely motionless as I enter you. You understand?"

She jerked her head forward in a nod. *"Yes, Master. Just, oh…please hurry."*

Instead he took his time, rubbing his hand over the offended portion, watching the juices run from her cunt, wet her thighs more. He slid the broad head of his cock through the trail of moisture down the back of one, and she let out a plaintive cry, but she did not move, only her pussy lips rippling, so eager she could not control the involuntary response.

Mark had never been so huge in his life, so full of heated lust, beyond the pale of any of the most powerful and violent of emotions. He was going to fuck her hard, make her feel so used she wouldn't be able to walk tomorrow, but she wouldn't need to. She'd be in his bed, after all, and to remind her she was his, despite her soreness, he would ease his morning-hard cock into her first thing, right before she woke, as gentle then as he intended to be rough now. She was all his. All gloriously his.

He would rub liniment into her abused muscles, bathe her himself, feed her breakfast from his hand. He would be a demanding Master, he knew, because that was what had always been in him. But beyond that, he knew there was an edge to that demand now, the need to test her in a million ways, reinforce with every action the message that this was what she had accepted with his collar, and he wouldn't let her go unless she took it off and gave it back.

"If you wake up in the middle of the night and you're thirsty, you will wake me and I will give you water from my lips. Your collar will be chained to the bed rail, and only I can release you in the morning to go to the bathroom. Often, right after that, I'll want you to come back to my bed, so I can start my day by fucking your cunt, making you feel my claim on you the first and last part of each day. Over the threshold of our home, all your basic needs will be met by me."

As he spoke, she trembled harder, and he knew with a surge of elation it was the tremble of a true submissive arousal, a little afraid of his words, but more because she was overwhelmed by her own uncontrolled reaction, her desire to be his in the ways he was describing.

He slid his cock in at last, feeling that wonderful, indescribable combination of tightness and sudden easing, only to have her muscles grip down on him again with the force of her response, making every forward inch a moment of heated heaven he wanted to prolong and yet push her past her limits at once.

She arched her back and he slid in to the hilt, uncovered, unprotected, and it underscored that they'd both made their decision. Her by stepping on the boat, him by refusing to send her back off on it.

She knew he'd not had anyone since his wife, and he knew she'd been celibate since the death of her husband.

The sound of pleasure escaped her lips before she could suppress it as he slid deep within her, and he sank his teeth lightly into her shoulder, just to the left of the collar. His thighs pressed hard into the back of her own, pushing up her ass cheeks as he made sure he was seated as deeply as possible, filling her.

She moaned again as he thrust home, hard and sure, seeking to brand as much as pleasure her. He did not flinch or hesitate, and the spiral of alarm that shot through her belly as she saw the kayakers had moved moderately closer, to get a better view, was dispelled forcibly by his next powerful stroke, which shoved her forward against the rail.

She shuddered, watched the kayaking couple, almost motionless as herself except for the tiny movements of the paddles to keep them in place, as the man and woman watched her and Mark perform the act they all knew. Nicole knew they must be seeing a momentary flash of her eye, the whiteness of her breast, perhaps the sheen of her knuckles, grasping that lower rail. He'd bound her so close to it she doubted that they could see that she was bound, but their choice to watch, to stay at a respectful distance and yet indulge in voyeurism, like nature watchers or an audience in a darkened movie theater, added to the moment in a way she wouldn't have expected. Exhibitionism was not an interest of hers, but perhaps it was calculated exhibitionism. This spontaneous, unexpected merging of beings, locked together in a four-way circle of sensual awareness, coupled with Mark's claim upon her, the kayakers like witnesses at a marriage, took it to an intensity level that had her legs shaking. So much so that when he entered her again, she had to tighten her hands on the rail to keep herself upright.

But he knew, as a good Master and a lover would, and his arm was there around her waist, giving her additional support, holding her up.

"That's it, Kitten," he murmured, sliding out, then back in again. Slow, deep, his hips moving in an easy controlled rhythm now, his legs pressing against the back of hers.

"Please, Master," she gasped. "Please let me move with you, against you...I can't bear it."

"Even if I say you must?"

She let out a moan of pure frustration and stayed still. His next thrust was harder, pushing her against the rail again, the rough wood scratching the tender skin beneath her breasts. Her whole body was a coil of tension, drawn back like the hammer of a revolver, ready to explode with a shattering, irrevocable violence, and his voice was the trigger.

"Move for me, sweet kitten. Fuck my cock."

Her hips lifted to meet his on the next thrust and that brought the lightest brush of his testicles against her clit, enough to start a firestorm. Nicole could not stop the cry that burst forth from her lungs with the same violence as the climax. Her body flushed with heat from the soles of her feet on the deck to her hairline. Lifting and lowering her hips furiously, she met his every thrust, timing it so that they drew apart with close friction and came back the same way. She took the full length of him every time, mindful to serve her Master with all of herself, in order to earn the reward that focusing on his pleasure now delivered.

He growled in her ear, his thrust shoving her into the rail over and over, his grip around her waist brutally tight. He had said he wouldn't be gentle, and now he proved it, hammering at her with all the strength and lust a male animal had, prolonging her own orgasm between blinding pleasure and the edge of pain. Her cries escalated into a long low cry of completion as he groaned his own release, emptying himself, his pain, his desire and his seed into her, making her his in truth. And still hard in her, still not sated, he wrapped his hand in the rope keeping her head pulled up and yanked it back further, jutting her breasts out under the rail into that near touch of sunlight, exposing them fully, making them quiver and shake for the watching couple as he pounded into her.

His legs made a loud slapping noise against her ass, his testicles tattooing against the opening of her pussy, so the aftershocks of her climax continued like a fist wrapped around it, milking every last reaction as her pussy learned to accept his presence within her past the point of endurance, into the area of complete physical and emotional capitulation. It gripped the quiet part of her mind in amazement, to realize there was that additional level. Strong Master that he was, she was sure he'd known about it, intended to push her into it, to see if she had it in her to reach that point, even as he struggled past his fears and anger to give her as much of himself as he could.

As her cries settled to soft noises, caught somewhere between wondrous contentment and the distress of an animal who was unharmed but realizing her fate was totally in the hands of another, he pressed his body against her back, and laid several kisses on her temple. As he did so, he released her binding, the rope sliding away, and he just held her, bent over her like that, encapsulated and surrounded by his body. She pressed her face into his neck.

"I love you, Mark. Master."

And Mark knew in that moment she would accept the painful road of winning his trust, though she'd done nothing to earn such a rocky path. She accepted everything good and bad about him. He thought he had to punish her, to be sure she was going to be there every day, every morning, come hell or high water. In this moment, body to body, heart to heart, he knew that, in order to keep her, he had to believe in her. Cherish and love her, trust her, with all the risk that step entailed.

The time for tests was over.

His breath was a soft sigh against her skin. "Ah, Kitten." And that was all he said.

Nicole almost smiled as she pressed her face more firmly against his strong jaw. A man of few words he was and would always be, unless he had a pen in his hand, or unless he spoke to her with his body and soul, as he had just done. She knew it would be all right, even if he didn't know it yet. She shifted her gaze, and the kayakers were quietly paddling on, now their faces the ones in shadows from the dying light.

Mark swatted a glancing blow on her flank and Nicole jumped, startled, turning her attention back up to him. He gave a half chuckle. "Sorry, darling. *That* was a mosquito."

She laughed then, so easy to do, everything so easy at this moment. It wouldn't be that way always, she knew. "Forever" relationships were cliffs one day, sunshine and waterfalls the next. Sometimes an arduous hike in the desert or a tedious climb. Occasionally a dangerous gorge to leap. As long as they were connected, hand in hand, no shields between them, she knew there was nothing beyond their ability to face. "Mark," she said softly. "What do you want?"

He was silent a long moment. "In a couple days, I want you to go home, pick up your things, and move in with me. If it's too far a commute from your job, we'll find a place closer. I'll sell this place. It had its time and place."

She nodded. "Will you come home with me and help me pack, so I don't have to be without you one more minute than I have to be?"

So you won't reconsider and I'll find you've changed your mind?

He grinned, tucked himself back in his jeans and fastened them. "Turn around, put your arms around my neck. Stop exposing yourself to the neighbors, shameless exhibitionist."

"You—" She turned, her mouth open indignantly, and he put his own over it, taking her good-natured jab in his stomach, overwhelming humor with an astounding level of urgency, given what they'd just done. As he kissed her, he bent, caught the back of her knees, lifted her up in his arms without breaking the kiss and turned them, headed back to the cart.

"My clothes…"

"We'll come back for them. They've served their immediate purpose and you're not going to need them for a while. I'm taking you up to the house." He kissed her nose, her mouth. "Putting you in my bed and keeping you there for at least forty-eight hours, until I've impressed upon you that you're stuck with me forever." His eyes became steady and intent. "I've made my decision, Nicole. I won't change my mind, God help you."

Based on the hardness growing under her hipbone and the heat in his eyes, she knew he meant it. The strength of his arms told her she was in for a rough and glorious, forty-eight hours. She was a little afraid, because she knew he had a lot he was unloading along with the lust, but as if he knew her fears, he stopped at the cart, continued to hold her in his arms.

"You're not the one on trial here, Nicole. I know that. You're the gift. I promise I'll try not to push you too hard to resolve my own fears. But Kitten, I'll be honest with you." He sat her down on the golf cart seat, smiled at her startled yelp at the cold vinyl on her bare backside. Then he took her hand, raised it to his lips, a lovely, fond gesture as she sat there, clad in nothing but his collar, his seed on her thighs. Heat swept through her at the look in his eyes. "I want you in so many ways I'm afraid I'll shatter you, trying to pull you as deep into myself as I can. I don't know if that need is a destructive obsession or not, but it's what I have to have. I think you're the key to me healing once and for all, and if you're the prize…well, I don't know if I can hold back."

"I'm yours, Mark. Trust in that and you won't shatter me." She spoke in a whisper, moved by his desire and his honesty, moved enough to feel her own desire growing within her to match his. "I'm yours, Master. In any reality you want me to serve you."

He leaned forward and kissed her. In this quiet, isolated space, with the noise of water and wind moving gently around her, the kiss turned desperate and reverent at once, a straining of souls to the surface of everything that they had experienced before, a desire to merge into one, to face whatever came now and after.

When he raised his face, his amber eyes only inches from hers, his voice spoke inside her soul.

"This one. Every one."

Enjoy this excerpt from
Snow Angel
© Copyright Joey W. Hill 2003

"So what do you want for Christmas, little girl?"

Constance Jayne Bradwell looked over her shoulder, startled and then amused to find Santa looking directly at her.

The Children's Home Benefit Party was one of the city elite's most popular Christmas Eve events. The organizers had wanted some of the hands-on volunteers here tonight to mingle with the wealthy attendees and answer questions about the shelter. She was told she had a pleasing appearance that would fit in well. She'd done her duty, mixing, mingling, making conversation, all the while wondering if any of them had the slightest inkling what it was like to face Christmas alone in the world, belonging to no one but yourself.

She hated this holiday, with its pounding messages of family, love and togetherness, a scream so strong there was no escaping from it. Another hour and she could go home, put a pillow over her ears and sleep until it went away. She tried not to watch the dancing couples, one woman's elegantly manicured hand resting on the shoulder of her husband, his hand around her waist. What would it be like to have that casual intimacy? Any intimacy at all?

It had been a long time since she'd had sex, and she was lonely enough to long for even the artificial intimacy it could conjure. Wouldn't it be nice to find a safe guy to take her home, let him inundate her with mindless physical desire, and make her forget what she really wanted? What would it be like to have a man guide her to the dance floor with a protective, possessive hand to the small of her back? Get an aspirin out of the medicine cabinet if she had a headache, rather than having to stumble there by herself, blinded by the pain? What would it be like to have someone else hold the reins for awhile, not because it was his job or volunteer shift, but because he'd made a willing commitment to make her his, to cherish and care for her?

It was a confusing yearning, as if she wanted a parent and a lover both. She'd always been terrified to let go of control of her life, and yet tonight she had an overwhelming desire to do just that.

"You can't tell me a pretty little thing like you doesn't want anything for Christmas. Come here."

Santa held out his hand. On an impulse, she set her rum punch on a nearby table and took his offered hand to help her up to his throne. Some of the wrapped packages around his feet had gotten scattered, so she had to pick her way carefully through them with her heels. Santa's other hand touched her waist to steady and guide her, then she was up the step. He sat back down, using their clasped hands and the hand on her waist to guide her onto his knee.

Well, they always said "knee", but it was really a man's thigh you sat upon, a very intimate posture. There was no doubt the person on whose leg she sat could feel the shape of her bottom, the division of her thighs, perhaps even the small apple-sized area of vulva and labia, the dress being a typical formal, thin silken cloth that hugged her curves and sparkled.

"Let me guess." She arched a brow. "It's getting late, so you decided to make a play for the only other person at the party without a date."

His lips curved into an appreciative smile. Hazel eyes tipped by dark lashes looked at her from the framework of the curly white wig and beard. Putting that together with the muscular thigh that felt capable of accommodating her as long as she wanted to sit there, Constance realized with some surprise that this Santa was in his late thirties.

It made sense. Ironically, there were no children at this event, so his efforts were geared toward adults, exchanging quips with the men as he handed out presents, and encouraging ladies young and old to take his knee for a moment's flirtation.

"Not necessarily. You looked sad, and I thought you might like to tell the one person at the party who's supposed to grant wishes what would make you happy."

He had a compelling voice, with the smooth, rich tones of a late night radio talk show host. It was a voice that inspired confidence and comfort, and Constance felt something in her chest tighten, as if his words had the ability to wrap around her heart and squeeze out thoughts she would normally have no intention of saying out loud.

"So, is this like a confessional?   Nothing I say will be repeated?"

"What's spoken in this ear," he tapped it with one finger, cocking his head, "is only repeated to elves and angels."

She'd asked it half joking, but his response was serious, and her attention clung to those beautiful eyes. She had an urge to reach out and touch his mouth, and decided she needed to go home before she embarrassed herself.

But the shallow, harsh noise of two hundred impersonal voices pressed against her, and his touch, kind and strong against the small of her back, his expression attentive, steady, roused things in her she couldn't ignore.

He was Santa, and she had a very special wish. Maybe wishes whispered into the ears of a symbolic Santa *would* get to the ears of an angel and, if she'd been very, very good, some small part of her desire would be answered. She'd believed it once.

Constance leaned back, her shoulder pressing into his chest so she was speaking into his ear, not to any party guests standing too close. He tilted his head closer and when she spoke, she inadvertently brushed his ear with her lips, her jaw line pressing against the silky cotton sideburns of the beard.

She closed her eyes, shutting out reality, giving herself the same courage that the screen of the confessional provided. A safe place to voice her sins, her fears, her deepest wants. His hand tightened on her waist, holding her to him, and the words tumbled out of her mouth.

"I don't want to be here. I want to be home with someone who cares about me. I want to wake up tomorrow with someone's arms around me. I want to hear someone whisper 'Merry Christmas' in my ear, and be able to believe, if just for that moment, that I'm the most important person in his life. I want to be swept away, taken over. For one night, I want to believe I can trust my happiness in someone else's hands."

She straightened up, looked into those golden green eyes. "Pretty tall order, hmm, Santa? Bet you don't have anything in those little boxes at your feet to cover that."

She pushed off his lap before he could respond and walked away, already feeling like a fool.

About the author:

Joey W. Hill is published in mainstream, paranormal and erotic romance, as well as epic fantasy. Most of her erotic romance falls into the BDSM genre. She has won the Dream Realms Award for Fantasy and the EPPIE award for Erotic Romance. Nominated for the CAPA award and the PEARL, she also has received many gold star reviews from Just Erotic Romance Reviews, multiple Blue Ribbon reviews from Romance Junkies, and a Reviewer's Choice award from Road to Romance. She regularly garners five star reviews from erotic romance review sites. In 1999, she won the Grand Prize in the annual short story contest sponsored by Romance & Beyond magazine.

Following the dictates of a very capricious muse, she often brings in unexpected elements to a storyline – spirituality into erotic romance, paranormal aspects to a contemporary storyline, an alpha male who may believably perform as a submissive... all with intriguing and absorbing results for the reader. As one reviewer put it: "I should know by now that Ms. Hill doesn't write like anyone else." All of her erotic works emphasize strong, emotional characterization and the healing power of love through sexual expression.

Joey welcomes mail from readers. You can write to her c/o Ellora's Cave Publishing at 1337 Commerce Drive, Suite 13, Stow OH 44224.

Why an electronic book?

We live in the Information Age—an exciting time in the history of human civilization in which technology rules supreme and continues to progress in leaps and bounds every minute of every hour of every day. For a multitude of reasons, more and more avid literary fans are opting to purchase e-books instead of paperbacks. The question to those not yet initiated to the world of electronic reading is simply: *why?*

1. *Price.* An electronic title at Ellora's Cave Publishing runs anywhere from 40-75% less than the cover price of the <u>exact same title</u> in paperback format. Why? Cold mathematics. It is less expensive to publish an e-book than it is to publish a paperback, so the savings are passed along to the consumer.

2. *Space.* Running out of room to house your paperback books? That is one worry you will never have with electronic novels. For a low one-time cost, you can purchase a handheld computer designed specifically for e-reading purposes. Many e-readers are larger than the average handheld, giving you plenty of screen room. Better yet, hundreds of titles can be stored within your new library—a single microchip. (Please note that Ellora's Cave does not endorse any specific brands. You can check our website at www.ellorascave.com for customer recommendations we make available to new consumers.)

3. *Mobility.* Because your new library now consists of only a microchip, your entire cache of books can be taken with you wherever you go.

4. *Personal preferences are accounted for.* Are the words you are currently reading too small? Too large? Too...**ANNOYING**? Paperback books cannot be modified according to personal preferences, but e-books can.

5. *Innovation.* The way you read a book is not the only advancement the Information Age has gifted the literary community with. There is also the factor of what you can read. Ellora's Cave Publishing will be introducing a new line of interactive titles that are available in e-book format only.

6. *Instant gratification.* Is it the middle of the night and all the bookstores are closed? Are you tired of waiting days—sometimes weeks—for online and offline bookstores to ship the novels you bought? Ellora's Cave Publishing sells instantaneous downloads 24 hours a day, 7 days a week, 365 days a year. Our e-book delivery system is 100% automated, meaning your order is filled as soon as you pay for it.

Those are a few of the top reasons why electronic novels are displacing paperbacks for many an avid reader. As always, Ellora's Cave Publishing welcomes your questions and comments. We invite you to email us at service@ellorascave.com or write to us directly at: 1337 Commerce Drive, Suite 13, Stow OH 44224.

NEED A MORE EXCITING
WAY TO PLAN YOUR DAY?

ELLORA'S
CAVEMEN
2006 CALENDAR

COMING THIS FALL

Discover for yourself why readers can't get enough of the multiple award-winning publisher Ellora's Cave. Whether you prefer e-books or paperbacks, be sure to visit EC on the web at www.ellorascave.com for an erotic reading experience that will leave you breathless.

WWW.ELLORASCAVE.COM

Printed in the United States
30416LVS00007B/193-261

9 781419 951848